Ballroom Blitz

by

Natalie Cross

Dancesport Mysteries, Book One

Ballroom Blitz

Cover Art by *Diana Carlile*

The Wild Rose Press, Inc.
PO Box 708
Adams Basin, NY 14410-0708
Visit us at www.thewildrosepress.com

Publishing History
First Edition, 2022
Trade Paperback ISBN 978-1-5092-4433-1
Digital ISBN 978-1-5092-4434-8

Dancesport Mysteries, Book One
Published in the United States of America

The music slowed to a close, and he gently lowered her back to the floor, his hands sliding along the sides of her body, trying to make the few beats last as long as possible.

He breathed heavily, deeply, his heartbeat racing faster than was probably wise.

This woman would kill him one day. He would probably let her.

His gaze met hers. Had he remembered to temper the fire within him? Her eyes widened. Was that a flicker of desire? A momentary tightening of her hand against his?

Finally, finally, maybe he could just incline his head a little—

And she pushed him away, standing up and moving back to the sound system all at once. She took a long, long drink of water from her travel mug. "Well," she said at last. "Your Standard isn't bad. Let's try jive."

Praise for *Ballroom Blitz*

"A rollicking good time that will keep you on your toes until the very end--no dance shoes required."

~ Anna T.

~*~

"Ballroom Blitz is a delight. Fast paced, funny, and sexy."

~ Maureen T.-W.

Dedication

For my beautiful girls.

Prologue

The ballroom still thrummed with the clack of heels and the slide of suede, though its last inhabitants had vanished over an hour before. Applause and cheering from the final-night party echoed across the hallway. The tables were strewn with hairpins, empty water bottles, and sweaty towels tossed with exhilaration before another heat. The perfume of sunless tanner and hair spray drifted toward the apex of the ballroom's ceiling, and it almost seemed that a few notes of a Viennese waltz still clung to the utilitarian white hotel tablecloths.

Rapid footsteps broke the waiting silence. Stilettos from the *click click click*, glimmering with crystals, a few of which scattered from the shoes with a brackish clatter as the heels struck the parquet of the ballroom floor. Heavy breathing, panting. "No!" A stumble as one heel of the red satin crystal-encrusted stilettos snapped. Sobbing.

Then another pair of footsteps, flats, fashionable. Something hard, with an edge that might draw blood. These footsteps were measured. No panic. No anxiety. Calculating.

The sobs intensified. "Please, please, please, no, I didn't do anythi—"

A gurgle, a grimace, a thud. The wash of silk from a bone-white evening gown susurrated along the cold parquet floor. The scent of copper flooded the air.

A grunt, a vicious exhale, an audible sneer.

Then the ballroom closed upon itself again. The tables, the cloths, the chandeliers, the lights. All waiting for its new secret to be discovered.

Chapter One

Anita Goodman bounced on the tips of her sneaker-clad toes as she unlocked the door to her studio. Seven a.m. Just enough time, never enough time. Clean studio. Mail. Hopefully time for herself, just this once.

One by one, the sounds staccato and rhythmic, she flicked on the lights in her studio. Everything tidy, everything clean. Just as it should be, at least in her professional life.

Wait. Damn it.

Anita scrunched her face and rubbed at the smudge on the mirror that spanned the entire length of the main studio. She had just cleaned it last night. How did it get smudged when no one was there? *Please don't let it be rats.* Moths didn't smudge mirrors, did they?

Anita stepped back, admiring the sheen she had given to the mirror with the sleeve of her black, slouchy cardigan. Perfect again. Moths be damned.

Her phone buzzed in her pocket like an angry, demanding swarm of bees. For the eighth time already that morning. He wouldn't stop until she answered.

She sighed with her entire body and slid the "accept" button. "Stop calling me."

"Anita!" Even his accent sounded slimy. "How are you?"

"Busy. Stop calling me."

Mikhail tutted over the phone, every sound he uttered jarring her last nerve. "Anita, please. We are adults. We can be civil."

"Civil? Civil is not dumping me for Tatiana Lurshenko three weeks before Keystone, dickhead." She put the call on speaker and tossed the phone onto the check-in desk. She needed to buy a damn punching bag. "What could you possibly want this early in the morning?"

"I know you're up, Anita. You've probably been up for hours."

"Yes. Because I have to do my own work and now yours, too." Dickhead. *Gadina.* Anita could swear in about eight languages and wanted to use every last one in her arsenal. "Just tell me why the hell you needed to call me at seven a.m. Are you rubbing it in that I now can't dance at Keystone?" Without a punching bag ready, she grabbed the broom and started speed-sweeping. She should have listened to Nigel. Never confuse a dance partnership for love.

Mikhail, that Ukrainian *gadina*, never swept the studio floor a single day they were together. Now that she was single again, she had the time and anger to keep everything tidy. At least in her professional life.

Oh God, he was still droning on about how breaking up was going to be better for her. She really should just hang up on him. See how he liked it. Breaking up with her by text? Was he eleven?

She swept the mail from underneath the slot in the door into a tidy pile, which she collected and dumped unceremoniously in her little office. Even all the way across the studio, she could hear his incessant prattle. She needed this to be over. She had wasted enough time on him and every man like him.

Her feet moved so quickly across the floor she might as well be running over broken glass. "Mikhail, just stop it. Tell me what it is you want so I can get back to my life. I am done. I have way too much to do today to deal with you."

He drew in a dramatic breath, and she rolled her eyes before taking a sip from her "Rumba Walk Away" mug.

"Anita, you still have some of my things. I need them."

She spat the coffee back into her mug in an accidental guffaw. "Like what?" She thought he had taken everything. Her dignity. The last three years of her life. Her business partnership with Patrick.

Wait, she didn't mean that. She had had to let Patrick go.

"My hair gel. Ani, you know it is very expensive. My mother, she sends it straight from E.U."

Frost chilled through Anita's veins. Her eyes flicked to the bottle of hair gel that he had left beside the computer, and she swiped it into the trash can. It wasn't her fault he couldn't keep track of his own stuff.

"I don't see it anywhere. Maybe Tatiana can help you with that." She stabbed at the "end call" button and screamed inside.

Life was not fair. Men were not fair. Men, with their stupid hair gel and their wannabe dance reality stars. She was done with them. All of them.

She did her yoga breathing, re-centering herself, and then tightened her ponytail. *Men.*

Her phone buzzed again, not quite as angry this time. Less bee-like and more mall massage chair. More composed now that she had trashed Mikhail's designer hair gel, because apparently that was a thing, she glanced at the screen, and all of the tension fled from her body, as fast as a Viennese spin.

A text from Patrick, just a GIF of a roly-poly, black-and-white sheepdog puppy with a Maine coon kitten perched on its head.

Maybe not all men.

Anita glanced at the clock. Read the mail or practice? Yesterday's mail had brought a reminder about the Keystone Star Ball, at which she would definitely not be performing sans partner.

No mail.

She warmed up with a quick boxing workout, letting the punches and kicks and jabs stretch and warm her muscles. The tension in her neck and shoulders unwound as she moved out of the boxing warmup and into her samba routine. There was nothing better in the world for relaxing into the music than a deep bass drumbeat. She spent so many hours making other dancers look good, but this was how she felt most herself.

If only she had time to do it more often.

"Looking good, there, Anita," said a familiar voice.

She halted abruptly and inelegantly out of the chassé turns she had been working on. Damn it, she had been in the zone for the first time in weeks. Who could have possibly—

Oh.

Standing on the edge of the dance floor, arms crossed over his trim muscular frame, curly dark-brown hair hanging in his face, Patrick O'Leary grinned at her. The dimple drew her gaze immediately. How did he possibly look so good in just track pants and a windbreaker? All casual, sexy Jim Halpert? It wasn't fair. It took Anita ages to get her ponytail at just the right tension, and all Patrick needed was a beat-up messenger bag slung across one shoulder. "You're dropping your shoulder on the end of that turn, though."

"Did you come home from New York just to insult me?" She got a puppy GIF but no actual warning? A girl needed time to prepare to see that face. She knew postcards were passé, but he could at least have sent an "SYS" text. "And I'm not dropping my hip."

He smiled lazily and cast his eyes toward the floor. "I caught an earlier train. I missed it here, I guess."

"Three months is a long time to be away." Anita crossed her arms over her chest. She would not find him adorable. Absolutely not. Why hadn't he written her more? GIFs do not a friendship make.

"Did you miss me?"

Yes. "No. Besides, what are you doing *here*? At the studio? I thought the world didn't really start turning for you until eleven a.m." She moved across the studio floor to turn the music to a local pop station and sipped at her coffee. There was nothing left, but she needed to do something with her hands.

"Toni has a cold. She asked me to cover her class." He sat down in the waiting area, pulling off his boots and changing into a pair of sneakers.

He had called Toni before he called her? "I'm sure the ladies will love that," Anita remarked. Patrick was eternally very popular among the Zumba regulars, who had very vocally missed him over the last few months. Not only did he have classic Irish-handsome features, like a brunet Chris O'Donnell, but he was also just a generally decent human being. A rare quality, as she could attest. If he wasn't her best friend, it would probably bother her, but Anita had been watching women stalk him with devotion since they had met in their high school ballroom dance club. She was more than used to it by now.

Strange, then, the pang in her chest. She rubbed at the area absently with her knuckles. She should really switch from coffee to green tea.

"Besides." Patrick stopped, his voice catching in his throat. "I, um, I heard about Mikhail." Her heart would not stop palpitating. A cold sweat trickled down her spine, leaving a delicious warmth in its wake. He had heard about Mikhail and had come home early?

She opened her mouth to reply, but no words would form.

The bell over the door chimed, and a pair of timid thirty-something ladies in black leggings and brand-new high-end sneakers entered the studio. Anita shook her head and pasted on her most professional smile.

"Good morning." Patrick grinned at them, disarming them with his warmth and charm. He was definitely good for business. "Here for the class?" They nodded shyly, and he stood to his full height, extending his hand. "I'm Patrick. I'll be your instructor. Have you done Zumba before?"

Anita's smile bloomed inside her chest, and she moved to the check-in desk, filling her empty coffee cup with water from the nearby dispenser. The morning seemed a little brighter, having Patrick home at last. Things always ran a little smoother when he was there.

****

She heard the final strains of the cool down music,

a collective whooping, and the slaps of high fives. Where Patrick went, the party followed.

Not that the party was for her.

She sighed over her paperwork. Tax forms. 1099, W-2. If only running a business could just be about the music and dancing, but it was a lot doing everything herself. She glanced at a yellow sticky note stuck to the bottom of her computer monitor that said *social media??*

It had been there for half a year.

She would absolutely not indulge in self-loathing. She had built this business almost entirely by herself. Even her beloved father had not initially been supportive, but look at her now.

In the reflected glow from the computer monitor, she could see deep purple bags beneath her eyes, tension in the set of her jaw.

It was far too early for self-criticism.

"Hey." Patrick smiled at her from the doorway. He had changed into a bright-yellow tank top with Zumba emblazoned in neon blue that hung loosely off his muscles, which were shining with sweat. How did he have time to get those abs? She barely had a moment to practice her dancing.

He held a towel to his forehead to mop up some of the sweat.

Lucky towel. "Good class?" She kept typing *G* instead of *S*. Over the years, she had gotten quite skilled at decidedly not acknowledging his innate hotness. *It's just Patrick.* The guy who had once let his dimple be colored peacock blue. So what if he had the body of an MMA fighter?

Anita clacked hard on the Enter key.

There was that sexy little dimple again. "Yeah. Those ladies have a lot of energy. I don't know how Toni keeps up with them."

"Toni drinks green juice three times a day and hasn't had a simple carbohydrate in four years."

"I always knew I'd be undone by my love of hoagies and soft pretzels." He stepped into the office and sank into the chair across from her. Even his sweat smelled good, like pine forests and mint, the scent compounded by the close proximity of the room. How frustrating.

"How was New York?" Maybe she could just avoid his gaze to distract her from his scent. What was wrong with her? She had known him for over a decade. Why was she suddenly noticing his abs and his pheromones?

No. No pheromones. Do not think about pheromones.

Anita busied herself with the tax forms, which could have been written in Cyrillic. She could have sworn she knew what she was doing three minutes before.

Had he come back early just for her? No, that was impossible. He had far more important things to do.

"It was good. A lot of work. Deadlines and schmoozing. The writing went well, though. A lot of inspiration in NYC." Patrick rested his hands on his well-toned thighs. "It was definitely weird leaving after Nikita's murder."

Her chest felt as though it had been submerged in an ice bath. Nikita. She had hardly been a saint, but the woman had been truly dedicated to Dancesport, and Anita had always appreciated her attention to detail.

"We were all stunned."

"Did they find out anything about her killer?"

"No. They thought it might be one of her *petits amis*." She shrugged. "So far nothing's come of it." She watched Patrick, who was leafing through the in box on her desk. Old habits. He had used to handle the mail for the studio. "Why? Are you getting into true crime podcasting?"

He chuckled. "I've got enough on my plate, thanks."

"I thought diversity of media was important for an influencer."

The corner of his mouth tilted upward, revealing just the slightest hint of clean white teeth. All the nerve endings on Anita's arms stood to attention, her mouth almost salivating. Was she coming down with something? She should find her thermometer. "You think I influence people?"

Anita rolled her eyes, chalking up the butterflies in her stomach to her lack of a proper breakfast. "Did New York change you?"

Patrick winked, exaggerating the motion like he was in a bloated blockbuster comedy. "You can't tell that I had my nose done? My plastic surgeon's online reviews were spectacular."

Anita rolled her eyes. Patrick had a terrific fear of needles. Besides, his nose was absolutely perfect. "Ha ha." Anita liked the comfort of knowing his face. Of all the people in her world, Patrick was the one she hoped would never change.

Patrick picked up the large envelope she had hidden underneath a pile of grocery circulars. The letters on the return address glittered in black and gold.

"The Keystone Star Ball, huh?"

Can't put anything past the man. Anita frowned.

"You're kidding." Patrick's eyes twinkled with mock shock. "You're not going to compete? You love the Keystone. You've been going since we were fifteen, and you dragged the rest of the ballroom dance club with you because you wanted the moral support." For some reason his kind smile stabbed her a bit in the heart, but he seemed to notice and softened his voice. That was the thing about Patrick. He could definitely read a room. "Not that you needed it."

"I'm competing in pro/am, and I have students who have registered as couples." She did not have time for disappointment. She was a professional business owner. Besides, disappointment caused wrinkles. "I don't have a partner for the open, and I don't have the time to find someone to practice the routines."

Things had been so easy back in high school. The girls all dressed in sequins and fringe, shellacking Patrick's curly hair into an impenetrable helmet. So much laughter. She was the idiot for dancing with Tyler, nationally ranked but more than a bit of a tool.

Live and learn.

Anita returned her attention to her friend, who was watching her with a curious expression.

Patrick shrugged. "I'll do it."

Anita barked a laugh. Of all the things he could have said. "Patrick, you don't have the time. You only teach when you aren't writing, *and* you haven't competed in over a year." Since he left the studio, but she refused give voice to her pettiness.

"I bet it's like riding a bike." He smiled in that hapless charming manner of his, stretching his long legs in front of him. "We've danced together a couple of times before, and it worked out. I seem to recall some bronzer and a little hairspray."

"A lot of hairspray." Anita smiled, mostly to force the memories of their few dances together from her mind. She was absolutely, positively, one hundred percent not going to blush in front of him. That show dance from the Ohio Star Ball...

Lock the door on that unhelpful line of thought and throw the key far, far away. A girl has to keep herself together.

She really didn't want to miss the Keystone Star Ball. There was going to be a memorial for Nikita Ivanovna, who had been murdered three months prior. Plus, she begrudgingly had to admit Patrick was an excellent partner. Especially when she could still see the outlines of his muscles through his Zumba tank. Was that a six- or an eight-pack?

Anita gulped and glanced at her computer screen, which had changed from her financial report to her screen saver. She needed a glass of wine and a hot bubble bath. "You're too tall for me."

Patrick leaned forward, causing his tank top to gape at the top and offering Anita a glimpse of his full set. Eight-pack, definitely. It was not fair to dangle carrots like that. "Anita, you are five foot seven, and you wear three-inch heels when you dance. You can handle it."

He had to be right, of course. As always.

"Seriously, what is the problem? You want to do this. I'm available. You can convince the coordinator to let me come out of retirement or whatever." His deep blue eyes looked almost wounded. "I'm not *that* bad of a dancer."

She frowned, staring at the screen saver on her computer. Photos of palm trees and jungle waterfalls spilling into crystalline pools floated softly across the screen. He wasn't a bad dancer at all. He had always been rather magnificent. Responsive, kind, careful. Sometimes when she watched him dance, she would wonder what it would feel like to partner with him, really work with him, all of the hours together choreographing and refining. Touching. Nobody had hands like Patrick.

But that had never been their relationship. It never could be.

She definitely needed to stop drinking coffee if it was going to affect her heart rate like this.

"Patrick, this is really important to me. Of course I want to compete again, but I don't want to fail. I am tired of partners who put themselves first, and the dance suffers. So I need a partner who's going to be there with me. Who's not going to slack off or show up at eleven thirty when I needed him there at eight." Mikhail? Tyler? Giorgio? Terrible taste in men? Check, check, check.

Patrick sat back in his chair and steepled his fingers. Those blue eyes that she knew so well looked so thoughtful, so caring. "I know how much this means to you. I can be that guy. I promise." His gaze found hers, and he held it for several long moments.

Anita blushed under his intensity. Something deep in her gut pinged, almost like a homing beacon or one of those sonar blips on a submarine. "Okay, then. We will start tomorrow at nine."

He grinned. "What? What happened to eight? I had

already mentally set my alarm." That lopsided grin was decidedly disarming. She needed to schedule some serious meditation ASAP if she was going to keep her composure through this.

"Toni has Zumba again tomorrow morning. The studio won't be free until then. Besides, I need today to figure out what we are going to perform, work out some basic choreo, and call the coordinator to tell her you're coming out of retirement. I'm not sure what we will do. We are starting way too late for the 10 Dance." She gathered one of the stacks of paper on her desk into a useless pile.

"Is it really coming out of retirement when I teach at the high school and still have the occasional private lesson?"

"Nina Rabinova does not count." Anita finger-combed her long, dark-blonde ponytail. "She takes lessons from everyone. Says she wants to 'perfect her dancer's body.' Though honestly, I think the only dancer's body she has ever wanted is yours."

Patrick feigned shock, a hand held to his chest in a very Scarlett O'Hara gesture. "Ms. Anita Goodman, what are you implying? I'll have you know, I am always the perfect gentleman with my clients."

"Uh-huh." Anita raised her eyebrows. "Much to their chagrin, I'm sure."

"Well, I'd love to sit here and banter, but I know you have a ton of work to plan for me to do." Patrick rose from the chair. "I'm going for a run. I need to check out the new Barney's Bagels down off Pine Crest."

"Does the running cancel out the bagels?"

"Absolutely. Otherwise, why bother?" Patrick

grinned wickedly, and Anita raised her hand in farewell.

The bell over the front door saluted his exit, and Anita sat back in her office chair and allowed herself an indulgent moment to lower her heart rate.

The Keystone Star Ball. In three weeks. With a partner who had been out of the game for over a year.

No. Not with any partner. With Patrick. Patrick.

A smile tugged at her lips.

Take that, two-faced Mikhail.

Chapter Two

Patrick was running early, but there was no way he would let Anita know he was actually that responsible. Besides, a man could not show up empty-handed when starting a new partnership. Well, dance partnership, but beggars could not be choosers.

To delay himself, he stopped off at Amore, his favorite café along Main Street, and bought a nonfat latte and a hot tea. He liked to present her with options. Or at least he had liked it, before he had escaped to NYC for three months. The distance hadn't been enough to erase her from his mind. His traitorous heart had lapped up the sight of her yesterday like a man finding a chain coffee store in the middle of the Gobi Desert.

He paused for a moment outside the small shop, staring far too hard at the white plastic lids. Was she still trying to switch to tea? Maybe she would rather have had something else, like an I Heart NYC keychain or a snow globe from Rockefeller Center. Maybe he had never really known her at all.

If he kept dithering, he would one thousand percent be late, and that would not set him up for success. This was his last chance. She had broken up with Mikhail, and this was it. If he couldn't figure out how to tell her how he felt now, he had to be done.

He timed his arrival at Lewis Dancesport Academy

precisely at nine, exactly as some of the stragglers from Toni's Zumba class were milling out of the studio.

"Morning, ladies." He smiled, tipping a to-go cup near his forehead as if doffing a hat. "Good class?"

"Missed you today, Patrick," Melanie Templeton said, the tilting of her lips not meeting her eyes. Of all the people who could have forgotten that he taught Zumba, why did she always remember? She was stick thin and had a brittle personality to match. Patrick knew she was married, but it didn't seem to stop her from trying to fondle him at every opportunity. Had she never heard of boundaries? "My legs were on FIRE yesterday, and I couldn't stop cursing you all night. Did you have to be away *so* long? No one ruffles our hair like you." Despite her assertions, her carefully coiffed blonde ponytail seemed shockingly kempt.

What was the minimum modicum of respect he needed to show without in any way encouraging her?

"Mel, you are so bad!" Her shorter and nicer friend Kim Somebody-or-Other swatted her playfully on the arm. Clearly Melanie had been recruiting acolytes during his time in New York. At least Kim was better at keeping her hands on more socially acceptable parts of his anatomy and was less fond of the midriff-baring top. "Toni is great as always. It was just nice to have a switch-up yesterday."

As if hearing her name had summoned her, Toni herself walked out of the studio, hefting her black sports duffel bag over her right shoulder and holding a ridiculously large water bottle in her left hand. She wore a fitted jumpsuit in three different neon colors that matched the beads in her long black braids.

Thank goodness for Toni. She had saved him

before, when he and Anita had just opened the studio and offered to rent the space for Zumba classes. They had been in the black that month for the first time. Now she was doing it again.

"Ladies, let Patrick by," Toni said smoothly in her Georgia drawl.

He raised a hand to her in thanks and waved goodbye to the ladies from Zumba. He could still feel Melanie staring daggers into his back. Well, let her stare. It didn't hurt him. He would never do anything about it.

****

Patrick placed the drink cups and his dance bag on the floor so he could change his shoes, because he had learned the hard way that suede soles had no place outside a dance studio. Toni had left an '80s pop song medley running on the sound system. The woman had excellent taste in music, less so in men. The Georgia girl had followed an ex-lover to Lewis, then had "lost the douchebag, kept the accent."

And yes, he was definitely thinking about Toni to avoid thinking about Anita.

"You're on time."

He glanced up from tying his shoe and felt his heart catch a bit in his chest the way it always did when he saw Anita. It wasn't just her poetry-inspiring looks, how she smelled of spring break trips to St. Barth's. No, when he allowed himself to think it at all—which was close to never, for the preservation of his sanity—it was the little familiarities that he liked best. The black open cardigan that molded to her curves in the most casually sensuous way, the way a dimple appeared in her frown, the look of utter joy and peace on her face when she was dancing.

This was his last chance to tell her. He had been in the Friend Zone long enough to know there was no escape. Not even three months in New York had been far enough. The moon wouldn't be far enough to forget her.

"I live to surprise you." He stood, dance shoes now tightly laced, and held out the two cups. "Nonfat latte or tea?"

She grimaced and extended a cautious hand toward the tea. "I'm still trying to switch. There was this really good article about green tea being better for you. I guess I just am not strong enough to quit that first morning cup of coffee."

"Then don't." He sipped the latte, the creamy bitterness coating his tongue. "Why deny yourself life's simple pleasures?"

Anita turned back to the dance floor, her tight, blonde ponytail whipping behind her. Patrick had missed that kind of whiplash. "We have a TON to do today. I thought we would start with Standard, do a test dance. If that works, great. If not, we can try Latin."

"Why not just do a showcase?" He leaned against the check-in desk, latte in hand. "Only one dance to learn and not screw up." She averted her gaze from him, but he could still see the way she bit her lip. Seriously, how did even the most mundane actions make him want to kiss her senseless? "Admit it. You want to beat Mikhail."

"Wouldn't you?"

"The great Anita Goodman, out for vengeance. Now that is a superhero movie I would watch." Why had he gone to New York again? He had not bantered with anyone like this in months. Sometimes, late in the middle of the night when he couldn't sleep because he couldn't stop thinking about the smell of her shampoo, he wished that he hadn't left working with her at the studio. Last year, finally realizing it was just too painful to spend all day working with her but not, frankly, all night, he had stopped teaching lessons and shifted more to writing. The lonely hours in front of the computer felt like penance of some sort. Or maybe purgatory.

Maybe this was his ticket out of purgatory? A chance to move things in a different direction?

"We don't have time for this. We need to start practicing," she replied primly.

So, no chance of a new direction, then.

Anita walked to the sound system and turned off the '80s power rock. "What do you think? Quickstep first?"

Interesting option, but he was in the mood for something more classic, maybe a bit overly dramatic.

"Nah, let's waltz." He did some arm and leg circles to warm up while she thumbed through the songs on her playlist.

The opening strains of Lifehouse's "You and Me" emanated from the speakers as she took her position across from him. "I approve the choice." He grinned as he bowed to open the dance. She curtsied pertly, then they stepped together, opposite hands raised toward each other.

Something was different. It wasn't the frame, the placement of his right hand on her back and their other hands entwined. It wasn't the electric thrill in his body that noticed every move she made, the way they seemed perfectly in tune. He had always felt that way when they had danced together.

No. Now it seemed almost as if she finally noticed it too and was subconsciously trying to ignore it.

Intriguing. Definitely intriguing.

He led her through a series of different waltz elements, turns, whisks, establishing the rise and fall of the dance. Through the connection of their bodies, he felt her relax into the music, into their rhythm. It was almost better than sex.

Almost.

He sang softly under his breath as they swayed around the floor, closing his eyes in an overly dramatic, and hopefully romantic, way.

"Are you seriously singing right now?" She giggled—giggled!—and he tucked her into a complicated figure, loving how she followed wherever he led. "You are not taking this seriously."

"I always take you seriously. Hey, keep your frame."

Her gaze flicked toward his. Was that surprise, pleasure? Whatever it was tilted her mouth and lifted the corners of her eyes in this incredibly sexy way that made him want—

Things he could not have.

The music crescendoed. Might as well have a bit of fun.

He turned her into and out of a series of turns, then into a Viennese spin. "Arabesque," he whispered. As commanded, she lifted her right leg in an arabesque, and then he put his hands on her waist and lifted her into the air. He twirled her for an eight count, his gaze riveted to her, stretched out over him like a willow tree. His hands burned where they touched her waist. If only he could transfer his strength to her, but he knew better. She did not need his strength.

The music slowed to a close, and he gently lowered her back to the floor, his hands sliding along the sides of her body, trying to make the few beats last as long as possible.

He breathed heavily, deeply, his heartbeat racing faster than was probably wise.

This woman would kill him one day. He would probably let her.

His gaze met hers. Had he remembered to temper the fire within him? Her eyes widened. Was that a flicker of desire? A momentary tightening of her hand against his?

Finally, finally, maybe he could just incline his head a little—

And she pushed him away, standing up and moving back to the sound system all at once. She took a long, long drink of water from her travel mug. "Well," she said at last. "Your Standard isn't bad. Let's try jive."

He bounced up and down on his toes. A dance they could do almost entirely in shadow position. Maybe she had finally felt that kick in the heart, too.

Chapter Three

Anita politely dismissed her last student of the night around nine-thirty. Fourteen hours of dancing and her feet were going to fall off right here, right now. She just needed to finish locking up, and then she could sink her toes into a warm bath filled with peppermint-scented salts. God, yes.

She yawned and turned the deadbolt, but the thunk reminded her. She had forgotten to sweep the floor. Just a quick sweep. That was all that she needed to do, and then she could go back up to her apartment, make a cup of herbal tea, maybe read a little of the Theresa Romain waiting for her. She could do that, right?

She pushed the broom around the floor. A waltz. That's what she needed. Music as motivation. Nothing better to stanch the ache than make cleaning fun. She really must be exhausted. Next she would be whistling and changing her broom into a magic wand.

What had she been humming? Lifehouse. It had been so good. So, sooooooo good. The strength of Patrick's muscles under her hands, the intensity of his gaze when he had brought her back down to the ground, the delicious burn of his arms around her waist.

Anita stopped abruptly in the middle of the studio, catching sight of herself in the mirror. Her ponytail was rumpled, her eyes bright and almost fevered. This wasn't her.

She had been off-beat with the jive kicks. She had been smiling like a moron during her evening group beginner's class. Unacceptable.

She was a professional. This was a professional agreement—that was it. Patrick had been her friend for years, and she had not had feelings for him in nearly all that time. Well, certainly not ones that she would ever admit to herself. It was the exhilaration of the dance. That was all. A moment of fabricated romance. She was just a little lonely.

Still, he had looked at her as though she was his first meal in a week, or a rainstorm in a drought. A harbor in the tempest.

No. She shook her head to clear her thoughts. She finished sweeping, turned off the lights, and headed up the back stairwell to her apartment. She would do literally anything for a glass of wine. Screw the peppermint tea.

Thump knock thump.

She whirled, her nerve endings suddenly on high alert. She had locked the front door, hadn't she? Of course she had. She had a distinct memory of turning the dead bolt, the steady thunk as the metal had settled into place. But had she? Or was it just something that she had done eight hundred thousand other times?

Thump knock knock thump thump.

Maybe she should have left on the lights. She tiptoed across the studio, stepping through the spiderweb of shadows stretching across the polished golden wood floor. She latched onto the firm metal handle of the broom she had carefully leaned against the wall by the stereo. At least it was something. A girl could not be too careful, but this was her studio, her livelihood. Like she would let it go without a fight.

How best to startle the intruder? If it turned out to be a raccoon or something equally mundane, she would never live it down.

She heard the sound once again, summoned her courage, and leapt out in front of the door, flicking on the lights as she moved, brandishing the broom handle in front of her like a crazed janitor.

Nothing. There was nothing there, not even a tree branch scraping the glass window of the door.

Anita set the broom against the check-in desk. Her heart would not stop pounding, the small hairs on her arms and on the back of her neck standing at attention like she had been electrocuted by sticking a wet finger in a light socket.

She moved cautiously closer to the door. Was she just a twenty-something spinster, hallucinating after a bizarre day? Maybe lusting after her friend of umpteen years was making her delusional.

Nope. Lusting after Patrick was worse than fear.

She exhaled forcefully. *Get a grip, girl.* She turned to go back up toward her apartment when the half-light of a streetlamp through the door caught a flash of white at its base. She froze in the moment, her hand on the wall, contemplating. It couldn't really be anything dangerous, though she remembered the stories of poisons sent through the mail, pipe bombs in packages.

She needed to stop reading the news before bed.

Jammed under the door, apparently with a great deal of force or anguish, was a single piece of plain white printer paper. Nothing too scary. Ordinary. *Get a grip, Anita. For real this time.*

She cast a cautious glance through the glass front

of the door. Nothing. No one. She was hallucinating. *Just do it quick and move on.*

Anita unlocked the front door, grabbed the paper, then set the deadbolt again. She went over to the check-in desk and tilted the paper under the tinted light from the vintage Emeralite desk lamp.

The handwriting was scratchy and slanted. It was written in pencil, too. Weird. Who used that after grade school?

I SEE YOU.

Weird. It almost looked like one of those letters with the alphabet cut out of various magazines, though whoever had written this was a lot lazier. Why spend all that time cutting and gluing when you could just write a creepy note with a first grader's writing instrument?

Anita smoothed the paper with one hand, then turned it over and over. There were no other identifying marks. It looked like the same plain white printer paper she had been using ever since she was a child, sitting and drawing pictures on the floor behind her father's giant mahogany desk.

She really just needed to go to bed.

Her heart rate beat only a degree above normal. Why worry over anonymous childish threats when they could not bother to be more specific? Out of sight, out of mind.

With a slight huff, Anita tossed the paper into the recycling bin, turned on the alarm, shut off the lights again, and headed upstairs so she could finally, finally soak her aching feet.

Chapter Four

Patrick yawned and stretched his arms over his head. Waking up early to practice with Anita had been critical. But seriously, when was he supposed to sleep? Last night he had to go to a new restaurant opening in Philadelphia and had not gotten home until the wee hours. Now he still had to finish his latest blog post, respond to a few different inquiries on his social media pages, and organize the photos from the restaurant opening. It was nine p.m. already, and he was exhausted. Clearly he had blocked out how physically taxing comp practice was.

Necessary, though. The way Anita had felt in his arms…

But she had blocked him out long enough for him to stop dreaming. Or at least try.

Patrick yawned again and went to the small kitchen to get himself a glass of water.

The ficus Anita had given him as a joke was looking a little peaked. She had told him it would suit his "bachelor pad," but he hated to think he couldn't even take care of a damn plant. Water. Plants just needed water, right?

He filled his glass from the stainless-steel fridge dispenser and glanced at the empty wall of exposed red brick in the living room, the lack of ornamentation.

"When are you finally going to move in, Patrick?"

Anita had asked a few months ago. Minimalism did not quite suit her. Her own apartment was a riot of color and throw pillows, cozy rainbow-colored cable blankets, and half-drunk mugs of tea on every available surface. She presented the world a buttoned-up, elite athlete, while inside she was a neurotic marshmallow.

He definitely had a taste for marshmallows.

Patrick's phone pinged with a social media notification, and his heart flopped uncomfortably. He had deadlines. He could not keep standing around musing over things that would absolutely never happen.

He had never intended to become an influencer. He had started his blog, *PhillyProud*, as a way to distract himself from his unrequited adoration of his beautiful and talented friend. As one does.

It had been a good time to leave the Dancesport world, though. Patrick was not a masochist. He did not want to keep going every single day to watch the woman he loved and the ridiculous partner she had chosen over him.

And seriously, Mikhail? After Tyler and Giorgio and a few other scattered dudes Patrick knew would never last, Anita had picked Mikhail? Apart from his decent technique, he wasn't terribly creative with choreography, and he had almost objectively "stupid hair." It was a thick black ball of too much hair gel, an environmentally unfriendly amount of hairspray, all styled into a ludicrously outdated pseudo-pompadour. It didn't deflate even after two hours of dancing, which proved to Patrick its direct impact on climate change.

Patrick could be forgiven for never wanting to be in the studio with the jerk, right? The feeling had definitely been mutual. Mikhail didn't trust Patrick—

which, all things considered, he shouldn't have.

Life was all about timing. One fateful instruction from his soccer coach to try dance to improve his footwork, and he ended up meeting the love of his life. Who didn't even really like to be touched unless they were dancing together.

Patrick yawned again, downed the glass of water, and did a couple of jumping jacks to wake himself up.

Work. He sat down at his laptop and pulled up his social media and email accounts. He had already pre-scheduled his posts for the next two weeks and frankly did not have the time to spend trying to write pithy comments on other people's posts tonight. As quickly as he could, he clicked through the emails, confirming a few deadlines on articles, updating an editor from the *Inquirer* on article progress, and sending out an invoice for a paid sponsorship with a men's clothing store that he had completed. Once he checked his messages, he could finally go to bed.

Unusual. Only one message.

It was from an account he didn't recognize, PHL29848, and the avatar was a photo of the Philly Phanatic. When had subtlety gone out of fashion? It wasn't like he used the Rocky steps for his brand logo. Whatever it was, it was not bound to be urgent.

Still, he had a duty. He had to be there for his followers, respond quickly to messages, or he would quickly find himself waiting tables again. Damn it, he desperately did not want to go back to that.

MISSING YOU...

No name, no photos, no links.

What the fuck? Was he hallucinating through his fatigue?

Nope, not a hallucination. Just an all caps direct message written in red font.

He clicked on the PHL29848's profile page, but it was mostly landscape photos of different Philadelphia landmarks and only dated back a week.

Whatever, he was too tired for spam. He deleted the message, made sure he blocked PHL29848 so whatever creepazoid it was couldn't follow him, and fell asleep within moments of his head hitting the pillow.

Chapter Five

The next day, the sun broke crisp and clean, the idea of snow left somewhere back in February.

Patrick knew better. A born-and-bred Pennsylvania boy never trusted March.

He jogged down the streets of his small town, past evidence of Lewis's gentrification, large two- and three-story Georgians and Cape Cods set back from the street and fronted with lawns that would be emerald-green in the summer. Especially after the last three months in the over-tangled bustle and smoky snow of New York, the country air restored him.

There, the high school where he had first seen Anita and first started dancing. There, the empty soccer fields where he had played nearly his entire childhood. His mother had always told him to get out of this town, that he was meant for something better.

She had never liked that he quit soccer, either. Sorry, Mom. Ballroom dance had helped him to see the world, and now ballroom dance had brought him back home.

Five miles into the run, he paused by Lewiston Creek. The creek was beautiful in the early morning March sunlight, the ice still breaking around the edges as the center ran brackish with dried twigs and leaves. When he was a boy, he and his friend Will Forbes would come down here to race boats made of bark and rubber bands. Simpler times.

Patrick stretched. His muscles ached and burned in a way that made him never want to stop moving. Endorphins. He should write a blog post singing their praises.

He was turning back toward the street when he noted a flash of blonde hair. Was that a Wildcats blue-and-white jacket? What were the odds? Okay, pretty good considering the geography, but still.

"Anita?" No answer, though a few yards from him twigs cracked, the sound almost as loud as a gunshot. "Anita? Is that you?"

Weird. She was supposed to be teaching an early lesson. They were not supposed to practice until later that morning.

Whatever. It couldn't be her. This town was full of blonde Wildcats. If they didn't want to talk to him, he should just ignore it.

Patrick fitted his earbuds back into his ears and turned his attention back to Todrick Hall.

****

The post-run hot shower shook his nagging sensation of being watched. This was Lewis, after all. Patrick just had not yet abandoned his New York wariness. Like sea legs, it would take a while to get back into the groove of leaving his small-town doors unlocked.

Coffee would help. Nothing like a local coffee shop to reset his perspective. Just a quick hit of caffeine and he would be good to go.

He pulled on black track pants and a dark-gray hoodie over his white T-shirt and slung his dance bag with his shoes, towel, water bottle, and shoe brush over his shoulder.

Downtown Lewis was not very large. Though his apartment was set back from the main street, it was less than a ten-minute walk to Amore, and the weather seemed promising that morning. The weather could turn at any moment into an icy, snowy beast, but so far, the sun had held, and Patrick could pick out tiny purple-and-white crocuses pushing up between a few of his neighbors' white pickets.

He pushed open the door to Amore and sighed in relief. Things were in his favor this morning. Not a huge line today and Kevin was the barista. He'd get to the studio early and surprise Anita.

The bell over the door clanged again, bringing in a gust of brisk March air.

"Patrick!" a female voice exclaimed, breathy as Marilyn Monroe.

Something in his stomach turned unpleasantly. He turned and waved brusquely at Melanie Templeton and her wannabe. *Be professional.* He gritted his teeth. *Do not make me late for Anita.* "Good morning, Melanie. Kim. Beautiful day, right?"

Melanie had on a full face of makeup despite the early hour and was wearing designer flats and athletic pants under what had to be a $1,000 overcoat. Her friend Kim was wearing a version of the same outfit, but the coat and shoes were almost certainly knockoffs. Where in the world had these two met? Melanie had told him her entire life story unprompted one morning, so he knew she had moved to Lewis with her husband about a year ago. Kim must have entered the picture while Patrick was in New York. The woman certainly hung on Melanie's every move. Poor kid.

Melanie grinned brightly at him, shifting her posture to accentuate her chest. "Didn't figure you for an early riser, Patrick." She had lowered her voice to more of a burr.

"Early bird and all that." He checked the line again—only two more in front of him. Maybe Kevin could catch his eye, put his usual on his tab.

"Isn't this the best coffee around?" Kim said. Her voice seemed slightly shrill next to her friend. There was something oddly familiar about her, but Patrick had known a lot of women like her in college and the Dancesport circuit.

"Well, Patrick knows all the best spots." Melanie's eyes traced his body, making him feel distinctly like a London broil. Patrick tried not to recoil. "*PhillyProud*, right? I'm a born and bred Philly girl, myself. Well, Ardmore. If you'd like, maybe I can show you some of my favorite childhood haunts, for the blog, of course."

Uh-huh, hard nope. "Thanks, but I grew up around here, too. Oh, look, my coffee's ready." Thank God for Kevin. The man was a genius and scholar and should be praised on mountaintops. Patrick handed him his credit card in exchange for the two to-go cups. He turned back to the other women and nodded, pulling his face into a smile. "Ladies, have a great day."

"You too," Melanie practically purred. She stretched her left hand, with an enormous diamond poised on her ring finger, and stroked his arm. "We really should keep meeting like this."

Kim scowled.

He was not getting into the middle of this. "I have to run." He exited the coffee shop without inviting further conversation and hurried down the street to the studio.

****

Anita had not gotten her typical eight hours of sleep last night. She desperately wanted to blame Patrick, as part of the problem had been a rather explicit early morning dream from which she had woken up sweating through her sheets, but it could not all be his fault. There had been the weird letter shoved under her door, too. Maybe she should have kept it.

She could have erased the pencil marks and re-used the paper. Office supplies were not cheap.

Whatever the reason for her lack of sleep, it was a Pat Benatar kind of morning for sure. Anita stood in front of the studio mirror, stretching out her neck, her arms, her hips, her ankles, massaging away the fog of fatigue.

She heard Patrick singing in a falsetto and turned to watch him lip sync like a contestant on a fake game show. He had his eyes shut tight, a coffee cup as microphone held to his lips, and a ridiculous grin on his face. Classic Patrick. She fought the smile, but something about the lines of his face mirrored something from her dream last night and—

Suppress. Suppress. Red Alert.

"You're not making fun of Pat Benatar, are you?" She crossed her arms over her chest and affected a wounded posture. Normal day, normal Patrick. No X-rated fantasies here. Nope.

"Nah." He smiled. "I've done a mean cha-cha to 'Invincible' once or twice."

"Is that for me?" She nodded to the coffee cups in his hands, and he handed one over to her. Their hands brushed, and oh my God, was she on fire? *Get a grip,*

Anita. She affected a bland smile. "Thanks. I swear, I'm going to give up the coffee eventually."

"You can't give up all your bad habits." Patrick perched on one of the chairs and pulled out his dance shoes. "Then you'll be even more perfect, and you won't let me be your friend anymore."

"That's not true. Who would remind me of my awkward teen years?" Sweet how he always remembered how she liked her coffee. She knew his order, too. Splash of almond milk, or an americano when available. One time at a competition in Vienna, they had ordered eight different types of coffee drinks and lined them up on the table. They had practically buzzed off the walls after that.

"You never had awkward teen years." He tied his shoes in neat, taut bows. He really did have the best hands. "Hey, is there Zumba this morning?"

"Not on Wednesdays. Why?"

Anita had never seen a person literally turn green, but Patrick's face had a definite hue. "I ran into Melanie Templeton and her friend Kim at Amore this morning."

Patrick had always liked lanky blondes, though she had not expected Melanie's patina to appeal. Anita rubbed at a pang in her chest. Maybe she was getting an ulcer. "Oh?"

"Yeah. She's a bit much, Melanie. I thought she was married."

Patrick had talked to Melanie? "I think so. Her husband does some sort of finance thing in Philadelphia. I understand he's away a lot. Toni told me she saw Melanie and some other guy looking very cozy at a bar in Devon a few months ago." Wow, she needed to tone it down. Anita never deigned to gossip or cattiness. Stupid weird letter thing. Still, she could not resist. Maybe if she could get a good night's sleep—

"Are you interested?"

"Hard pass."

The tension in her shoulders eased. "Well, you haven't really dated anyone in a while, right? After Gabriella, there was, what? Eva, Emma, Tatiana. You broke up with Tatiana a year ago, Patrick." She fiddled with the dials on the stereo system. It did not matter who he was dating. Of course it didn't. She needed to ask, that was all. As a friend.

He did not reply. She turned, and her breath caught in her throat. He was so close to her. When had that happened? Suede soles were quiet, but seriously, was he part angel?

"I'm doing just fine." His gaze fixed on hers. An intoxicating heat rose deep within her at his proximity. Had she ever noticed before how beautiful his lips were? "Unless you want to talk about yourself, Anita."

Shut it down, shut it down. She had to dance with him. She could not be fantasizing. "We're wasting time gossiping," she finally said. "Let's start with cha-cha."

Chapter Six

The day that had started with a promise of spring warmth had chilled into the threat of an ice storm. Anita belted her dark-blue winter coat against the descending frost and headed out of the studio to her little hatchback. She had set the alarm, hadn't she? It wasn't OCD if there was a potential threat. She could not miss Wednesday night dinner with her parents for anything. If someone wanted to leave her another weird letter, they could stick it through the mail slot.

Singing along to Hozier on the radio, Anita pulled in front of her parents' stately Tudor mansion fifteen minutes later. Her family home was set deep into the Pennsylvania woods, with a circular driveway leading to the dark oak front door. Her mother must have heard the car in the driveway—she had already opened the front door and was leaning against the jamb. Marina's dark-brown curly hair was silhouetted from the warm light within the house, her smile so bright that the starlight illuminated it. Anita stepped straight out of the car and into her mother's arms, the scents of garlic and cinnamon and warm bread wrapping her up like a cozy cable blanket. They moved as one through the front door.

"It smells delicious." Anita unbelted her coat, the warmth of the house in sharp contrast to the outside. Marina hung the coat from one of the elegant iron S hooks in the white-tiled foyer.

"Ah." Her mother waved away the compliment. "Just a little bread and soup."

No place like home. Anita followed her down the short hallway to the kitchen, dominated by a large white marble island and gleaming stainless-steel appliances. Bread and soup to her mom meant avgolemono and olive bread, both of which were Anita's favorites and Marina painstakingly made from scratch.

Her mother's internal Cypriot mainly manifested when she cooked or entertained. Patrick had practically been a second son in high school and college. Marina would stuff him full of grape leaves, loukoumades, kebab, and pasta.

Seriously, she needed to stop thinking about Patrick. If only for the sake of her dreams.

"Where's Dad?" Anita asked, standing at the kitchen island. She had slipped off her shoes at the front door and loved the way the cool, gray cork floor felt under her stockinged toes.

Marina shook her head with a laugh, and she opened the refrigerator for a bottle of wine. "He took a job teaching at Drexel two days a week. The man does not know how to retire."

"But on a Wednesday? That's my dinner day." Anita pursed her lips slightly as her mom filled two glasses with Sancerre. It wasn't totally out of character for him to miss a golden opportunity to harangue her into considering med school again. Like she would.

"I reminded him. He says he will try to make it home by dessert. He never remembers how long the train takes from Center City."

Anita swirled the golden liquid in her wineglass,

then lifted it to her nose and inhaled deeply. Her mother had impeccable taste in wine. Besides, the alcohol might soften the tension in her shoulders. "Mmm, what's for dessert?"

Marina winked, a wicked grin crossing her features. "It's a surprise."

That meant chocolate, the cure for basically any ill. Thank goodness for her mother.

"Come on." Marina picked up her glass. "Dinner's on the table. You must be hungry after working all day."

They sat together in the breakfast nook, surrounded by tall glass windows on all sides that let in the view of the verdant and elegantly landscaped backyard. There in the corner was the apple tree that did not grow apples but had branches long and lean. Anita used to recline in those branches to read. And there were the rosebushes Patrick and their ballroom club friends Tina and Louise had once chopped too eagerly, deadheading the robust blooms and causing Marina to blanch like a ghost.

"How's work?" Marina asked.

Anita sipped at her warm, citrusy soup. Heaven. Weird letters and uncomfortable emotions about her best friend were easier to shove down deep when well-fed. "It's good. Busy. There's a Saturday dance I have to coordinate next weekend. Toni's been at me to add more Zumba and athletic classes, and Ricardo is pretty much booked solid."

Marina broke off a piece of olive bread. "Isn't the Keystone coming up soon? You must be disappointed, since that awful man left you high and dry." Her mother never could quite bring herself to say Mikhail's name. Anita suspected it stemmed from the time he declined to eat her homemade souvlaki because she could not guarantee it was gluten-free.

She should definitely have known.

"It isn't Mikhail's fault, Mom. He found another partner. And we wanted different things, anyway." She pushed her spoon around the bowl of soup.

"Still." Marina huffed and refilled her daughter's glass. "You love the Keystone. I'm sure some of your students are going. At least you can do that."

Anita swallowed, the soup burning the back of her throat slightly. Of course, her mother would have asked. If only her dad had been there to demean her life choices. "Well, actually, Mom, I—I found a partner for the Keystone."

Marina's spoon clattered in her soup bowl, and she nearly pushed her wineglass into the loaf of bread. "You did?! That's wonderful! Who is it? Tell me all about it."

"Um, well, it's—it's Patrick." Anita could not meet her mother's eyes. How had Anita Goodman come to need such pity from her best friend? She had worked so hard, had been nationally ranked in high school and college. "He volunteered, you know. I think we are going to do Latin. I mean, his Standard is excellent, but he has more of a feel for the Latin choreo, and—"

Her mom's warm hand covered her own, and Anita finally lifted her eyes. To her surprise, Marina's face was lit by an enormous smile, and tears glistened in her almond-shaped eyes. Her legendary smile creased her entire face from lips to forehead to pixie ears.

"This is the best news I have heard in a very long time, my Anita." Marina slapped the table and raised her eyes to Heaven. "Thank goodness! Finally. You have a partner you like, who likes you. This is excellent news!"

Anita whipped her hand away from her mom and hid it on her lap. "Wait, what? I've always liked my partners, Mom."

Marina waved a hand and rolled her eyes. "Oh, please, Anita. I am your mother. I know."

"Mikhail and I were practically living together."

"He was using you, because you are better dancer than he." When Marina was on a roll, her accent deepened. "Don't deny, you never really liked him. I do not know why, but you never think you deserve someone good, and you use these other men to deny the fact that Patrick is in love with you."

Anita sat dumbstruck.

"Don't look at me like that, love." Marina sipped her wine. "I think you think you know it, too. Which is why you never agree to dance with Patrick before. You are scared. But love, love like that, it is the only thing worth having in this world. But you have to take risks for things that are worthwhile. Love should not be convenient."

Anita's mouth had gone completely dry. Where was the bottle of Sancerre? She could not deal with the deluge of maternal wisdom with an empty glass. Besides, she was wrong. One hundred percent wrong.

Her parents had met when he was a study-abroad exchange student at Cambridge, and they "were like struck by thunder," according to Marina. She followed him back to the United States, married him, and finished her own education in his hometown of Philadelphia. She had gotten a job as a second-grade teacher to support him through medical school and residency.

Not everyone had such a fairytale romance. Anita had certainly never cracked the code.

"Mom, no. Patrick is my friend. Keystone is in just three weeks. It's insane. He is insane, for agreeing to do this. It has absolutely nothing to do with love." She had at least liked her other partners. Hadn't she? Tyler had a slight mirror obsession, and Giorgio had refused to wear deodorant, but those were not really deal breakers. Particularly if someone did not have time to date outside their profession.

Marina rolled her eyes dramatically. Anita had never been to Cyprus, but her mother certainly did an excellent caricature of herself. "My darling Anita, you are so smart, but you have always refused to see what is right in front of you. Any way you wish to see it, this is a good thing. You will go to Keystone, finally realize you are perfect for each other, and then finally your father and I will have our grandbabies." She clapped her hands together once and did a small *opa* dance in her seat.

Anita sighed. At least soon there would be chocolate. There was no use arguing with her mother when she got on a rant like this. It only made things worse.

****

Anita put the plastic container of pie and the plastic-wrapped piece of olive bread on the passenger seat in her dark-green hatchback. Her mother's leftovers were the world's greatest invention.

"Are you sure you don't want to take anything else?" Marina had put on a thick dark cable sweater to walk her daughter to her car. Anita tucked her chin into the collar of her coat. The temperature seemed to have dropped twenty degrees just in the few hours she had been at her parents' house.

"No, I'm fine." Anita kissed her mom's cheek. "Thank you for dinner. I'll see you next week." She needed at least a week, if not another decade, to put the idea of Patrick being in love with her out of her head.

Anita turned on the car and rolled back down the circular driveway to the street. It was nearly pitch-black, the moon barely a sliver and the stars hidden by thick clouds that had appeared with barely any warning. Most of the time she enjoyed being farther away from the city's bright lights, but on a night like tonight, she wished for a little more illumination. Anita shivered despite her woolen coat and the car's seat heater. She never quite understood what was meant by a devil moon, but this was certainly a contender.

She turned left out of the driveway and noted distant headlights moving quickly behind her in the rearview mirror. Kids joyriding. Every year, sadly enough, there were terrible accidents on the roads surrounding Lewis. They tended toward the dark and serpentine, and it was particularly easy to misjudge turns when the weather was unfavorable. Or when people had been drinking.

Anita yawned and directed her car into the proper lane. She needed a better night's sleep. She would absolutely not dream of Patrick tonight.

Curses, why had she even put that thought in her own head?

Lights flashed in her rearview mirror. The car again. Why were they driving so fast? It was aggressive, too fast for the sharp curves and poor visibility.

Anita checked the speedometer. She was going eight miles over the speed limit. "Go around me!"

They did not. The car kept accelerating closer to her, then braking and dropping back. The cycle repeated. Nearing her, almost close enough to tap her rear bumper, then backing off, the glare from their headlights receding.

Assholes. She did not need to deal with this. She put on her right blinker and pulled into the shoulder. Let them pass her. If they were in such a rush, they could flip on Dead Man's Curve in a quarter mile.

The car roared past her, its engine growling like an angry hippopotamus.

Good riddance.

But then the car stopped about fifteen feet in front of her, its brake lights bright-red eyes.

Anita slammed on her own brakes, pushing with both feet. Her little hatchback squealed in protest. Shit, she could not afford new tires. What kind of asshole—

Her voice caught in her throat.

The car's rear lights stared at her through her windshield like a goblin in a Halloween movie.

Shit. Anita hated horror movies.

If only she knew more about cars. It was big, like an SUV? It was impossible to determine the color in the dark night, even in the gleam from her own headlights.

If only she could find her phone. She scrabbled on the passenger seat for it, but her hands stilled. The red-and-white rear indicator lights were getting brighter.

Her breath in tight pants, her gaze glued to the rear bumper of the SUV.

What the fuck?

In the middle of the deserted road, the SUV backed up until its rear bumper was level with her front bumper.

Of all the times to be stranded by herself.

Her phone. There it was. She grabbed it off the seat, never so grateful for its giant pop socket with waltzers in silhouette as she was now. Where was the emergency call button?

There. There. She found it.

She inhaled, her muscles contracting, her breath shaky, but she could do this. She poised one finger over the tiny green phone icon. Just one more inch backward, and Anita would call. One more inch. "Come on, dickhead," she whispered.

Then, almost as suddenly as it had stopped, the SUV's engine roared, and the tires squealed on the pavement before rocketing down the road at what was clearly an unsafe pace.

Anita dropped the phone onto the passenger seat beside her plastic storage container and put her head between her legs.

What the hell had that been?

Chapter Seven

Nina Rabinova waltzed literally into the studio, accompanied by a gush of frosty air and a gigantic white fur stole. "*Zdrasvoote*, my darlings," she said in her thick Russian accent. "It is like Siberia today! The only thing to warm ourselves is vodka and dancing." She held up a large bottle of high-end Russian vodka, a festive and wicked grin on her face.

Patrick turned Anita out of the figure they had been practicing. Thank goodness for Nina. Anita needed a break almost more than she needed another cup of coffee. Or maybe a glass of wine. Anything to erase the nightmares of that SUV stalking her.

Nina draped herself dramatically along one of the seats. For the first time all day, Anita smiled. Nina was of an indescribable age between forty and seventy, with jet-black dyed hair pulled into a severe topknot, and a complete lack of wrinkles making her look like a creepy china doll. She accentuated this appearance by drawing on thick black eyebrows and painting her lips crimson. She always dressed for her lessons as if she was about to teach ballet in a long black ruffled skirt, thick rhinestone bangles, and a black leotard, usually underneath some riotously colorful overcoat. Today was no exception, the white fur stole notwithstanding. The coat had so many splashes of color it was practically a piece of modern art.

"I didn't know they still made those." Patrick nodded at the stole and coat. He had both hands on his hips in a clear posture of he-who-is-exhausted. Sweat dripped beneath the collar of his exercise shirt and beaded around the muscles in his chest. *Damn*. Anita's mouth went dry.

Nina sashayed over to him and drew one crimson-red fingernail down his bemused cheek. "Oh, my darling Patrick, of course they do. They are the only thing to keep a lady warm on a cold December night." She winked one heavily-mascaraed eyelash at him. How did she manage not to glue her eyes shut? "Well, not the only thing…"

Patrick smiled and deftly moved out of range. Spry fellow. "Good to see you, too, Nina."

"Ricardo isn't here yet," Anita told Nina. She grabbed a towel and dabbed sweat from her forehead.

Nina scrunched up her face in mock distress, not removing her gaze from Patrick. "Men are never on time. Patrick, what are you doing here? You are back from New York? I thought you didn't teach anymore." She pursed her lips at him. "You just do not want to teach me?"

Oh my goodness. If Anita only had a camera to capture Patrick's facial expression. He definitely excelled at keeping it neutral, even when someone was clearly fawning over him with abandon. He had certainly had a lot of practice. Anita went to the stereo and turned on Yerba Buena.

"Oh, Nina." He leaned forward to kiss her hand while catching Anita's eye with a crooked smile. "It is too much of an honor to dance with you."

The older woman seemed to melt under his

attention. Her grin started at her feet and spread upward like a flame, illuminating her features. Anita's discomfort melted at his kindness. Definitely not all men.

"You are such a gentleman," Nina simpered. "Please, Ricardo, he wait. You dance with me." She held her arms open wide to Patrick, and he moved forward to hold her in dance position, ever the professional.

This was going to be fun to watch. Last time Nina had danced with Patrick, she had attempted unsuccessfully to get him to reenact the famous "Dirty Dancing" lift. If only Anita had popcorn.

Instead, she turned the music to a foxtrot and leaned against the check-in desk to watch the show.

Patrick gently moved Nina around the floor, continuously trying to correct her dance posture by trying to reposition her head away from his shoulder. "Frame!" Anita called out wickedly. A smile tilted the corner of her mouth at Patrick's rude gesture behind Nina's back.

The doorbell rang as another gust of cold air fled into the studio. Ricardo Vega shook the chill out of his thick gray-white mane. He watched the couple for a moment before turning to Anita.

"I didn't know he was back," he said to Anita. She nodded gleefully. Poor sweet Patrick. He could be such a good sport.

"Just for Keystone." Ricardo was eyeing her in an odd manner. Anita straightened and affected her business owner stature. "Did you send in your entries yet?"

Ricardo nodded, his eyes darkening. He always had

at least thirty entries, and there was nothing he hated more than paperwork, almost more than Mikhail had hated it. "Thanks for entertaining Nina. I got caught behind a bus."

"No problem. She's harmless."

Ricardo arched his dark-gray eyes at her. "No one is harmless, Anita. Be careful."

There went her good mood. The image of the SUV's rear lights flashed across her mind, the twin red flares burning like cigarette butts. Ricardo wouldn't know what had happened, would he? She scoffed. Of all the people she knew, Ricardo was the least likely suspect. He would never have wasted his time scaring women in hatchbacks on the winding country roads outside Lewis. He was too busy seducing cougars in wine bars.

"Ah, Ricardo!" Nina clasped her hands together causing her bangles to chime. Anita had missed the end of the dance with Patrick. At least he looked a bit worse for wear. "You have not been missed. Let me just dance with Patrick, and I will conquer Blackpool!"

"*Spasibo*, Nina." Patrick bowed slightly, as any partner would do to close the dance.

Anita could have predicted Nina would not take it as routine.

"He even speaks Russian!" Nina practically fainted with delight. Ricardo rolled his eyes, then pulled Nina back onto the floor to start their lesson.

Anita's mind churned. What did Ricardo mean? No one would target her, would they? She hadn't done anything.

She also clearly had not noticed Patrick standing beside her, but her insides were suddenly on high alert.

"Hey." Patrick nudged her. "Want to run out for a coffee while they practice?"

She glanced at him, smelling of his intoxicating mix of pine and mint and cinnamon. It both soothed and exacerbated her wrought nerves. "Definitely."

****

They walked the two blocks from the studio to Amore. Anita closed the lapels of her coat against the chill in the air.

"Here." Patrick stopped in the middle of the sidewalk, taking off his scarf and tying it around her neck casually. His fingers thrummed against the bare, tender skin. "Can't have you freezing, now, can we?" His touch lingered for just a beat too long on the ends of the scarf, holding her gaze with his own.

"We should hurry back." Even to her own ears, the words sounded hollow, forced. For the briefest of moments, she wondered why he couldn't leave his hands there forever, close to her face, close to her. Why didn't she deserve this? Because this was Patrick, he of the eternal four-leaf clover. Right. And she was just…just Anita. Anita, who couldn't hack medical school. Anita, who never quite made world champion. Patrick deserved more. She swallowed the despair in an audible gulp. "Can't miss a moment of practice."

Patrick released his hold on the ends of the scarf. Anita thought she might fall over onto the side of the street. "Absolutely right. Time is ticking. Though I think we have a decent jive and paso. Everything else is gravy." He smiled broadly at her, that smile that was so perfectly Patrick. There was something wonderfully nostalgic and magnetic about a person who reminded you of who you used to be and accepted unconditionally who you were now.

Anita pulled herself together and followed him into the coffee shop. Being more than dance partners had never worked out for her. She could not make the same mistakes. She could not lose Patrick as a friend. She needed to nip this weird attraction she was feeling right in the bud. It was almost the weekend.

Chapter Eight

Weekends at Lewis Dancesport Academy were hectic, to say the least, and lasted from Thursday night until Sunday afternoon, particularly in the weeks leading up to a competition. The studio buzzed with anticipation, the constant hum of music, the tapping and gliding of footsteps.

Anita loved it. Usually.

Less so when she had a partner who featured very prominently in some seriously hot and heavy dreams with two weeks before Keystone. What on earth had possessed her to host a master class on Saturday night?

For most of the day on Saturday, she hoped Hanna and Markus would cancel. Maybe there was a collapse of the Lincoln Tunnel or something. And also no, because that would be an epic tragedy and may have been a movie Patrick had forced her to watch in high school.

"I forgot how busy things get around here on the weekends." Patrick helped her sweep the floor after the last student on Saturday afternoon. Anita tightened her ponytail, fixing it more firmly to the nape of her neck. She had an hour before the professionals were due to arrive, and still she needed to run out to pick up the catering for dinner and set up a drinks table. Nonalcoholic, of course, during the class, then wine and beer for afterward.

She could definitely use a glass now.

"But it brings in good business," Anita replied, mentally checking things off her list. "I have to stay relevant somehow."

"There is always improving your social media presence. You could upload dance tutorials, photos, create your own hashtags." Patrick arched an eyebrow at her. "Not to harp, but I was looking at your metrics and—"

"Yeah, yeah, yeah. Everything you just said is literal gibberish." Anita busied herself with straightening the corners of the silver-and-gold tablecloth.

"Well, let me help." He rubbed his hands together eagerly. "I have time. We've worked out most of our dance routines, except for the rumba."

The rumba. Dance of love. Anita strangled down the wave of lust that tore through her at the thought. She would postpone that choreo as long as possible. "Don't you have to write? Deadlines and such?" She flailed her hand in the air with a vague demonstration of "such."

He shrugged. "I finished some this morning after we practiced, and I'll have time tomorrow."

"Oh, I have a lesson scheduled with Nigel in Center City tomorrow night." She pulled plastic wineglasses out of her decorations box and set them neatly on the drinks table. "Can you come with me? It will be good to get his opinion."

"Absolutely." Patrick flattened the tablecloth over the refreshment table. "Now seriously, what else do you need done tonight? I'm completely at your disposal."

Help? He couldn't mean it. Anita smiled warmly,

feeling the tension even in her eyebrows lessen just the slightest fraction. She hadn't had actual, meaningful help in ages. Mikhail had often told her party planning was "not my forte."

Tool.

"Do you mind running out to pick up the catering? I have a few more things to set up here before Hanna and Markus arrive."

"No problem." He picked up his phone and car keys and headed quickly out the door.

Anita watched him go, slightly ashamed at how thrilled she was that he was helping.

Of course, she could have asked Ricardo or Toni, but they were so often busy with other things, particularly on the weekends. Her mother was supportive, but on weekends, she and Dr. Goodman were usually out on one of their circumscribed activities.

Besides, it was better to do a thing yourself to make sure it was done properly.

Once in a while, though, help was wonderful. It almost made her feel like she was on vacation. Not that she had taken one of those in eons.

Anita finished setting up the refreshment table and turned to get a few more chairs and another flat of bottled water from the storage closet.

Thump bump skreeeeeek.

She turned sharply. The sound at the door. How? It was practically the middle of the day. Okay, more early evening, but still far from the witching hour. Her hands balled into fists, she quickly approached the door and flung it open.

Nothing. No one was there, just a few pedestrians

on the other side of the street window shopping in the late afternoon on Main Street.

Anita rolled her eyes. Workaholism was driving her insane. Either that or she needed to call an exterminator. Ew.

Knock knock.

This time, though, it was coming from the small practice room on the other side of the check-in desk. They did not use it often, mostly for overflow or for private lessons while there was a group class in the main studio. Anita had been wondering if she should try to rent it out for yoga.

No one would be in there.

Okay, she had to check it out. It was her responsibility, her duty.

Please don't be rats please don't be rats please don't—

Anita gasped.

STAY AWAY

Someone had scrawled the words in what looked like dark-red lipstick across the mirror in large, jagged strokes. It was so angry, so pointless.

Tears rose to her eyes. *Don't cry, don't cry, don't cry.*

But her body did not obey.

"Stay away from what?"

There was no answer in the silent studio, just the occasional beep and hum of a passing car out on the street, and the rush of March wind rattling the windowpanes.

Anita wrapped her arms around her knees and sobbed.

****

Patrick returned fifteen minutes later with the catering only to find Anita, blanched white, scrubbing furiously at the mirror in the practice room. "Anita?"

She spun around and brandished the glass-cleaning bottle at him. She must have recognized him, though, because her bravado almost instantly deflated, and she crumpled onto the floor.

He rushed toward her.

"What the fuck happened?" He had never seen her like this. Never. Never once had the goddess fallen apart in front of him. *Please don't let her be sick.* Then, which was almost worse and made him want to vomit and scream and hurl blunt objects—*please don't let it be me*. Don't let her rethink this partnership. "Are you okay?"

"Yeah, I'm fine, I just…" Her sides heaved. He knelt beside her, a hand on her shoulder. If only he could suck the pain away. "I'm sorry, someone wrote 'stay away' all over this mirror, and I freaked out. It's stupid, I'm sorry." She sniffed, not looking at him.

"Don't be sorry." He glanced at the mirror. She had almost finished cleaning it. He could see a few streaks of red, but the words had been erased. "That sounds horrifying. Who would have done that? Did they break into the studio?"

She shrugged, the gesture so helpless that it made him want…he didn't know. Something. A white horse, maybe. Or a large cup of coffee. "Hey, Anita," he said softly. She looked up at him, her eyes brimming and red-rimmed. How could he resist? He stroked her cheek with his thumb. "It's all right. I'm here now." Her skin was so soft, so warm, wet from her tears but brimming with life underneath it.

He needed to stop, to shove it back down like he always did. This was not the time, no matter how badly he wanted her. He always wanted her, *had* always wanted her.

Anita sniffed, nodding. "Thank you. Really." She met his eyes briefly and tried to smile. "I feel like I'm being silly. Maybe this wasn't even meant for me."

"Well, Ricardo is a bit of a cad." Patrick tried to smile. Of course, it had been for her. But why? The worst thing she had ever done was date assholes. That did not mean she deserved to be threatened.

No one deserved that.

A niggling memory of his recent social media messages stalled him, but Anita's laugh, an unintended bark that rang in his ears like chiming Christmas bells, shook it away.

He needed to focus on her. Not that *that* was difficult. "Or maybe they meant stay away from the cheap liquor? Come on, I'll get the studio ready for the master class. Why don't you take some time for yourself?"

Anita paused. "You don't have to do that, Patrick. This is my studio—it's my responsibility. You don't work here anymore." The soft way she said the last phrase broke his heart a little.

"I know." He couldn't tell her how he regretted leaving almost every single moment. He took a deep breath and held her hand in his. It was so warm. Every time he touched her, it felt new and exhilarating. Which was awful at this exact moment because she was so upset, but still. She needed him. He could do this. "I'm still your friend. And I'm here. Let me help."

"Okay," she agreed. Several quiet moments passed.

If only she would just meet his gaze. "I'll just run up and take a quick shower. Hanna and Markus will be here in about half an hour."

"Perfect," he replied. He swallowed down the unrequited love. "Don't worry. Everything is going to be all right."

****

Anita walked down from her apartment, hair freshly washed and blown dry, in a backless black dress with long sleeves and a skirt that hit just below her knees. She hopped down the staircase, pulling on her four-inch black stilettos.

At the bottom of the stairwell, Patrick leaned against the banister, gaze on the studio floor, where Hanna and Markus were preparing for the master class. Warmth flooded through her. He had waited. Just like prom, only she had stupidly never gone to prom with him.

He turned toward her, and his eyes widened. Was it appreciation? A flush rose to her cheeks. God, she was acting like a damn teenager. *Get a grip.* Just because he was so kind and thoughtful and helpful when she actually needed it.

"You look incredible," he breathed.

Oh. She blushed, unable to stem the rise of color. His blue eyes sparkled, twin sapphires guiding her home. "I haven't put my hair up yet."

"Don't." He reached out a hand and lightly touched the end of her locks, blown into soft waves. It really was criminal how handsome he was. "You're perfect."

Chapter Nine

Patrick woke up early the next morning, groaning. He had to meet Anita at seven at the studio to practice before she had to leave for church with her parents. He wanted nothing more than to go back to sleep. He wouldn't say no to a Jacuzzi or a massage, either. No use worrying about things that could not be.

What was actually happening was that someone was trolling him with fake social media accounts. Like he did not have enough to do.

At first it had just been the one cryptic message, *MISSING YOU*, but now had devolved into more-disturbing missives. Emojis like a peach and a fire strung together with the kissing face. One had just been all hearts and signed with the emoji with Xes for eyes. At times it seemed like someone unfamiliar with how to creep people out on the Internct and, at other times, was directly on point. The latest message last night had just been a photo of a mouth with a painted-red finger poised over it, almost as if he/she—who was he to judge—was either shushing him or about to suck on the finger. Neither was welcome.

Then there were the comments on his blog posts.

OMG Patrick, you are soooooooo funny lol We need to meet IRL

You were there, too????? I thought you would see me

You are so hot I think about you all the—

Maybe if the grammar were better, he would be less freaked out by it all. Or maybe more freaked out.

He had deleted every single message and comment and blocked the accounts, but they kept coming. And coming. Not that he was not used to weird internet traffic, but this was fairly classic cyberstalking.

Which was all he needed while trying to prepare for his first professional competition in over a year, with barely three weeks of practice.

Practice. The studio. Anita sobbing last night and the smell of glass cleaner permeating the air. It couldn't be related, right? The shit he was dealing with seemed completely, totally unrelated to her drama.

And yet.

Damn it, he had an endorsement deal with a designer menswear company pending, and he could not get bogged down in internet trolls.

Maybe he had gone certifiably insane. He yawned and stretched again, then headed for the shower. Busy, busy, busy.

****

"Nigel!" Patrick exclaimed, opening his arms wide. The older man had not aged at all since Patrick had last seen him over a year ago. He stood about half a foot shorter than Patrick, with bleached blonde spiked hair, thick black eyebrows, and a small diamond stud in one ear. Despite the fact that he had definitely entered his sixth decade, Nigel Walker was still fit and trim and wearing his signature white button-down shirt and black dance trousers.

"Patrick!" Nigel greeted him warmly, returning the embrace.

"You two are adorable," Anita commented, standing at the edge of the dance floor. "Like Lucy and Ethel."

"You should have warned me, Anita." Nigel kissed her on both cheeks. He hadn't tamed his thick Leeds accent in over thirty years of living in the United States. Patrick had a feeling the choice was deliberate. "I didn't know you had finally found a partner."

"It was a last-minute decision." Anita sat down in one of the folding chairs and changed into her practice shoes. "Patrick's doing me a favor."

"You're dancing at Keystone?" Nigel sipped at his ever-present liter-sized coffee cup.

Patrick sat beside Anita and changed into his own shoes. "Anita hasn't missed it in almost twelve years. I didn't think she should have to miss it just because Mikhail is an ass."

"Hey!" Anita protested, standing up, looking unimaginably regal in her asymmetric tunic over her black tights. Patrick guessed she had recovered from the shock of last night. Then he realized he had tied the laces of his dance shoes together and bent to untangle them before she noticed. "Just because it didn't work out between us, it's not particularly anyone's fault. Mikhail wasn't an ass."

Nigel caught Patrick's eye, and the two grinned at each other. "Sure, love." Nigel turned to the stereo. "Whatever you want to tell yourself."

****

Nigel had them move through the routines they had already choreographed. He upgraded a few of the moves and had them smooth out some of the transitions. "Not bad," he finally said. "What about rumba?"

After finishing their paso doble, Patrick was panting heavily and went to grab his towel to dry his hands and forehead. Did they really need two chassé capes and the leap? He needed to up his cardio over the next couple of weeks.

"Well? Rumba?" Nigel repeated, looking between the two of them. "I haven't got all night."

Patrick glanced over, but Anita was studiously looking anywhere but at him.

"We—we haven't done it yet," Anita replied.

Patrick wondered if Nigel's eyes were going to pop straight out of his face. "You have less than two weeks until Keystone, and you don't have a routine? For the rumba? Are you out of your minds?"

"We've been a little busy." Anita scuffed at an unseen mark on the floor with the toe of her shoe.

Patrick wisely kept quiet. Since that first waltz, she had avoided being so close to him unless absolutely necessary. The other dances could be done more in shadow position or generally have less intimate contact. But the rumba...the rumba, in certain circumstances, could be like sex on the dance floor.

From his position in the unrequited Friend Zone, Patrick tried not to read a lot into Anita's reluctance to stage the rumba. Nigel, though, clearly had no such compunctions.

"That's no excuse, Anita. Patrick, get out here. We solve this now." He scoffed. "Honestly, you call yourselves professionals."

Patrick moved back onto the dance floor and took his stance by Anita.

"Hey, not my fault," Patrick whispered to a stone-faced Anita.

She looked everywhere but at him. "Hey." Patrick nudged her. "Is there something in my teeth?" He grinned broadly at her, knowing he had stuck a piece of gum between his incisors. Caught unawares, she finally smiled and seemed to relax.

"Right. Let's start together. Patrick, invite her to dance by reaching for her face. Anita, hesitate, but then reach around his back. Swivel, swivel, swivel, long leg through his, yada yada. Go!"

Patrick saw Anita stiffen, but the music was starting. There wasn't time. "What do you think he means by the yada yada?" Patrick whispered to her. Her eyes flicked to his. He heard the classic rumba beat, 2-3-4-and-1, and reached out for her. "No, seriously. Does he mean this?"

Patrick scooped her off the floor and into a lift where he wrapped her around his back and then quickly rotated her into a cartwheel, all while anchoring her hips with his hands. Anita burst out laughing when he set her on the floor.

Nigel turned off the music. "Cute," he said dryly. "You don't have time for cute. Back to positions!"

****

Anita tried to involve herself in the precision of the movements instead of her proximity to Patrick, but her body was not cooperating. It didn't help that Nigel had chosen Enrique Iglesias. Still, though, Patrick was being…so *Patrick,* Anita couldn't help but ease into the game of the rumba. The push and pull, the enjoyable seduction, the way he seemed to know exactly where she would be, ready to catch her or spin her.

If only sex could be like dancing.

Before she could realize it, the hour was over. The music abruptly stopped, and Anita became suddenly, desperately aware of her hands on Patrick's temples, and his hand encircling her thigh, which was wrapped around his waist. *Shit.* She disentangled herself from him, ignoring the hum in her skin where he had touched her. He needed to keep those amazing, soft, sensuous hands to himself. Even if they did arouse a lot of weird and unusual feelings within her.

Nigel clapped his hands briskly. "There. You have a rumba, easy peasy lemon squeezy." He rolled his eyes. "Took you both long enough. See you next week. We'll spit and polish. Off you go."

"Uh," Patrick said sheepishly. "All right if I use the bathroom really quickly?"

"Course, mate." Nigel sipped again from his bottomless cup of coffee. He moved closer to Anita, who was trying to calm her breathing and change her shoes. Neither task was going well. "This is a good idea," he said softly to her.

"What? He's just doing me a favor." She drank from her water bottle. "He's retired, remember?"

"Looks very unretired to me."

"Nigel, there's no way we can win. We've been practicing less than a week."

Nigel looked at her discerningly. She had never quite gotten used to that look from him, despite having known him since she was twelve. She was never sure if it was belief in her talent, or disappointment that she had not fulfilled his expectations. "You're selling you both short, love. He's good for you. I don't know why you didn't do this sooner."

Anita's hackles rose. "It's not like I was wasting

my time. I made top ten without Patrick. I competed all over the globe. Without Patrick. Mikhail and I were invited to Blackpool twice."

"Yeah, but you could have won at Blackpool with Patrick." Nigel caught her eye. "Don't look at me like that, love. You know I'm right."

Patrick rushed back across the floor toward them. "Sorry, did I miss anything?"

****

Anita folded her legs into the passenger seat of Patrick's semi-ancient sedan, zipping her white fleece jacket closed.

"I'm starving." Patrick turned the key in the ignition. "Do you mind if we grab something to eat here before we drive back?"

"Oh, I'm not really hungry."

He glanced at her in mock horror. "We just burned practically four thousand calories. Are you really not hungry?"

In defiance of her earlier assertion, her stomach rumbled. She grinned despite herself. "I don't know. Maybe a little?"

He tapped the wheel happily. Some men never lost their boyish enthusiasm. "Perfect! I never get the chance to show you around down here. Cheesesteaks?"

Anita rolled her eyes. "Absolutely not."

"You are a born and bred Philly girl, and you will not say yes to a Sunday night cheesesteak? Next thing you'll tell me is that you're a Patriots fan, and then we can't be friends anymore."

She held up a hand. "Do not go there. I have a mean right hook."

He held up his own hands in a gesture of surrender.

"I'm sure you do. But come on, there's this great place down in Fishtown."

Anita felt herself wavering as the heat in Patrick's ten-year-old car finally kicked on, spraying warmth from the vents. "I don't know. Do they have chicken cheesesteaks?"

He smiled. "I'm going to pretend you didn't say that."

****

Twenty minutes later, Anita snorted with laughter at an outdoor picnic table strewn with grease-stained napkins and checkerboard deli paper.

"That absolutely did not happen." She grinned as Patrick licked cheese spread off his fingers. "Daniela, she of the 'oh' "—here, Anita pursed her lips mock-seductively and affected a fairly accurate Brazilian accent—" 'in Brasil we would *never* do that.' "

"Yup." Patrick grinned. "Daniela absolutely did. Completely flaunted over this guy at the bar for at least half an hour—in front of me, of course—before finally realizing it was not, in fact, Johnny Depp."

Anita snorted again before reaching for her bottled water and one of Patrick's potato chips. "Can't say I miss her."

"Yeah, me neither." He wiped his hands on a napkin. *Damn, those hands.* When they danced together, the way his hands felt on her body…

Anita flushed, but Patrick did not seem to be paying attention to her. Thank goodness. He had a wistful, sort of lost expression. Something sad and broken in those blue eyes.

"I'm really sorry, Patrick." Anita moved her hand near his, but not quite touching. "First Daniela, then

Tatiana, and Nikita…"

"Nikita?" He scrunched up his face in confusion.

"Yeah." Anita squirmed in her seat and took her hand back from where it had been on the table. "I still can't believe that happened at the Jersey Classic. She was a nice woman." Anita waited, but no response. She wasn't wrong, was she? She had heard enough gossip. "It was awful how she was killed."

"Yeah. I mean, I only met her once or twice, but she seemed like a nice lady."

Anita's brain short circuited, and she almost dropped her iced tea all over her shirt. "Wait, what do you mean, you only met her once or twice?"

"Umm, there isn't that much mystery in that statement, Anita." Patrick took a large bite of his cheesesteak.

"But weren't you two, like, having an affair?"

He almost spat out his food. Patrick's eyes widened, and his brow furrowed. "Are you joking? Of course not. Who told you that?"

Anita held her water against her cheeks to try to hide the blush. "I don't know. It was just, like, a rumor that was going around. So-and-so saw you together, thought you looked—cozy, I guess."

Patrick sighed. "I interviewed her, about a week before she died. The *Star Trib* wanted a piece on the competition. We met for drinks in Princeton the night before so she could answer some follow up questions. That's really it. I mean, yeah, she called me a few times afterward, but nothing happened. I keep things professional."

Anita frowned. She never paid attention to the ballroom gossip. Why had she listened to the shit about

Patrick? "I'm sorry, I wasn't trying to offend you."

"You didn't," he replied curtly. "It's just been a long week." He shivered. "It's freezing out here. Maybe we should get back home."

Anita nodded and bit her lip as she helped clear the plates. She had messed that up right and proper.

****

They drove home in silence, ostensibly listening to an old Snow Patrol CD on Patrick's ancient sound system. Anita kept her eyes out the window, watching the shadowy trees and outlines of homes pass.

"Are you okay?" Patrick finally asked.

Just rethinking everything she thought she knew about her friend. "Of course," Anita replied instead. Maybe if she counted mile markers she would be less inclined to say something stupid.

Beside her, she heard his slow inhale and exhale before he continued. Great, now he was going to ream her out and tell her all the reasons he no longer wanted to dance with her.

But he wasn't Mikhail. She chanced a glance at him, his familiar profile outlined in the headlights of passing cars. How could she know someone for so long and not really know them?

"Are you mad I didn't tell you I had met Nikita?"

Anita barked a laugh. "Seriously? I thought you were mad that I had listened to the gossip."

"Everyone gossips, Anita. I have to admit, I was a little surprised you believed it." He glanced at her, the crooked smile casting a bright flashing light on his super sexy dimple. Anita's breath caught in her throat, and she bit her bottom lip. She had a sudden, almost uncontrollable urge to lean over and lick that dimple.

When they were sixteen, he had let her paint it peacock blue before a comp.

Which was clearly evidence that lack of sleep and being stalked with weird messages had driven her batshit crazy. She sat on her hands. She could do impulse control.

Patrick did not seem to notice. "At least it didn't feel like you were accusing me of murder," he teased.

Anita licked her lips and stared out the window. "Patrick, I don't think I've ever met anyone less capable of murder than you."

"Well, that's the nicest compliment I think I've ever had."

He pulled the car in front of the studio and turned his dark-blue eyes to hers. It really was unfair. They were so warm, so inviting. It did not seem right how Patrick could seemingly hug someone just by looking at them. "Should I walk you inside?"

Yes. "No, I'm all right." But she could not move from the seat, her hand frozen on the handle of the door. She had a full menagerie caught in her chest, threatening to burst out at any moment.

He placed one hand on her shoulder, an old, friendly sort of gesture, but a pulse of electricity frizzled down her back. Her eyes were drawn to that sexy little dimple, always painted peacock blue in her mind.

Keeping her shit together was exhausting.

Before she could give herself time to rethink it, she leaned over and pressed her lips right over the dimple at the corner of his mouth. The little divot tasted like cheesesteaks and potato chips and salt and a thousand other warm and sexily comforting things that were one thousand percent going to torture her all night long.

Damn it. Cover, Anita. Cover.

Patrick's wonderful face was too close to her own. Was he angry? He must be angry.

He didn't look like it, though. His dark-blue eyes had clouded over, and his gaze was fixed on hers. If looks were fire, she would need a specialized burn unit.

Was he going to kiss her?

Red lights flashed warning in her brain even as her heart warmed.

She had to shut this down. But she wanted it so badly. The knot of repression that she had wound so tightly simply begged to be ripped open, laid bare.

Patrick was not Mikhail. Patrick was more than Mikhail, more than Giorgio, more than Tyler. He was the best man she had ever known.

She did not deserve him.

But damn it, he was now very, very close to her, his breath hot against her skin.

"Thank you." She might have croaked like a frog, but the words popped some balloon of tension in the air. She pulled back, unable to meet his gaze. His breath, so warm and inviting with the promise of a thousand mornings of French toast and crossword puzzles under quilted blankets, caught in his throat, and he made some sort of strangled sound. He was not for her. "Um. Bye."

With that witty rejoinder, she pushed open the car door and cursed herself in eight languages as she unlocked the studio, relocked it behind her, walked up the twenty-two steps to her apartment, and then she crashed face-first into her brightly colored comforter.

Chapter Ten

Monday passed in an odd blur of activity. Early Tuesday morning, Anita's phone exploded on her nightstand with text messages. Anita blearily looked through them, groaning. Ever since she had kissed Patrick's dimple, well, fine, ever since he had come back from New York, she had not been able to get her eight hours. She was frustrated, exhausted, and had bags under her eyes the size of the Keystone Star Ball trophy. It did not bode well for competition.

Neither did the fact that Toni kept missing Zumba classes. Anita checked through her texts. The excuse this morning was that she said that she had missed the last train out of Philadelphia and wouldn't be back in Lewis before class. Super. Add that to the list of the things she had to do today.

Yoga would even her out. That's what it was for, right? She closed her eyes in namaste, focusing on her breathing, but Patrick kept intruding on her thoughts. Odd things, like his sweat that smelled of cinnamon and mint, the feeling of his strong and steady hands when they danced, the feel of his skin against her lips, the way his mouth curved ever so slightly that just made her want…

Anita opened her eyes. Namaste be damned. Now he had ruined her morning routine.

Anita sighed and finger-combed her long blonde

hair. She had once read a book about a stalker who had switched her target's shampoo for hair remover.

Great. It was surely a short step from breaking into her studio to scrawl cryptic messages to hair remover in her shampoo.

Nobody would have broken into her apartment, right?

Anita glanced around her bedroom. Everything seemed in order. Well, as ordered as it ever was. There were only three paperbacks and two ice-cold mugs of tea on her nightstand. She was just being paranoid.

A shower. Warm water, start over—

Oh my God, what would Patrick look like massaging soap onto his chiseled abs glistening with water droplets?

Shit.

A run, then. She would run him and the weird lipstick letters and creepy SUVs out of her system, and then everything would be back to normal.

Right.

****

Anita walked the last half mile back to her studio and apartment, panting heavily. March was so far ending on a blustery but behaved streak, and she could feel the warmer April air starting to push through the cold front. She had just enough time for a quick shower and breakfast before comp prep with Patrick. Once she caught her breath, of course.

She leaned against the wall of the studio, one hand on her ankle to stretch her quads. Through the glass-paneled door, she could see Patrick leaning against the check-in desk, arms crossed over his neon green Zumba tank and glaring at something on his phone. His brown hair was spiked with sweat, and his tanned muscles appeared far too tense for someone who had just spent an hour shaking it to Flo Rida and Pitbull.

He looked up as the bell clanged, but the narrow suspicion in his eyes softened as he registered her.

"Hey," she said quietly. They had not talked about how she had kissed him. *It had just been a friendly peck. Nothing to get worked up about.* Her runner's high dissipated like mist on a hot summer day.

"Hey." He was definitely not himself. He danced on the tips of his toes like he was being chased by a horde of angry crows. He treated his phone, which previously had seemed surgically attached to his hand, as if it was going to give him herpes.

She leaned against the check-in desk across from him. "What's going on?"

Patrick hesitated, then ran his hands through his hair. He tousled it adorably, though she had a feeling that wasn't his intention. "Look, I didn't want to bother you with this. I know you're dealing with a lot. I'm sorry."

As if she could not feel more selfish. "Patrick." Anita moved toward him and placed a friendly hand on his arm. He felt so good, so like home. "I want to hear everything going on with you. You're always there for me. We're friends, right?"

Patrick looked at her, a curious expression on his face. She brushed her cheeks with one finger to remove whatever was offending him. *Friend* wasn't a four-letter word.

A long moment passed. Anita's stomach churned. This was her fault somehow. The kiss had been a mistake, the whole partnership had been a mistake.

At length, Patrick broke the standstill.

"Okay. This is going to sound crazy. Someone is trolling me on social media. I didn't think it was a big deal, but it's just getting weirder and creepier, and I'm not sure if I should tell the police." He deflated and sank into a chair, his hands in his hair.

Her breath hitched, but she couldn't show her relief. He wasn't mad at her. Not what she had anticipated, to say the least. She sat beside him, trying not to lean into the comfort of his aroma. "Would you show me?"

Patrick looked over at her, his blue eyes dark, cautious. Without a word, he retrieved his phone and then sat beside her. He held the screen of his phone toward her and scrolled through apps with his phone. He finally stopped over a photo.

"Ugh." She recoiled, then drew closer. It looked like late-night drunk sexting. Not that she had a ton of experience with that. "What even is that?"

"I think it's a torso with a tattoo of a heart by the belly button," he responded. "I had the same reaction at first." He glanced at her face and snickered.

"What?"

"Your reaction to the word *torso.*" He giggled. Giggled. Of course the man giggled at her. "Isn't your dad a doctor?"

If her dad had his way, she would have been a doctor, too. It wasn't her fault the sight of blood made her want to vomit. "So what? They just randomly sent you a picture of their creepy tat?" It was a lopsided heart, too. That was rough. Someone had pissed off the artist.

That stopped the giggling at least. The phone

engrossed his attention again. "It started with weird messages full of suggestive emojis from burner accounts. I thought it was some internet troll playing a prank. But now there are these photos, and the messages have gotten darker and creepier." He showed her the words preceding the heart tattoo picture.

You're Mine, Now and Always.

Oh, for Heaven's sake. A lopsided tattoo and an uninspired creepazoid greeting card.

"Classy," Anita said, her voice dry. "What other sorts of things have they been saying? Are they going to send you a pony for Christmas?"

Patrick grimaced, and a flush swept up his neck. "It's not funny. I've seen "Play Misty for Me" three times, and it just does not end well."

He had a point. She was more familiar with "Swimfan," but still. She knew well the mind-fuck of unwanted attention.

"Patrick—" Even after seeing his evidence, she could not shake a nagging tension in her shoulders. The words crowded themselves inside her, begging for release. She just had to open the floodgate. "It's not just you."

His gaze found hers. It was hot and so intense she simultaneously wanted to lean into it and run as far as she could. She could roast a marshmallow in that heat.

"What are you talking about?" His voice was low, dark. She shivered.

"You remember the mirror with the lipstick? Well, that wasn't the first thing that happened." She told him about the letter, the car that had followed her home from her parents' house the week prior. His face grew darker, more pensive. She withdrew farther into herself.

She should have dealt with it on her own.

He tapped his phone against his leg. "You don't think these incidents could all be related, do you? What are the odds there is more than one stalker in Lewis, Pennsylvania?"

Anita shrugged. She opened her mouth and then closed it again. She missed his dimple, the little trio of fine lines around his eyes that crinkled when he smiled.

Now he just had a look of determination, a soldier about to head into battle. "We should call the police."

"Can they do anything?"

Her last experience with the police in Lewis had been in the sixth grade, on a very short tour of the facility. The sheriff's office consisted of four deputies and the sheriff herself. Their duties primarily entailed tracking down Mr. Jeffers, the eighty-year-old man with rapidly advancing dementia who had a predilection for wandering Main Street in his boxers.

It did not inspire confidence. Particularly if nothing was really wrong.

"It's better than nothing. We can call John Flaherty." Some of the lightness of his features had returned. She did not know whether to be grateful or disgruntled.

"John?" She raised a single eyebrow and cocked her head at him. "John Flaherty?"

His excitement was nearly palpable. "Yeah, he joined the sheriff's office after he got out of the service. It's perfect."

Perfect, right. Their best hope was an eighth-grade arsonist turned cop.

One more thing to add to her to-do list.

On the bright side, the dimple had returned. Patrick

flopped into the seat beside her again, spraying her with sweat.

"Dude, you need a shower."

"No one says *dude* anymore, Anita."

"I'm saying it right now."

He was grinning at her. Full-on, eyes sparkling, boyish hot guy grinning at her. A delicious heat spread up her spine.

"It's not my fault Melanie and Kim invited an extra twenty people when they found out I was teaching this morning."

The heat turned to ice. "Melanie? Wow. She, uh, gets up early."

He did not seem to notice. "Those ladies have way too much energy that early in the morning. You would like them."

Not likely. Anita pulled at her damp running shirt. She smelled like an eighteen-year-old boy's college dorm room. No sweet Patrick scent for her.

"I'm going to take a shower." She shook her head, trying to shake out the image of Melanie Templeton hanging on Patrick's arm, laughing at his jokes, sticking her cleavage under his nose. If she had the chance she would—

She heard the distinct sound of his steps on the stairwell behind her.

"Can I help you with something?" She was not sure where the edge in her voice had come from, but she could not take it back now.

"Any chance I could use your shower?"

Anita's feet halted abruptly. Patrick in her shower. Water and Patrick. That eight-pack—

The heat had returned and now spread all the way

from the backs of her thighs to her shoulder blades.

"Why can't you use yours?" She choked, her mouth so dry it was like she had eaten sand. *No, no, no, no, no.*

Patrick leaned one hip against the handrail of the stairs. "They have the water off at my apartment until eleven. Besides, you have all the good products."

Her voice would not work, so she made a feeble gesture toward her door and tried not to melt into the floor.

****

Patrick tossed two slices of whole-grain bread into the toaster and turned the front burner on the stove to low to scramble eggs. He could hear Anita singing show tunes off-key in the shower. No, he could not look at the door. It would not be ajar. She would not be reflected in the bathroom mirror, surrounded by highly perfumed steam.

He looked anyway.

Masochist. He was a masochist, that was the only explanation.

Reality was that she had practically barricaded the bathroom door, and she would never allow herself to appear in front of him less than fully attired. Even when they had traveled for competitions, she had never let him share her hotel room, no matter how broke they were. Part of it probably should have been because they partnered with other people, but Patrick still took it personally. After a while, Patrick had stopped asking.

Not stopped dreaming, just stopped asking.

While the eggs cooked slowly, Patrick cut up an avocado and an orange he found in the fruit bowl on the kitchen counter. He checked the coffee in the French press and poured cups for the two of them. If he couldn't see her naked today, at least he could cook her a decent breakfast.

It would be easier to ignore if she had not kissed him. Just a peck, but it was a terrible bone to throw to a starving dog. He had barely been able to think of anything else. Not that she wanted to discuss it.

Time was ticking, and his plan to tell her how he felt was going exactly nowhere.

Through the closed bathroom door, he heard the blow dryer running.

"Breakfast is almost ready!" Patrick called.

Anita nudged the door open. She was already dressed in her usual daily outfit of gray sweater, leotard, and leggings—unfortunately—but her damp hair framed her face like a lion's mane. The smell of grapefruit and hibiscus clung to the steamy air.

He definitely deserved a medal for not just pushing open the door and grabbing her then and there. Hibiscus flowers. That's what she had smelled like when she had kissed his cheek.

"You made breakfast?" Anita had a blow dryer in one hand and toothbrush in the other. *Sexy little multitasker.* He really should stop standing there, staring at her like an idiot with a silicone spatula clutched in his fist. *Great job, O'Leary.*

"You need to eat. Blow dry your hair later. Eggs aren't good cold."

She shrugged and joined him at the table, accepting avocado toast, fruit, and scrambled eggs on her vintage mismatched plates. "I don't think anyone has ever made me breakfast."

He forked a spoonful of eggs into his mouth.

"You're missing out. We should have been dance partners ages ago." He gestured at her with his fork. "I also make a mean Bolognese."

"And by 'mean,' that implies 'barely edible.' " She smiled at him in that mocking way of hers that he loved, the way that tilted the corners of her eyes wickedly, then bit into her avocado toast. Ah, to be toast.

"Well, I *order* a mean Bolognese." Patrick nudged the coffee toward her. "But I can definitely do breakfast."

They ate in companionable silence for a moment or two. This was the dream. Mornings sipping coffee and chatting after nights of rocking her world. Which he definitely would never say out loud, because this was not 1994.

Anita sipped her coffee. The steam haloed around her head. "Did you call John yet?"

"No." Not because he had forgotten, which he kind of had. He had been thinking other things. "I thought we could call together."

Anita nodded, tensed, and sipped at her coffee.

Inhaling deeply, Patrick put his phone on speaker and dialed.

"Pat O'Leary?" came an incredulous tinny voice over the speakerphone. "I saw your name, and I was like, who is shitting me?"

"Hey, John," Patrick replied a little too loudly. He was never sure of speakerphone etiquette. "How are you?"

"Good, good, you know, can't complain. Hey, I was going to call you. Do you still know Anita Goodman? My fiancée wants us to have a fancy wedding dance or something, and she's been at me to call her."

Anita smiled. "Hi, John," she said softly. "This is Anita. I'm here with Patrick."

"You two are together!" John whooped. "I always knew it. I mean Patrick had a *serious*—"

Patrick quickly moved to cut him off but caught Anita's bemused glance. That fire had barely been doused. "No, we aren't, like, *together* together. Just friends. Still. But we are having a problem right now that we wanted to discuss with you."

"Oh," John said over the phone. "Gotcha. Work related. What's going on?"

Anita and Patrick proceeded to tell the deputy everything that had occurred over the last week while John listened quietly. "Do you have pictures or copies of these messages?" he finally asked.

Patrick blanched slightly, as did Anita. "Umm, well, no," he replied. "At first I thought it was a prank, so I deleted everything and banned the scam accounts."

"I don't either." Anita's voice was hoarse. "I didn't even think to take a picture of the message on the mirror, or the license plate of the car. I recycled the letter. Stupid."

"Not at all." John's voice was tinny over the speaker. "Happens to the best of us. The problem is, without evidence, there isn't much we can do."

Patrick's buoyant mood at the pseudo-date with the love of his life ebbed. This was a small-town police department, not "CSI." They couldn't recover deleted files or get DNA off a social media photo. The odds were slim John or anyone else had even been trained to get metadata off a photo.

"Look, so far it just sounds weird and creepy but kind of harmless and bumbling. Keep an eye out, lock your doors, and if anything else comes up, keep it and call me back. Send me a copy of today's message. I'll see what I can dig up."

Which would likely be a big fat nothing. Patrick worried more about Anita. Her stalking seemed more perilous than someone's misdirected love letters.

"Thanks, John." Patrick sighed. "Take care."

"Tell your fiancée I'm happy to help." In her voice, he could hear how Anita struggled to maintain her professionalism. It must be exhausting to wear a mask like that all the time. "I'd love to choreograph something for you."

"Thanks," John replied. "But don't get too excited. She's a huge U2 fan and, for some reason, wants our song to be 'The Sweetest Thing.' "

The phone beeped twice, and the call ended. Anita's face had gone ghost sheet white.

Patrick concealed his snicker behind a cough. "Isn't that song about how Bono forgot his wife's birthday?"

She nodded. "Oh well, bigger fish to fry and all that."

She looked so lost.

He would give anything to knight-in-shining-armor her. If only she would let him. "You all right?"

Anita paused. "Yeah. Let's practice. I need to shake this off, and I have lessons soon."

"As you wish." Patrick nodded gallantly, sweeping into a bow.

Chapter Eleven

She sat in her car, inhaling the scent of cheesesteak and fried peppers and onions. Across the street, she could see him through the large glass windows of the dance studio. His head was back, laughing. He was so fucking handsome, it hurt. It burned.

"To be frank, I'd have to change my name," she whispered, letting her lips linger over the punchline. He would love her jokes. Throaty, deep belly laughs that would turn into a smoldering gaze. He was turned on by a good sense of humor. That frigid dance bitch could barely crack a smile.

She could cut a smile into her face. Yes. That's what she deserved. Pretty little heart-shaped mouth stretched like the Joker. Who's laughing now?

She crumpled the greasy sandwich paper in her hands and threw it into the back seat. She had had to drive all the way into the city to pick it up, but he had posted about how it was the best cheesesteak in the city #PhillyProud, and she knew she had to try one. She thought about how she would talk to him about the differences between Tony Luke's and Geno's and how she had always thought the best was from this hole-in-the-wall in Wayne. He would like that, she knew.

Not like that bitch. Her lips drew into a thin line as she watched the blonde dancer spin and swivel and shake her ass in Patrick's handsome face. "Selfish cow," she spat. That bitch did not appreciate him. It was not fair.

Patrick. Even his name was sexy sweet.

He would see her soon enough.

****

"That's all for this week!" Patrick clapped his hands, and the couples all turned out to take their bows. "You guys all did great. Make sure to email me if you need help with your routines for Keystone, but I expect to see all of you there."

The bell in the Lewis High School gymnasium sounded, and the kids in Patrick's dance elective chattered animatedly among themselves.

Some things never changed. He watched one of the girls, Lana, holding court. She reminded him so much of Anita in high school. The gentle leader. Back then Anita had glowed.

She still did. It just required a bit of polish to find the shine. Mikhail's leaving and Nikita's murder had dulled her. Too much work, not enough time to enjoy herself. Patrick closed his eyes. If only…

"Hey, man," said a voice from across the gymnasium. Patrick turned to see Will Forbes, one of the high school coaches and an old friend from varsity soccer.

Will was also the only child of Lewis's beloved Sheriff Forbes. And had apparently grown some sort of weird facial hair.

"You have a thing on your chin." Patrick gestured vaguely with his hands toward his own face.

Will grinned and ran his fingers over the strip of hair on his chin. "Really? I kind of like it. Gives me a soulful vibe."

"Just tell me it doesn't require its own comb and products."

Will rolled his eyes. "Says the 'influencer' who gets free products. Share the wealth, dude."

"No one says *dude* anymore. This isn't Malibu."

"I say it like I see it." Will shrugged. "How's the class going? The kids all talk about it. You are beloved, if you can believe it."

Patrick returned to packing his dance bag. He always had to bring extra shoe brushes when he taught at the high school. Anita and some of their dance friends had donated proper footwear, but none of the kids ever remembered shoe brushes.

Will scratched at his facial hair. "You free? School is out, and I could use a drink."

When he had been competing internationally, Patrick would not drink for a week or two leading up to the comp. Best physical form and whatnot. He was older and wiser now. "Why not?"

****

They ended up at the Caf, a dive-y sort of bar across the street from the high school. Patrick was pretty sure it had not been updated since the 1970s. The ancient jukebox was covered in a thick film of old cigarette smoke and spilled booze, and the neon lights flickered persistently like a mosquito that refused to be swatted. Four o'clock on a school night was clearly not its busy time.

He noticed a blonde woman in a Phillies hat nursing something bright blue with an umbrella, a risky choice in a place like this, and the two ageless school librarians perched precariously on two of the red leatherette barstools, already two Yuenglings deep and spitting laughter.

"You guys still come here?" He followed Will to a table in the middle of the room by the bar. No surprise that the silverware stuck to the table.

Will had a craggy, handsome sort of face that straightened out when he smiled. "Yeah, my boyfriend doesn't get it either. But it's cheap and nearby." He signaled the bartender, a guy of short stature and long white hair that he tied back in a ponytail. The bartender filled two pints with Yuengling and left them at the edge of the bar.

Foamy goodness, yes please. Patrick brought them over to their table. "How's life, Will?"

Will sipped the beer and licked the foam from his upper lip. "Not too bad. Job's good, Bobby and I are getting along pretty well. Can't complain. Small-town life, am I right?"

Patrick tugged at the collar of his shirt. No matter how far he tried to escape, Lewis pulled him back. Not just Lewis, of course. "How about your mom?"

Will barked a laugh. "The ballbuster? She's amazing. She's been lobbying the township for extra money so she can finally have a detective on staff."

"Do we need a detective in Lewis?"

Will shrugged again and downed half of his lager. "Beats me. The world is changing, right? Listen to any true crime podcast, and you'll see nefarious activity everywhere. My mom was telling me about some drug smuggling thing over the Maryland border she's worried about, and even ballroom isn't safe, right? I heard about that poor woman in New Jersey." Will polished off the rest of his beer and signaled the ponytailed bartender for a second. "You'd think people who did ballroom would be chill, like you and Anita."

Patrick sipped thoughtfully at his beer. The two librarians at the bar were now slapping each other jokingly and calling for Bushmills. "Would you really call Anita chill?"

Will snickered and went up to the bar for his second pint. "Trouble in paradise?"

"What are you talking about?" Patrick looked over Will's head at the black-and-white TV behind the bar. He thought all rabbit-ear TVs had died the death of disco.

Will hit him on the shoulder. "You and Anita? You two having problems?"

A lump settled in Patrick's stomach. Maybe he should drink some more beer. "We're not together."

Will whistled loudly, drawing the attention of the librarians. Much as Patrick had tried, he never could tell the difference between them, though one had pointier eyebrows than the other. Pointy Eyebrows leered at Will. "Forbes!" she called out, slurring the *R*. "Who's your handsome friend?"

"Maeve, it's Patrick O'Leary." Will gestured with his beer. "Remember Patrick? He did ballroom dance and soccer."

Patrick nodded to the ladies, who were shimmying in an uncoordinated way. Were all former teenagers reduced to their high school hobbies?

Pointy Eyebrows' friend wolf whistled.

"Maybe we should go," Patrick whispered.

"They're harmless," Will replied. "Besides, you've barely touched your beer."

Patrick sipped at the beer, which tasted suddenly stale. There was no way the librarians were involved in sending him those photos, right? Will was right. One bad turn, and he saw suspects everywhere.

Pointy Eyebrows and her friend had gotten their shots of Bushmills and were ninety percent of the way to passing out on the bar.

Will nudged Patrick's attention back. "So what do you mean you and Anita aren't together? I heard it from John Flaherty."

Damn it, John. Though maybe some rumors might kick him out of friend purgatory. "We're not. I promised to dance with her at this thing in Harrisburg in a couple of weeks. That's all."

Will raised an eyebrow. "That's all?"

Patrick said nothing in reply. He focused on the black-and-white TV with the rabbit ears, though the image was too grainy to see any detail. Will watched him for a few moments, tapping his fingers on the sticky wood table.

"You know, I read some of your stuff from New York," Will finally said. "My boyfriend wants to plan a trip now."

New York. Patrick had gotten more work done in three months there than in three years in Lewis. And had hated almost every minute.

"It's a great city. I got a lot of really good feedback. I can give you guys a list when you go."

Will tilted his head curiously. "So if it was so great, why are you back? New York has a lot more opportunities for a guy like you."

He was not sure he was actually going to say the words until they left his mouth. "Honestly, I have no idea." He squeezed his cheeks between his palms, reveling in the pain. His mother was going to be right.

He was wasting his potential.

Will polished off his second beer, then picked up Patrick's and poured it down his throat as well. He patted Patrick companionably on the back. "You have really got it bad, don't you, dude?"

"No, everythin—" Patrick sighed. "It's fucking torture, man." He covered his eyes with his hands, pressing the palms into them. "I honestly thought it was awful just being near her and not being with her, but I was wrong. It is a thousand times worse to dance with her, to touch her every single fucking day for hours on end, and she still does not want me. I think the woman could work at Guantanamo." Shit. Had he really just said all of that out loud? He glanced around the bar, anywhere but at Will. The librarians were hanging onto each other's shoulders, barely propped against gravity. The woman in the Phillies cap was staring at them.

She probably wanted to know why the has-been Patrick O'Leary was having a breakdown in a dive bar.

If the floor could swallow him now.

Will nudged a shot glass full of amber liquid in Patrick's direction. He took it gratefully, though he was not the biggest fan. Toss it back anyway. Deal with the burn. It covered the ache in his chest.

"What are you going to do?" Will asked. He had gotten himself another Yuengling and took a long pull.

Patrick sighed. "I'm going to leave. I can't keep doing this."

Will raised both of his eyebrows and pursed his lips. "Are you still going to compete?"

The alcohol pulsed through his system, mocking his heartbeat. Would it be the same when he was not with Anita? "I promised her. I can't break my promise."

****

Neither of them noticed the blonde woman in the Phillies cap snap a photo before she slipped out the door.

Chapter Twelve

"Holy shit!" Anita cried and leapt backward four feet. Hot tears prickled at the backs of her eyes.

There on the doorstep of the studio was a dead bird, its wings splayed at an odd angle and its little head twisted off its body.

"Poor little robin." Anita extended a hand toward it but then recoiled. It was clearly dead. A headless bird could not come back to life, and though she was a more than fair seamstress, this was beyond her capacity. It still hurt her soul, though.

"Hey!" she heard Patrick call.

The day had dawned a warm spring morning, and Patrick had clearly taken advantage of the weather by walking from his apartment. His thin leather jacket casually accented his musculature. *Not a helpful line of thought.* Spending so much time together lately had clearly addled her brain.

He smiled when he saw her but then followed her gaze.

"Holy shit, is that a robin?"

"I think so." She shivered. "I don't know what happened. I've seen birds hit the window and get stunned before, but that doesn't rip their heads off." She needed to find a shoebox and an old washcloth. Bird funerals had been her specialty at one point.

"I guess we should clean it up?" Patrick's voice

shook.

Anita swallowed her dread. Her father, the great Dr. Goodman, would be *so* proud she was facing her blood phobia. "I'll go get a bag and some gloves."

"Let me do it."

She sighed in relief, but it was short-lived. He hesitated at the entrance to the studio, then turned back to her. "Actually, did you take pictures yet?"

"Ew, of course not. I'm not going to take a picture of a poor dead bird." Anita couldn't stop staring at the thick rope of blood and gristle where the bird's head ought to be. No creature deserved that.

"It's for John." Patrick took out his phone and knelt beside the body. "He said he needed evidence."

Evidence. Right. She should program her phone to remind herself to be smart. Except she still was not quite sure how to set reminders on her phone. "You think it's related to the other stuff?"

"It's too weird not to be related." He finished snapping the photos and texted them with a loud whoosh. "Did you see anyone outside the studio this morning?" he asked, stowing the phone in his back pocket. Which meant she looked at his back pocket and what it covered, and oh seriously, she needed to pull herself together. She was not turned on by the death of an innocent. Patrick looked at her expectantly. "What about your security cameras?"

Riiiiiiight. She shook her head and glanced up at the bare edges of the door frame. "I don't have security cameras. It's a dance studio in Lewis. If someone really wants to take my water dispenser, I say have at it." She made a note to herself to do an internet search for how to install security cameras.

Patrick just shook his head. Great, now everyone was disappointed in her. "Look, I'll clean this up. You do what you need to do."

She crossed her arms over her chest. "It's my studio, it's my dead bird. I will clean it up."

The corner of Patrick's mouth twitched upward. "As you wish."

Anita opened her mouth to retort, but instead Patrick's phone sounded a too-loud ping. Even she knew how to turn the volume down on a phone. Well, she had put it on vibrate once two years ago and then never figured out how to turn it off. Same difference.

"It's John," Patrick said, staring at the text. He chortled once and held the screen up for Anita to see. "He wrote, 'Gross, put it in a plastic bag, will swing by later.' " Patrick shrugged. "Who knows? Maybe this is a lead."

"You watch too many detective shows." She sipped at the coffee cup Patrick had left on the check-in desk, but it had gone cold and tasted more than a little bitter. A great start to the day. "Do you want a cup of coffee? I'm going to make a pot. They must have used a different blend at Amore this morning."

"I can make it if you want to get the body."

Ugh, right, the body. She was an independent woman. Responsibility sucked. "Great, thanks."

She heard his footsteps in the apartment above her as she plodded around her studio collecting supplies. Plastic bag here, cleaning gloves there. *If I move more slowly than I ever have before, the body will decompose naturally, right?*

Shove it down. Repress. Lock the door and throw the key deep into the back of the freezer.

It did not hit her as she scraped the little carcass into the plastic bag. Nor when she pushed all the air out of the bag and pressed the seal closed.

It was only when she smelled the fresh coffee Patrick had prepared.

She ran inside the studio, her head buzzing too loudly to do anything else. *Shit, shit, shit, shit, shit.*

She curled up underneath the desk in her office, head buried in her hands. The room was too hot, too close. Seriously, could she just get in a deep breath? She wiped at her eyes with the backs of her hands, then pulled them away to gaze at the streaks of tears across her skin.

"Anita?"

She couldn't look at him. Not now. Not like this.

A waft of warmth and pine and mint surrounded her, wrapping her up like a cozy cardigan. "Anita?" he repeated.

He placed one hand across her shoulders, but that was it. She could not hold it in any longer. She wrapped her arms around him, buried her head in the soft fleece of his jacket. She was going to die. No one could survive this, this aching need, this unending want, this loneliness.

But then he wrapped his own arms around her body, holding her close, tilting his nose to the top of her head, and the sobs eased.

He was so close, encompassing her but not stifling. No one had ever held her like this before. Maybe her mother, but no one else. Her blood heated, tingling.

She pulled back from him enough so she could push the heels of her hands against her eyes.

Patrick did not let her go. She found his gaze, dark,

flames licking the glint of gold in those heavenly blue eyes. It was too intense, too primal.

She needed to shut this down. She shifted slightly, biting her bottom lip, and Patrick's gaze dropped to her open mouth.

What was happening? She couldn't—couldn't do this. This was Patrick. *Patrick*. Sweet, funny, caring, sexy AF Patrick.

She wanted him.

God help her, she wanted him.

She brought her gaze to meet his, the smolder in her meeting his fire. Her heart ceased its Wagnerian pounding and fluttered instead, a caged bird flapping to be released.

A rush of images flooded through her, and she pulled herself out of his warm embrace. *Bad idea, bad idea, bad idea.*

It was a long few moments before she regained control of her heartbeat, her breath. She really needed to find the air conditioning. Power bill be damned.

At length, she steeled her spine and turned. Patrick still sat on the floor where he had held her. His handsome features were contorted with…confusion? Regret? Anger?

She desperately hoped it was not disappointment. "I'm sorry." He was her best friend, and that was all she could muster. She squirmed, pulled the sleeves of her well-worn cardigan down over her hands, scrunched the cuffs into her fists.

Patrick would not look at her. Why should he? She was a mess. She had shown her vulnerabilities, and now he would leave. Tears threatened again, but she stifled them. It wasn't her fault someone had murdered a poor defenseless bird on her stoop. But this was wrong. She could—no, she *needed* to be better. Stronger.

She sniffed and crossed her arms over her chest. Bit by bit she would reconstruct her armor. "I'm sorry you had to see that." Good, that sounded better. Less like she was apologizing for shoving him away instead of kissing him senseless.

Now she needed that thought out of her head.

Which was a lot more difficult now that Patrick was looking at her again. He had his hands on his knees, his pose contemplative.

"Are you fucking kidding me?" he finally asked, his voice low, almost dangerous, like a sexy growl. It sent a thrill of heat through her again. She bristled.

"I beg your pardon?"

"Are you seriously apologizing for needing a mini breakdown after cleaning up a dead bird?"

Oh, right. Good, he had not been about to kiss me a few minutes before. Great. Perfect. World in order again.

"You should not have had to see that." Lame, but not quite as lame as a sorry-I-almost-jumped-you apology.

Patrick shook his head and stood to his full height. She loved how tall he was, not dwarfing her but not at eye level. Just the right amount of tilt.

Focus.

"We're friends." He hesitated on the last word but reached out and took her hands in his. *Friends. Right. Good.* Anita inhaled deeply to calm her breath. "Whoever did this is doing it to both of us, right?"

Anita nodded. Was it hot in there again? Maybe it was just something in the way he held her hands, just the way he held her when they danced. Gentle but firm. A leader.

But he was right. Damn it, he was right.

She pushed the sinking feeling from her stomach and pulled her hands from his. "Of course. We need to split up."

Patrick laughed, and a frisson of—hope? embarrassment?—coursed through her.

"Have you seriously never seen one horror movie? Nature documentary?"

Wait, what? She had once done five pirouettes in a cha-cha routine and had not been this dizzy.

Patrick was still laughing. "Anita. When there is a threat, you do not want to get separated from the pack. Stronger together."

"Oh." The word escaped her, thrust from her mouth by a crush of conflicting images and emotions. She and Patrick spending more time together. A lot more time. Close. Dancing, whatnot, close. Close to those eyes, those hands…

She couldn't breathe again. She managed to find a chair and crumpled into it.

Patrick knelt before her, a huge grin creasing his features. That dimple, damn it, that dimple was definitely going to be the death of her.

"We are masters of our own destiny." He just looked so boyishly charming, so completely enticing. Her fingers itched to trace the outline of that dimple.

Instead, she nodded.

He clapped his hands together, the noise louder than a gunshot. "Perfect! What's on our agenda for today?"

She could hardly remember her name, let alone her

agenda.

"Umm—" Practice, but there was no way in hell she wanted to think about their rumba routine right now. "I—I still have to get some stuff ready for the party on Saturday night. Oh, and dinner with my parents, but I don't think I'll go." It would take time to research security cameras. And how not to lust after your best friend and dance partner. It was going to be a full night.

Patrick's eyes widened in apparent horror. "Dinner with Marina and Bill? You can't not go to that, Anita. I'll come with you."

And for the life of her, she suddenly could not think of a reason why not.

Chapter Thirteen

She remembered why not the minute they arrived.

"Patrick!" Marina's smile was as wide as her arms as she raced to envelop Patrick. "Ah, I did not believe it at first when Anita told me, but then I realized I must have known." She took his hands in hers and leaned in, whispering conspiratorially. Great, now they were allies. Perfect. "I made pastitsio."

Patrick groaned. "I have missed you so much, Mrs. Goodman."

"Bah." She threw the compliment away with a carefree wave. It had been a smart move on Patrick's part. Her mother loved nothing more than a compliment on her cooking. "You must call me Marina. After all these years, we are friends, no?"

"As you wish, Marina." He winked, actually winked, and offered her mother his arm to lead her into the house.

Anita stalked in behind them, slamming the door. They did not notice.

"Oh, it is so chilly tonight! Smells like snow." Her mother practically glowed under Patrick's attention. Her father must be in absentia, as was becoming usual.

"I doubt it's going to snow, Mom." Anita felt nauseous and sullen and distinctly like she was the unfavored child. After the experiences of the morning, her day had significantly gone downhill. "It was sixty-five degrees at lunchtime."

"You never can tell here in Pennsylvania." Marina flipped her recently blown-out hair over her shoulder.

Anita fought the urge to go home. She had no interest in watching her mother flirt with Patrick. It had been difficult enough sitting beside him in the car on the way here.

"You must tell me how you are doing, Patrick," Marina gushed. "You are like a son to me. You know, Bill and I tried and tried to have a son"—she winked at him wickedly—"the trying is the fun part, after all."

"Mom!" Anita said sharply. She slipped out of the heels that had been a mistake. Her bathtub at home called to her.

If Patrick really wanted to spend time with her—

Nope, shutting that right down. Anita swallowed a wave of bile.

"Anita?" Marina stared at her from the kitchen, two glasses of red wine in her hands.

Great. She was standing barefoot in her parents' foyer, daydreaming about Patrick and bathtubs. Or decidedly not daydreaming about Patrick and bathtubs.

She must be coming down with something.

"Everything okay, love?" Marina asked.

"Yeah, yeah. I've just, you know, lots going on lately." Anita cursed herself for stammering. Her stomach turned over, and she tried to swallow the heat creeping through her body. It would be easier if Patrick wasn't leaning against the doorjamb of the kitchen, his body languorous and that wicked dimple calling out to her like a homing beacon.

"Poor dear," Marina cooed, moving toward her daughter. "Come, have a glass of wine and eat. Good food will make you feel better."

God, yes, wine. Anita followed her mother into the kitchen. At least her dad wasn't there to put the cap on the evening.

****

"What's wrong?" Patrick asked. Marina had gotten up to put away the dinner plates and fetch the dessert, leaving the two of them alone, if only for a moment.

"Nothing." Anita sipped again at her wine. It was only her second glass. He did not need to make a federal case of it. It was not like she had needed to contribute much to her mother and Patrick's conversation.

She wanted to be home. Home in bed. Alone. Definitely—probably?—alone.

It would help if her body stopped flushing every time Patrick looked at her, though right now she was freezing and half wished he would put his arm around her. Seriously, did her mother always live with the house this cold? She could barely drink her wine for her lips chattering.

"Who would like cheesecake?" Marina announced, carrying in a large, clear glass cake stand bearing a beautiful four-inch-high cheesecake drizzled with chocolate glaze and adorned with fresh raspberries.

Anita's stomach flipped. *Oh no.*

"Wow, Marina, you are absolutely a gourmet." Patrick accepted a large slice from her. Anita gulped, holding a hand to her mouth.

"Oh, please, Patrick, your mother's cooking is also excellent."

Her mother offered her a slice of cheesecake, but Anita held up a warning hand. Marina cocked an eyebrow at her daughter but said nothing.

Good. Marina tended to force food like a love language. She was too full of wine and pasta and her body too exhausted trying to fight its attraction to the man sitting beside her. The man charming her mother, which was possibly the most attractive thing she had ever seen.

"She is vegetarian, yes?"

"Mostly," Patrick said, a large piece of cheesecake on his fork. "But on special occasions she will make meatloaf. The things she can do with a carrot are inspiring. You know me, though. I never could give up a good cheesesteak."

Patrick smiled sideways at Anita, which literally made her stomach flip. Seriously, what was going on with her? He was just a guy, just her oldest friend in the world. Exactly. Yes. She really should ask Toni about dating apps because she clearly—

Her stomach flip-flopped again dangerously.

Oh no. No, no, no, no.

She raced to the bathroom, hand clutched over her mouth, and just made it.

It was a good thing she had not taken the cheesecake.

Sweat pooled on her forehead. She ran cold water over a washcloth to drape across the back of her neck. Anita sank onto the floor, the A-line skirt of her light-blue dress fluttering around her. She closed her eyes and cooled her forehead against the chilly porcelain sink.

A gentle knock. "Anita?" Marina called through the door. "Are you all right?"

No problem. Totally normal. "I'm fine, Mom!"

Good. Project confidence.

Her stomach flipped again. If only her body would cooperate.

"Can I come in?" Her mother did not wait, just nudged open the door. Anita could not meet her gaze but took the glass of ice water and pressed it to the nape of her neck. "What's going on?" Her mother's voice was soft. Tears pricked in Anita's eyes.

"I don't know. Maybe the salad I had for lunch was contaminated or something." She melted into the familiar warmth of Marina, the well-loved scent of cinnamon and vanilla and clove. "I'm sorry, Mom."

"Don't be silly," Marina replied. She swept tendrils of hair off her daughter's face. "You're sick. I hope it wasn't the pastitsio."

"I doubt it. You and Patrick seem fine." She had not eaten much that day. There had been the weird bitter coffee from Amore, but that couldn't be it. She had barely sipped it, and whoever heard of salmonella from coffee?

"I'm sorry you do not feel well, my dear. But I am glad you brought Patrick."

"I can tell." Anita sipped at the ice water. Thank goodness her stomach was finally settling.

Her mother opened her mouth to say something, but Patrick interrupted.

Anita's hackles raised at the sheepish way he had his hands stuck in his pockets. "What's wrong?"

"Umm, sorry, but the thing is, it's kind of snowing."

****

Snowing was an inadequate term. The blizzard had come on with gale-like ferocity, the wind whipping the fat flakes into loops and whorls. Anita watched the world opacify from her spot on the couch.

"I hope Dad's okay." She needed a new cold washcloth, but her limbs were leaden. She might die on that couch, simply leach into the white fabric where she had once perched in a very uncomfortable prom gown. A fitting end for a professional ballroom dancer.

Marina paced the floor. It looked exhausting. "He texted me twenty minutes ago. He will stay in Philadelphia with Dr. Stearns this evening. The roads must be terrible."

Despite the regularity of its inclement weather, southeastern Pennsylvania did not manage it well. The potholed freeways froze with black ice, drifts piled on the thin shoulders, or freezing rain would solidify old pipes and bring down electrical wires. The thought of driving in a blizzard like this—Anita gulped again.

Marina finally paused in her rapid pacing. "I will find you clothes. You will stay here tonight."

Heat rushed through her like a whip of adrenaline. *Patrick? In the room down the hall?*

She was definitely going to be sick again.

"Mom." Anita struggled to get into a seated position, dislodging her cool washcloth in the process. "We can wait an hour or so. Maybe it will clear up."

Her mother scoffed. As if she could have expected anything else. "Don't be silly. It will be a fun sleepover, like old times."

Chapter Fourteen

Patrick knocked softly at the door at the end of the hallway, with a small, vibrant-striped acrylic tray in one hand. Like mother, like daughter.

"Come in," he heard Anita grumble. He smiled despite the situation. The daughter of a doctor made a terrible patient.

She was slumped in bed, a washcloth pressed against her forehead. She looked pale and faded, like a plastic toy that had been left out in the sun too long.

His treacherous heart leapt anyway.

Her room had not changed much since high school. She still had the same fluffy white-and-blue printed comforter, the same cheerful display of stuffed animals in a little rope hammock in one corner, a white bookshelf overflowing with awards statuettes and crammed sideways with books.

"Hey you," Patrick said softly. Anita grumbled and threw her arm over her face. He should make her chicken soup. Or buy chicken soup. He wouldn't want to poison her further.

Next she put the pillow over her face. "Oh my God, Patrick, I am so sorry. I don't know what happened. Why didn't I check the weather before we left?"

"Were you distracted by something? Keystone in a week? Dead birds?" He placed the little tray on the white bedside table. "I brought you some crackers and ginger ale."

She removed the pillow, looked over at the tray, and immediately replaced her shield. "You should not be so sweet to me."

"Why would you say that?" He hesitated for only a moment, but it was just too tempting. He perched on the edge of her bed, far enough away to maintain the illusion of friendship. Almost.

She sniffled and moved the pillow halfway down her face so only her red-rimmed eyes were exposed. "I'm gross. I'm a huge mess. A—a disappointment."

"You never disappoint me," he said quietly. She was wearing a soft gray T-shirt that sloped across her shoulder and exposed her collarbone. If only he could press his lips there, run his fingers along the smooth surface from the arch of her shoulder to the base of her throat.

He should see about turning on the air conditioning in her room. He absolutely, positively could not feel up the woman of his dreams while she was sick.

She bit her lip. "Did my mom get you everything you need?"

"Yup." Great. A distraction. He could do distractions. "A pair of your dad's old sweatpants, very fashionable and figure flattering." He gestured to the time-worn black sweats. "I find the moth holes in precarious locations particularly daring."

There it was, that smile that increased her angelic features. *I could light my whole apartment with that one smile.*

She sipped at the ginger ale, her lips wrapping around the straw.

Patrick licked his lips and exhaled. Distractions were good. "I see Marina has maintained the shrine."

The corner of her mouth twitched. "I really should find something to do with those trophies. It's a bit ridiculous."

"You don't want to display them at the studio?"

"And have everyone remark on my success at the Emerald Ball when I was seventeen?" She rolled her eyes. "I hope I didn't peak then."

"Hardly."

She arched an eyebrow at him.

Heat crept up the back of his neck. High school Anita had been magnetic. Grown-up Anita was—mind-blowing.

"I don't think I've been in your bedroom since we were in high school." Not since—

"The night after Keystone senior year." Her voice was hoarse, breathy.

His own caught in his chest. She couldn't remember, could she?

"You wore that red dress with the feathers, and that little circlet of rhinestones in your hair." He could picture her so vividly. They had danced Standard together that year, and even now, he could remember his seventeen-year-old self, one side of his body pressed against the girl he loved unabashedly, twirling her like Fred and Ginger. He had never wanted it to end.

"You remember what I wore?" She had now completely set the pillow aside, and her spine was straighter.

He licked his lips. Was he reading this wrong? Maybe it was just the desperate knowledge that he was going to be gone in a few weeks. He could not continue to hide everything from her.

"I remember a lot."

That night, still in their makeup and spray tans, they had sat side by side on the floor, watching an episode of "Grey's Anatomy." He was not one to relive glory days, but there were some moments that lived in a halo.

The thrill of victory still coursed through them. They had been eating pretzels and small bowls of cherry water ice. The feel of her soft hair against his cheek, his teenaged hormones raging but knowing, knowing that this was one moment he could not screw up. There had been a look, a moment. One crystalline perfect moment.

Which of course had been interrupted by Marina. Never to be repeated.

He really needed to stop living in the past.

Anita regarded him with an odd expression. Did she remember that near kiss, too? Did she also regret that he had never made his feelings clearer earlier? So much wasted time.

Without fully thinking, he brought a finger toward her face and moved a strand of hair behind her ear. He heard her breath catch, saw her bite her lip the tiniest bit. He could not look away from that spot on her lip, the slight swelling of it, and inched slightly closer to her. One more inch, just one more inch—

"Patrick," she said huskily. "I think I'm going to be sick again."

She pushed past him and ran toward the bathroom. Patrick followed her and held her hair away from her face while she threw up. He found her toothbrush, gave her a glass of water to drink. He walked her back to bed, tucked the comforter around her soft but clammy body, refreshed the cool washcloth for her forehead.

Without a word, he waited until she was asleep, then silently left the room and went back to the guest room to be tortured by his dreams all night long.

Chapter Fifteen

Early the next morning, the hiss and clomp of the snowplow woke Patrick from his furied dreams. The world otherwise was always so quiet after a blizzard, even the animals stilled by the frosty precipitation. He pressed his arm over his eyes and groaned.

Sleeping down the hall from Anita was not a good way to get a full night's sleep.

The tang of coffee wafted up the stairs. Thank God for Marina. He pulled Dr. Goodman's worn sweatpants over the black boxer shorts he had worn to bed. He stretched, yawning, then performed his morning round of sit-ups and push-ups to get the blood flowing. Nothing like a little exercise to push the possibility of his best friend being poisoned out of his head. Or the way she had looked at him last night.

Possibilities and wasted time.

He pulled the navy-blue polo over his head as he walked downstairs. Marina was already dressed for the day in a dark-green cabled sweater and jeans. "Patrick!" She smiled as he entered. "Thank goodness the power didn't go out."

He nodded and yawned. "These March blizzards are the worst. Hopefully the roads won't be too bad. Is Dr. Goodman okay?"

She waved a hand at him. "That man, he is too much. Told me he and his friend Dr. Stearns drank

Japanese whiskey and played Scrabble until they both passed out. Honestly, you would think they were old enough to know better."

Patrick gratefully accepted the coffee she poured into a thick ceramic souvenir mug from Rehoboth Beach. "I hope I am never old enough to know better."

She shot him an arch look. "Now, Patrick, what do you like for breakfast? It is so long I get to cook breakfast for someone. Bill and I usually have something small, but on a snow day?" She clapped her hands enthusiastically. "Best day for a long, lazy breakfast."

"I'm fine with anything, Marina." He had stuffed himself the night before. Might as well continue the feast. It would be smoothies and poached eggs on toast for the next few days. "You are a wonderful chef."

"Bah." She blushed prettily, the gesture eerily reminiscent of her daughter. "If only my Anita would learn. Now, you go make yourself at home. I will make you something good."

Taking out his phone, Patrick moved into the living room with his coffee. He opened his photo app first. Distractions definitely helped. Anything to dull the memory of Anita curled up against his chest, her heat rushing through him.

Focus, Patrick.

No untoward messages today. Maybe his stalker's power had gone out in the storm last night. Small favors.

He hummed to himself as he gazed out the window, the carpet of white snow covering the front lawn, broken only by the small lumps of the snow-covered hydrangea bushes. He posed in front of the large front bay window, angling his phone for the perfect selfie. That would do. He typed, *winter wonderland?* He added the appropriate hashtags and hit Post.

Anita slumped into the room with a groan and flopped onto the sofa, clutching a throw pillow to her stomach.

The grin crept across his face, but he wrapped it in concern. "You look like shit," he said, mostly to make her smile and to distract himself from the way her pink-and-purple-striped pretzel pajamas clung to the curves of her legs, and especially from how her soft gray T-shirt was falling off her shoulder. Was she wearing a bra? He tugged at his collar. Maybe he should give himself a snow facial to cool off.

She did not smile. "Puke green is not my color. I just don't know what happened."

"I do." He shoved the niggling suspicion aside. "Clearly, I think you are allergic to me."

"Don't make me roll my eyes. It makes my headache worse."

"Breakfast is ready!" Marina trilled from the kitchen. Anita paled and shot up from the couch, her hand over her mouth.

"Was it something I said?" Marina asked, drying her hands on the skirt of her apron.

He kept his eyes focused on the path of Anita's retreat. It couldn't be. No. It had to be just food poisoning. Didn't it? "Might just be the two of us for breakfast."

****

She sat at her kitchen table, testily tapping her fingers against the marble counter. Of all the days for a blizzard and power outage. And she had forgotten to charge her phone. Foolish. Foolish.

Not as foolish as that blonde bitch. Never trust a drink that's given to you. She would be out of commission at the least, dead at best. Though she did not want the bitch dead yet. Make her lose everything she thought she had. Then. Only then.

Finally, finally, the buzz of electricity. The clock above the microwave started flickering twelve o'clock over and over. She reached quickly for her phone, dead in the night while the snow had blanketed her home. She shouldn't have neglected to pay the plow guy, but it was fucking March. So she couldn't get out of her driveway today. There were other ways to check on him. What if he was stuck in the snow, too? She could walk to his house with hot Irish coffee, fresh cookies. He would like that. She was a good baker.

She opened her photo app and checked his posts first thing, as she always did.

Her eyes widened, and she loosed a guttural scream so loud and vibrant it shook snow from the bushes outside her window.

Winter wonderland??

She had been reconnoitering that house for the better part of a month. How dare he?? She hissed through her teeth. What had happened? Had the drug not worked?

She screamed a string of a thousand obscenities into the void of her kitchen.

That bitch would pay.

Chapter Sixteen

Patrick moved his partner through the basic steps of the tango, slow slow quick quick slow. The older woman stumbled a couple of times and readjusted her posture but was still leaning so heavily on his frame he felt like he was trying to prop up the leaning tower of Pisa.

But he had promised. Anita needed to rest. He wasn't an idiot. He could cover the lessons. He was sure nobody would even show up with the inclement weather.

It hadn't deterred Lydia Swann, the septuagenarian in front of him who was indulging a Fred Astaire fantasy.

"Great job today." He forced a smile instead of wincing at the pain in his rotator cuff. She beamed with pleasure, the smile lighting her soft brown eyes. He needed to pull his shit together. Lydia had been his second-grade Spanish teacher, of all things. She just needed more practice.

"You're such a good teacher," she gushed. "Ricardo and Anita are wonderful, of course, but sometimes it is good to have an outside perspective."

"Absolutely." Patrick turned her into a bow to the right and a bow to the left. Thank goodness that was one hour down.

While Lydia changed back into her winter boots

and coat, he walked over to the check-in desk and took a large drink of water. He had forgotten how exhausting it was to teach all day long. At least he wouldn't have to add in a workout tonight. Maybe some yoga for once. He leaned into a deep back stretch. How did Anita not live on ibuprofen and ice baths?

"Hey there, snowman," a female voice lilted from the door. Patrick's heart sank. The woman should have a red alert bell around her neck.

Melanie Templeton slunk through the door, her white winter coat unbuttoned to show off the cleavage pushing through the deep V neck of her cherry-red, too-small cable cardigan. She had on tight white jeans tucked into a pair of brown, expensive-looking shearling snow boots, and her hair was long and flowing over her shoulders. Patrick assumed somehow she had missed the power outage, if her blow dryer worked.

"Of all the gin joints, am I right?" Her voice was lower, affectedly husky, than it usually was.

"Hello, Melanie, we weren't expecting you. Zumba was canceled today."

"I saw the light on." She gestured vaguely. "Thought I might, I don't know, take a chance." She runway-walked toward him. Snow and slush in the shape of the treads of her boots followed her steps. He needed to find the mop.

He caught a sharp whiff of too-strong perfume. While he had gotten distracted by the snow melting on the floor, she had closed in on him faster than Nicolas Cage in "Gone in Sixty Seconds."

She smiled. "Where's Anita today?"

"Not feeling her best." The hairs on his arms stood

to attention. Had she known he would be alone? She did not seem aware of what had befallen Anita. "Where's Kim?"

Melanie lifted her hands in a sultry, shrugging manner. "I guess we're alone, then." Her bee-venom lips tilted into a seductive sort of smile.

Patrick thought he might throw up. "Is there something you need, Mrs. Templeton?"

She laughed, too shrilly. "Patrick!" She swiped at his arm playfully, the shoulder of her winter coat sliding off her shoulder, revealing more of her décolletage and the sharp contrast of the cherry-red sweater against her pale skin. "I've told you before, you have to call me Melanie. Do you give private lessons? Maybe I should try." She dropped her eyes and pushed her mouth into a pout. "I'm very good with my hips."

A jolt of nausea. Maybe it was her perfume that was poison. "I'm just helping out a friend. If you want a private lesson, I'm sure Anita can help you when she gets back."

Melanie, her eyes glimmering, moved directly in front of him. Her perfume smelled strongly of jasmine and bitter orange, the scent suddenly flooding his nostrils as she bent her head and exposed her neck in front of him. Everything about her was designed to seduce today. How had she known where he was? She couldn't have done this, gone out the day after a blizzard, without the distinct motivation of finding him.

Social media.

He had posted a photo of the snow-filled parking lot behind the studio, himself frowning. *#noparking #snowday.* Idiot. He was a complete idiot. He might as well have stuck a giant red button on his head saying,

"Hey, Stalker, I'm right here."

"What do you want, Melanie?"

She locked her gaze on his and drew one finger up his arm. His blood chilled.

"I think you know," she said huskily. Had the lights in the studio dimmed? "We're both adults, Patrick."

"You're married." He gently took her finger and removed it from his arm.

"He doesn't matter. What matters is this, us. I know you feel it." She moved to put both arms around his neck, pressing her body toward his, but he stepped away.

The bell over the door chimed, and Melanie whirled, a mutinous look marring her face.

"Patrick!" Nina Rabinova drawled in her thick Russian accent. Today she was dressed like a psychotic skier, a thick white puffer jacket and slim white leggings with bright neon pink boots. Her hair was tied up in an elaborate neon pink swirled turban. "I am so sorry I am late. The snow! The ice! The plowman came too late." She cast a sharp glance at Melanie. "I hope I'm not interrupting."

Patrick had never felt so grateful for her dramatic entrance. "No trouble at all." He looked at Melanie. Her face grew steely with displeasure, and she haughtily tugged her coat back into its appropriate position. "Not interrupting anything at all."

****

Later that night, Patrick sat in Anita's office, searching through his social media accounts. It had to be in here. Somewhere.

He was just being paranoid. Of course. Just

because Melanie had expressed interest in him didn't mean she was the stalker.

It wasn't hard to find her public accounts, the photos of her from college, one among a group of nearly identical girls in too-tight sweaters and too-short skirts. A sorority? Wouldn't surprise him. The photos of her and her husband, stiff in formal wear, on a yacht, were more concerning. Her husband's eyes never met the camera. Where was he? Patrick clicked over to Mark Templeton's account and noted nearly daily pictures of meals and whiskey cocktails. Daily until a couple of weeks ago.

She followed *PhillyProud* and Toni, but not the studio. She probably couldn't find the studio page. It was buried so low at the bottom of the algorithm it would take an excavator to locate.

Patrick tsked to himself. The studio's social media presence was abysmal at best. Wasn't there a dance this weekend, a comp next week? The least he could do would be to help Anita zhush it. Maybe spend some time leaning over her shoulder, helping her edit photos.

He was pathetic. He knew it and knew there was very little he could do about it.

Patrick sat back in Anita's office chair, hands cradling the nape of his neck. Melanie couldn't be the stalker. Interest and sexual harassment did not necessarily equal stalking. He had traced some of the burner accounts that had left him messages, but none seemed remotely related to Melanie.

He heard the bell over the door chime, and he tensed. He could not recall how long he had been sitting there, but night had fallen sometime in the interim. The tension relaxed when he saw who had entered.

"Hey." Anita stood in the doorway of the office, her face drawn but a little rosier than when he had left that morning. A twinge of something primal, some instinct to protect, clutched at him. "Thank you for today."

She would not have needed help if he could have kept the stalker away from her. "No trouble. You feeling any better?"

"Finally." She reached into her handbag and pulled out a plastic container with a blue top. "My mom wanted me to give this to you."

He rubbed his hands together eagerly. "Your mom is the best."

"Funny, she said the same thing about you."

A beat. Patrick's gaze dropped to her mouth. The last time they had been in this office, she had been in his arms. Long dormant arousal heated his stomach.

But this was not the time. She was still recovering, even if she looked better on her worst day than many people did on their best. Curvy and lithe and—

Staring at him like he had three heads.

She broke the silence first. "So, what are you doing?"

His mind went blank, so he surreptitiously glanced at the computer screen. Right. Melanie. Stalker. "Social media. Speaking of which, you really need to bulk up your website and accounts."

"Do I, though? There's just always so many other things to do."

"Better things, you mean." His chest tightened. His mother didn't think his career was legitimate, either.

"No." Anita moved toward him, standing so close he was having trouble remembering anything. Not his name, not his job. Not even really what they were talking about. It was impossible to focus on anything but her intoxicating smell of lilies and hibiscus. If he could bottle that, he might be able to take it with him when he had to leave. "Not better, just less—complicated."

"It's not rocket science." She was so close. Her lips parted slightly, and for an instant, just an instant as any longer would be absolute torture, he imagined what it would be like to kiss her. To press his lips against her mouth, slide his tongue against hers, breathe the same air she did.

I need a cold shower. I need to move to Greenland.

Holding himself stiffly, he leaned forward and kissed the top of her soft mane of hair. "I'm glad you're feeling better. Sweet dreams, Anita."

Chapter Seventeen

Anita doggedly pushed through the next day and a half, drinking water or bone broth nearly constantly to stay hydrated. Work. She needed to work.

How had one single sick day set her so far behind? Their comp routines were fine, but she knew they lacked the oomph, the extra sizzle that the judges wanted. And her own students seemed to have all completely lost their minds. One of them had brought in a costume for her approval that was three sizes too small, another couple had forgotten half their routines, and even more stumbled halfheartedly through their steps. Not to mention Nina Rabinova, who kept asking if Patrick would be coming back to help with her comp prep.

It was unsurprising she was starving, sore, and about to have a serious diva breakdown before the Saturday night party.

Normally, it was such a good idea. It enticed more people to the studio. The wine bar helped loosen inhibitions, and people were more willing to try new moves and different partners. Social dancing was key to the studio's success.

But not when she was still fighting to keep up and had zero prospects of help. Toni had plans as usual, and even Ricardo had not promised to make it. She was on her own. Damn Mikhail.

She grabbed a granola bar from the emergency stash in her desk and unwrapped it as she went to fetch a box of party supplies from the closet. *I can do it alone. I can.*

Maybe not when she was hallucinating the smell of Chinese food. Her stomach, only recently tolerant of more than milk toast, churned and grumbled.

Anita picked up a stack of boxes and hefted them, the granola bar balanced between her teeth, and tottered back toward the studio.

A pair of tanned hands caught the top box just as it started to slide off the stack. Patrick, his blue eyes dancing in merriment, winked at her.

Anita huffed. Perfect. "Look, Patrick, I don't have the time to talk to you right now. The party starts in two hours, and I have seven hundred things to do—"

"Three fifty." He bent over and opened a box. "Maybe three forty-nine."

She was definitely delusional and far too exhausted for a math lesson. All she could muster was a helpless shrug.

Without ceremony, Patrick led her into her office, where three takeout Chinese food containers, a bottle of water, and chopsticks were set out on a piece of paper towel.

At least she was not hallucinating about soy sauce.

"What is this?"

He propelled her by her shoulders toward the desk chair and gallantly pulled it out for her. "Eat. Rest a bit."

It was so tempting. But—

"There's too much to do." Anita swallowed and shook her head. But was that orange chicken? And maybe sesame green beans?

"Let me help." He smiled at her, that sexy dimple practically begging to be kissed. "I'm not taking no for an answer."

Then he was gone.

****

Anita emerged from her office picnic twenty minutes later, stomach full of orange chicken, green beans, and brown rice but lighter than she had felt in days.

She walked onto the dance floor and gasped. He had gotten an inordinate amount done in just twenty minutes. He had set up the refreshment table and now was halfway through adjusting the fairy lights and stringing the bunting above the mirror.

He grinned when he saw her. He stopped her by holding up a single finger, then hit the play button on the stereo. Anita couldn't help but laugh as she heard the Jacksons crooning "Blame it on the Boogie." Her laugh intensified when Patrick started grooving.

"I can't believe you did all this."

"There's still a lot to do, but you need to take time for the classics." Patrick turned the music up louder.

He held out a hand to Anita, and she just could not help but start moving her hips, her shoulders. She hadn't danced the hustle in ages, but she did love a good nightclub dance.

They both started to move around the empty dance floor, laughing, lip synching. Patrick whipped her around in a series of spins, and she could not find her spot. But she didn't care. Nothing felt like this. Nothing felt so freeing and powerful as losing herself in the rhythm of a song. All of the stresses and trials of the last few weeks melted away, and at the end of the song, there was Patrick.

Patrick, who used to share junk food in empty ballrooms with her after competitions.

Patrick, who remembered every single dress she had ever worn.

Patrick, who adored her mother.

Patrick, who was panting and grinning at her with a smile so broad it seemed to lift him off the ground. *Yes.* Her body begged her. *Yes.*

His smile changed as his eyes fixed on her mouth. She moved her hand from his shoulder to cup his stubbled jaw. *Oh God, yes.* Her body thrummed and heated, and this had to happen. She was going to shatter if it didn't and—

"We'll have to play this tonight at the party." She sounded breathless, wanton. She tried to force herself to pull away, but her brain was definitely losing. It was his eyes that loosened her resolve to stop. The glints of gold in the deep blue oceans. The air between them crackled and sparked and swelled. She leaned in, tilting her face just so.

Yes. Yes.

"My God, you two are the most adorable thing."

Anita leapt away from Patrick and turned, plastering a smile on her face.

"Toni! What are you doing here?" Her voice was too shrill. She bustled over to adjust the bunting by the check-in desk. She couldn't look at him. That was all. Nothing had just almost happened. She had not almost made a huge mistake. Ballroom and romance did not succeed for her.

Toni stood against the short wall dividing the

studio floor from the changing area chairs, arms crossed over her chest and smiling knowingly. She was wearing a black-and-red jumpsuit that hugged her curves and had tied it with a thick black belt to accentuate her waistline.

"Patrick said you needed help getting ready for the party tonight," Toni replied evenly, her gaze flicking from Anita to Patrick. "I've never been to one of these shindigs before. Looks like fun."

How much had she seen? It was just a dance, that was it. It was completely unrelated to the temperature in the studio dropping about thirty degrees. Anita wrapped her arms around her body, holding in the warmth.

"I'll go get the catering," Patrick finally offered. But Anita could not look at him, could not watch him leave. She opened several folding chairs, then gazed helplessly around the studio.

Anita felt the other woman's eyes on her. *Shit, shit, shit, shit, shit.* She had owned this studio for two years and never been unprofessional before. "You'll like the party," Anita finally said, if only to break the silence. "We play a bunch of nightclub and other dances, and there's a good mix of levels. Everyone is very friendly."

"Patrick certainly is." Toni stopped moving chairs and now leaned against the mirror, one hand on a hip. "Come on, sugar. Spill."

It was definitely colder in the studio. Anita checked the thermostat, which was set to sixty-eight. She just had to call a repairman in the morning. That's all.

Toni was still watching her.

"There's nothing to tell." Anita unloaded a

container of plastic wine cups onto the refreshment table, then moved to the small refrigerator for the bottles of wine she had stored. Yes, wine. But no. She could not have anything to drink until afterward. No one wanted a hostess who reeked of booze.

"Come on, hon. If Patrick had ever looked at me that way, I would not be able to say that there was nothing to tell." She loosed a long, low wolf whistle. "That boy is smoking."

"He's my friend." Anita choked. The sign on the door advertising the party was crooked. She could fix that at least.

Toni chuckled. "You're selling the both of you short. I'm not saying you need to marry him, just enjoy it. Did you ever enjoy anything when you were with Mikhail?"

"Of course." Not that any examples sprung to mind. She had enjoyed that one time when Mikhail had gone back to the Ukraine to visit his family. Though that was probably not what Toni had meant.

"Really? So you are telling me that dancing with that gorgeous, sweet, kind man who clearly has an enormous thing for you does not make you want at least to jump his bones? Try him on for size, just once?"

Anita tried not to hesitate. Really, she did. She tried not to picture waking up beside him on a Sunday morning, her legs entwined with his. The way he would probably bring her breakfast in bed, let her watch what she wanted on TV. The way it would feel to slide her tongue against his, feels those incredible hands on her body, his weight on top of her…

But it was Patrick. She would disappoint him in the end, and he did not deserve that.

She sniffed back her tears and straightened her smile. This was a part she knew how to play. Even if it killed something inside of her.

"Absolutely not. I've danced with a lot of good-looking men. It doesn't mean I was attracted to all of them. There is nothing between me and Patrick besides a friendly dance agreement."

"Food's here," Patrick said stiffly.

Anita's blood turned to ice.

He carefully placed the catering box on the refreshment table, then turned back to the door. "Looks like things are good here. Bye." He slammed the door closed as he left, the bell jangling angrily.

If only the studio floor could have swallowed her whole at that moment. The Chinese food he had brought churned within her.

She covered her face with her hands, pressing the palms into her eyes. She just needed to count her breaths, that was all. Just one, two, three.

A comforting hand alit upon her arm. Anita glanced at her friend.

"Patrick is a good man." Toni's voice was soft, calm, reassuring, but stern. "If you really are not into him, which by the way I don't think is true, but if you aren't, you need to be kinder to him. This isn't you." That bombshell dropped, Toni unpacked the catering box.

A moment passed, then another. Anita could not find her breath again, but she had to. She had to. There was no one else.

She straightened her posture, lifted her chin, squared her shoulders, and got back to work.

Chapter Eighteen

In the end, Patrick blamed his masochistic heart.

He was absolutely not going to go back after he left. He wasn't. He was an independent, smart, handsome guy who could have lots of women. Lots. Sure, clearly not the one he had been pining over for more than a decade, but still. Enough was enough. He could take a hint. He was not the puppy dog panting and yearning for a distant owner's touch. He was an influencer, a private businessman, a semi-retired professional ballroom dancer, for fuck's sake.

He repeated this mantra multiple times to himself while he showered, shaved, brushed his teeth, dressed in a slim-fitting, light-blue button-down and trim black pants that moved well on the dance floor but weren't too showy. He said it while he polished his social dance shoes, buffed the soles with the metal shoe brush, and he reminded himself of it as he collected his jacket, dance bag, and keys by the door to his apartment.

So he really had no excuse for showing up to the dance party, none at all.

Except his heart hated him.

There were already almost forty people there, about a third of them dancing, the rest milling about at the edges of the floor, chatting or drinking wine or helping themselves to crudités or cheese and crackers.

It didn't take long to find her. Anita was always the

most beautiful thing in the entire room.

She had left her hair down tonight, parted in the middle, but had a sparkling crystal hair clip tucked above one ear and dangling crystal teardrop earrings. She wore a slim cream-colored top with a wide black-and-white-striped A-line skirt that dipped to her mid-calf, and her black Latin dance shoes with the straps that wound up her ankles.

His heart caught for so long in his chest he worried he would have to call 911. He had to stop doing this to himself.

He offered his entrance fee to Ricardo, who was manning the front desk/flirting with two older women, but Ricardo refused his money. "Trust me." Ricardo raised an eyebrow and nodded toward the large contingent of women in the group. "We're outnumbered here. We should be paying you."

Indeed, the moment Patrick stepped away, he was mobbed. The loudest of the throng was Nina Rabinova, dressed in a fire-engine red Latin dance costume not cut for her figure. He tried to glimpse Anita but couldn't through the sudden deluge of hairspray and heels and perfectly manicured fingers trailing along his arms.

For the next forty-five minutes, he indulged these women. Nina, Kim, Melanie, who tried to grab his ass and kiss his ear before slipping a hotel key into his pocket in a highly un-subtle movement. He ditched it in the trashcan beside the drinks table.

Then, finally, somehow, there she was. Halo intact.

He knew at some point in his life he had known how to breathe.

"Hi." Her voice was soft, almost breathy. His heart ached, both at her proximity and the memory of her words. *It doesn't mean I was attracted to them*, he had heard.

"Hey." He had a mantra. He was sure there had been something, some reason he wasn't supposed to be there. Something about independence? No, maybe it had had something to do with fortitude. Or fortune cookies?

Who cared? She was amazing, and she was right in front of him. If he was a man dying of thirst, she would be his salt water.

"You're popular tonight."

"So are you." He could see how the other men looked at her. Curious, wanting to see if the ice goddess was as cold as she looked. Damn them all. He had held her hair back when she was sick, let her cry on his chest. No one could take that from him.

There was only one more week. Once the competition was over, he would be gone.

Anita bit her lip, and her posture tensed. "Look, thank you for coming. You didn't have to."

"I said I would." He drank her in. One more week. A lifetime of missed chances and possibilities. He could not let this one slide. "Would you dance with me?"

She tilted her head, and he thought she was listening to the music, trying to decide if he was worthy of it. "Why not?" she replied and moved into his arms, enveloping him in her scent, her warmth. She pressed her body to his, keeping her frame but still their hips kissed to hold the shape needed.

Heat bloomed throughout his body, but he could not give in to it.

Without a word, the rest of the ballroom fading, he swept her into a sweet and sad and romantic waltz.

They swayed together, the rise and fall of the dance a parallel to their story. He wished the boundaries of the dance frame did not prevent him from leaning his cheek to hers, feeling her head against his shoulder. If he could write his adoration of her in a song, he would dance it as a waltz.

For the rest of his life, he would dream of this moment, the scent of hibiscus and lilies perfuming his skin, the swish of her black-and-white-striped skirt against his legs.

He would have made it last forever.

But this was real life. And it crashed against him too soon.

The waltz had ended, a lively samba now in its place, but somehow they were alone on the dance floor.

He needed to stop time. He could not see beyond the arc of Anita's eyes, the fullness of her mouth.

Then it struck him, a lightning bolt. *There's nothing between Patrick and me.*

He stiffly turned her out into a bow and led her off the dance floor. She was technically still the follower. If he never let go of her hand, he could lead her up the stairs to her apartment. Who was he kidding? He never wanted to let go of her hand. It fit inside his like it had been made for him.

He knew he was staring, but he could not help it. What would it be like, to have her body wrapped around his, arching against him in ecstasy?

A slow clap shattered his thoughts. Clearly the universe had other plans.

"Well, well," came a thick eastern European accent.

Great. Just fucking great. Of all the people in all

the whole damned world, Mikhail materialized from the crowd of people, stupid hair and all. He was wearing a black Oxford shirt unbuttoned to his nipple line, with tight black dance pants, and of course his hair was styled in some bizarre pompadour. He sported a thin pencil mustache above a goatee like a tosser. "You are looking good, Anita."

It was all Patrick could do not to scream.

"Hello, Mikhail."

"Hi." Patrick deliberately stuck his hand between them. To shake, of course. "Good to see you again, Mikhail."

"Yes, yes." The other man spoke curtly, not removing his eyes from Anita. "Will you dance with me?" He held out his hand, commanding. He had such—stupid hair. The warmth in Patrick's body dissipated when she removed her hand from his and placed it in Mikhail's.

They moved onto the floor into a flirtatious cha-cha routine, something easy and clearly well-rehearsed and deep in muscle memory.

Patrick couldn't watch. He didn't want to see their familiarity, the way Mikhail would touch her hips, her back, Mikhail's possessive gaze. Was she touching his chest? That wasn't fair. Patrick's pecs were much better than—

This was ridiculous. He needed a drink.

He made his way across the floor to the bar but found himself underwhelmed by the choices. When he had helped Anita with the studio, at least there had been whiskey at the Saturday night party.

"Not a wine drinker?" Melanie appeared at his elbow out of thin air. This night was just getting better and better.

Kim was standing beside her, smiling like a furry feline. At least Melanie couldn't make another awkward pass at him with her friend right there.

"Not usually." He selected a bottle of red and filled a plastic goblet with it.

"I love wine." Kim looked surprised she had said anything. Melanie shot her a cutting glance. Kim registered then ignored it. "There's a great wine bar in Wayne that we go to sometimes."

"Fun." Patrick sipped his wine. He could not look away from Mikhail and Anita on the dance floor. Mikhail was typically overacting, his gestures overly grand and pompous. This was what Anita wanted? How had she ever had sex with that walking greasy mannequin?

Melanie was whispering something to him. Somehow she had ditched Kim and was standing again far too close to him. "Sorry?" he said, realizing she was waiting for a response.

"I was asking if I could dance with you." She placed her long fingers on his arm.

Anita and Mikhail had moved off the dance floor. Was she leading Mikhail toward her office? The staircase to her apartment was through that door.

"Patrick?"

"Um, sure," he finally replied, unable to come up with an appropriate excuse.

The song turned to Amy Winehouse foxtrot. Nothing to this. He could manage, right? And keep Anita in his sight. He bowed to Melanie, who blushed and actually tittered. Yeah, this was definitely on his list of ten worst ideas, next to mixing mints with diet cola and overindulging at sake bars.

"You are so good at this," she breathed. She ran her hands up and down his arms and pressed her body close to his.

"You need to keep your dance frame." He pulled away and demonstrated. "This is mine, this is yours." He repositioned her head and shoulders, ignoring the way she kept eyeing him hungrily. At least she was not draped on him like an afghan. "Now, keep a slight tension in your hands, and just follow me. It's slow-slow-quick-quick." He started moving her through an easy slow eight count.

"I'm doing it!" she squealed. "I feel just like Jennifer Grey!"

"Yes." He moved her through the next eight count. "But keep your dance frame."

"You know," she said, clearly deciding she understood the rhythm of the dance and so had liberty to flirt again. Which he would have corrected if he was not looking for Anita. "I haven't had to work this hard for anybody in a long time."

"Maybe you shouldn't work so hard. I hear it gives you wrinkles." Patrick turned her to see if Anita and Mikhail were in the office or had gone upstairs. He couldn't tell from this vantage point. He needed to move her closer to the office.

"Oh, Patrick." She broke her frame yet again to trace her fingers up his arm. "You are so funny. We could be such good friends."

"You're married." He couldn't see Anita. Had she really taken Mikhail upstairs, left the guests at her own party? What was she thinking?

He felt Melanie move closer to him, pressing her

body closer to his. *Shit. I really should be paying more attention.*

"Patrick." Melanie's expression was deadly.

"Dance frame." Patrick tried to reposition her, but she would not follow his directions and wrapped her arms around his neck.

"My husband, he's terrible to me. He doesn't understand me. And let's be honest, he's not all that great in bed." She moved the hand on his shoulder closer to his neck, trailing a finger along his hairline. He tried not to recoil. "I think we could be so good for each other."

How long was this fucking song? "Keep your frame." He finally managed to readjust her hands. Oh, thank Heavens and all that was good and holy, the song finally ended. Perfect. He clipped a bow toward her. "Thank you. Enjoy your evening."

She haughtily put her hands on her hips. "Really? This is how you're going to treat me? What about that key?"

"Mrs. Templeton, I am not interested in your proposition. Thank you for the dance, and goodbye."

He could feel the anger smoking from her, but he was done. He had done his duty, danced with the clients. Anita was gone. She had left with Mikhail.

Patrick felt his heart plummet through the floor. This was it. He couldn't keep doing this to himself. He had to go while he still had a modicum of self-respect, even if it meant breaking a promise. She was never going to choose him. Enough was enough.

****

Anita crossed her arms over her chest. If he could just get it through his thick skull.

"Anita, please." Mikhail's hair barely moved, and he was typically expressionless. How the hell had she ever found him attractive? He reminded her a bit of an oily penguin in his black outfit. "Patrick? You will never win."

"I never really won with you." She never should have listened to him, never should have taken him to her office so they could "chat." "I can't do this, Mikhail. I have party guests." She moved toward the door, but he put a hand on her arm to stop her. She ripped it away from his grasp.

"I miss you." He contorted his face into what he clearly deemed an acceptable expression of contrition.

Fuck him.

"Really? Do you? After you completely ditched me for Tatiana Lurshenko? Where is she, by the way? How does she feel about your little decision?"

Mikhail stiffened and removed his hand from her arm. Ah. There it was. "She's ditched you, huh?"

"Her ex is planning on going to Stuttgart and invited her along," he replied haltingly. "After Keystone."

Anita crossed her arms over her chest and straightened to her full height. "Sounds like kind of a familiar ploy."

He scoffed, tossing his hair which of course did not move. How had she missed all the red flags? "You are a mess. I don't know why I am here."

"Me neither." She gestured grandly. "There's the door."

He stalked out. Anita rolled her eyes. Had he always been such a cocky, preposterous asshole? How had she spent three years of her life with him? She had to stop making the same mistake. Dance partners did not make good romantic relationships.

Like Patrick.

She could not find him in the crowd. At least tonight there was no surprise milonga with an Argentine tango group from New Jersey. But he wasn't there.

She could not still the disquiet in her chest. Had Patrick forgiven her for what she had said? When they were waltzing, she had not even found breath to speak. It had been simultaneously the longest and shortest dance of her life.

She just wanted the chance to apologize.

She forced a smile at some of the attendees but then focused on the clock. Only thirty minutes left. Very little good ever happened after ten p.m., so everything needed to shut down.

For the first time ever, she started encouraging her patrons to get out as gently as she could. If only she could just turn off the Saturday party playlist and hide underneath her desk with a bottle of wine and some Bon Jovi.

It took less time than she expected to clear her guests. She didn't realize she was looking for Patrick until she was alone, and he had not reappeared.

Shit. Just shit. Damn Mikhail and his shitty ass timing.

She finger-combed her hair into a loose knot at the nape of her neck but didn't tie it. Bon Jovi and cleaning. Perfect combination.

She had just grabbed the recycling bags when the bell over the door chimed.

"Sorry we're—"

But it was Patrick. Patrick, his features encased in stone and shoulders stiff.

Her mouth went dry. That shirt did him a *lot* of favors. "What are you doing here?" she managed. "I thought you'd gone home."

"I promised I'd help. I like to keep my promises." He brushed abruptly past her and fetched a pair of cleaning gloves and an extra trash bag from the storage box.

Ouch. "Well, thanks." Fine. She did not need him. The tears threatening at the backs of her eyes were from exhaustion.

She worked alongside him in tense silence for a few minutes, the only sounds the '80s rock ballads. She stole glances at him as he worked, as he meticulously sorted the trash and recycling, emptied half-full glasses into a bucket.

What have I done?

Before long they had finished with the general clearing. "I'll take this out." He heaved four whole trash bags over his broad muscular shoulders.

"Thanks."

Not how she pictured the evening. What had she pictured exactly? Not this. Not this angry hate cleaning.

He reentered the studio and went directly for the broom.

If she screamed it was not her fault. "Did you have fun tonight?" Was that her voice? It sounded strained, like a cheerleader about to find out her boyfriend was dumping her. Anita's blood roiled.

"Sure." He finished sweeping the dance floor and leaned the broom against the mirror. "I forgot how much work it is."

"Yeah." Anita snapped the gloves from her hands. He would know if he had just taken the time to be there over the past year, if he hadn't left her alone with Mikhail. "I need to wash my hands."

"Good idea."

This was not okay. She had never angered anyone merely by the act of washing her hands, but Patrick glowered, literally glowered.

She had never seen anything she hated more.

"What's going on?" She despised the desperation in her voice and crossed her arms over her chest.

"I don't know." He leaned against the door to the washroom, watching her. Infuriating.

"You're acting like you're mad at me."

"Why would I be mad at you, *Anita*?" He shoved past her and moved across the dance floor.

Her heart dropped at every step of distance. "Did I do something?"

He whirled, running his hands through his thick mop of hair. "I don't know!" He stood there, hands at his sides, pleading. His voice softened a little, but his face looked wracked. Damaged. She nearly swooned. "Look, just tell me. Tell me you and Mikhail are getting back together and my services are no longer needed."

"What?" She stifled a laugh that was more of a sob. "Are you insane? I'm not getting back together with Mikhail."

"Well, what was I supposed to think when your ex shows up in the middle of the party? You're always saying how good he was for you."

God, his face was so wounded and his eyes so deeply blue, cerulean like the ocean…lust crept up her body from her toes to her legs and higher… She needed to be away from him. "You're an idiot." She needed something, anything, to distract her. She fiddled with the dials on the stereo system.

"I'm an idiot?" He placed a hand on her arm. She tried to ignore the sudden jolt of electricity that shot straight through her body, tried not to fall over at the intensity. "What did you see in that guy? He never cared about you. His dancing is rote, and he—he has stupid hair."

"No!" She removed his hands from her body, ignoring the chill as skin left skin. "How dare you question my life, my choices? It's not like you've been here, Patrick. When you left last year, I was on my own. I built this business back after you left. I was the one setting up for the parties, hiring teachers. You didn't want any part of it when you switched careers." Her breath caught in her chest, broke like a sob. "But I knew you needed to go. I knew you needed something more. So I let you go. And maybe Mikhail was never that great at actually helping, but he was here." Not what she needed, never what she really wanted, but there.

Despair. That's what it was. That was the feeling of him being so close to her, yet so far away, the distance too vast to cross.

"And then you show up, with your cheesesteaks and your Pollyanna attitude, and you ruin my routines and disagree with my choreography, and you make me want things I can't have." She clenched her fists at her sides. She could not look at him, but then could not look away. "After this, Patrick, you will go back to your life. You will go back to being an influencer, to your popularity. You will follow your dreams. And I will still be here." Doing tax forms. Cleaning. Making it work. Her voice broke. "So don't question my choices, who I dance with, how I run my studio. I am not your problem."

The air thickened between them. Anita bit her lip and unsuccessfully fought back tears. This was it. She had ruined their friendship, all by telling someone else that there was nothing beyond friendship. With lies. She was a damned liar and—

"Are you finished?"

Patrick's face was still, set in stone, inscrutable and so undeniably appealing and charming and—oh my God, this was the last time she would ever see it.

A sob caught in her throat. She had to let him go. It was only fair. He needed, no, he deserved more.

"Are you finished?" he whispered again, and she nodded.

Then, instead of him leaving, he was there, wrapping his arms around her, pressing his face against her hair. Everywhere he touched, her body thrilled and warmed, like a marshmallow over a flame. "I'm so sorry, Anita. You're absolutely right. I'm a huge idiot."

Relief flooded through her, and she tightened her arms around him. "Me too," she replied, her voice soft, just a breath.

But the air shifted.

He was so close to her, his scent intoxicating. Her body tensed and curled where he touched her. His fingers brushed her hair back along the curve of her ear and rested just below her jaw.

Lust pooled and tensed deep in her belly like a vortex.

How had she ignored this for so long? Without

meaning to, she arched her back, tilted her face toward him. She was close enough to lap at that sexy little dimple, draw it between her lips, impress her mark upon him.

He was staring at her, a curious expression on his face. Had the moment passed? Like so many other fleeting moments. Possibilities and timing.

But she did not want it to pass. Not this time. Every nerve ending in her body wanted this, wanted him.

"Pat?" she pleaded, not sure if she was begging for him to kiss her or to stop this, stop her from stepping over—

But then he pressed his lips to hers, and she couldn't think, couldn't breathe.

Her body roared and bucked at the overwhelming sensations before melting farther into his. The taste of mint toothpaste and smoky whiskey intoxicated her, thrilled her. *More.* She wanted more. She wanted everything.

She slid her tongue between his parted lips to taste, to savor. He made a small sound at the back of his throat that sent chills and heat flashing through her. He tightened his grip on her, deepening the kiss, stretching her into a deep backbend, but she followed. She would follow him anywhere. Her whole body smoldered, the burning deep within her yearning for more, more of this, more of him.

She nipped at the tantalizing dimple, teased it with her tongue.

"Anita," he moaned into the base of her throat, his breath warm and inviting. She sucked in her breath as he nipped and licked at her collarbone.

A distant part of her brain tried to regain control,

but she flicked it away, cupped Patrick's stubbled jaw in her palms and took more of what she wanted.

Her Patrick, wonderful Patrick. Shockingly good kisser Patrick.

She buried her hands into his dark-brown curls, moaning, begging. But she could not break the kiss. There was urgency in it now. Something tender and swollen teased to a breaking point.

More.

He grabbed her hips, lifted her off the ground, pressed her up against the mirror. She wrapped her legs around his waist, the folds of her skirt sliding sensuously against her legs. He ran one hand along her naked skin from her ankle to her thigh, his fingers sparking electricity. Unconsciously, she leaned into the sensation, arching into his hands, into his body, feeling the hard length of him against her. *Yes.*

He panted her name and traced his tongue along her collarbone, teasing, licking, nipping her shoulder underneath the strap of her dress. The hand on her thigh, the pressure of his body between her legs was too much and never enough.

"Anita?" His voice in her ear now, low, seductive. A delicious tension coiled in her muscles. "Can I take you upstairs?"

Yes. Yes. Why wait to go upstairs?

She met his gaze then, fire meeting flame. This was it. She could not turn back now.

She reached for him—

But an explosion of shattering glass roughly shook her free.

Chapter Nineteen

Patrick tapped his fingers repeatedly against his leg. His fingertips tingled with the sense memory of how her hair had felt sliding through them not so long ago. Minutes? Hours?

It didn't matter when she wouldn't even fucking look at him now.

But he couldn't leave her. As John Flaherty had said, someone had just taken a baseball bat to the glass doors of the studio. Neither of them was safe.

"I don't have security cameras," he overheard Anita tell the deputy. Her voice trembled. "I never thought I would need them. It's Lewis. The biggest thing that happened last year was when the girls' basketball team rescued a cat from Gazebo Park."

Patrick's fists tightened. Stupid. He was just stupid. Why hadn't he thought to put them in after the dead bird? He had recognized the threat, brought it to John Flaherty, then did absolutely nothing. Nothing. He was an idiot.

A lovestruck idiot.

John Flaherty nodded at Anita and closed his notebook. He was dressed in the patrol uniform for the Lewis police department, but he was the only investigator on the scene. Maybe they really did need a detective in town.

He needed to do something, anything. He texted

the photos he had taken of the wreckage to the deputy. Lame. Lame. He was ridiculous. Of course, she would not want him when he could not protect her.

"Thanks, Patrick," John called, holding up his phone. Anita stood rooted in place, arms across her chest, her gaze fixed at the outline of spiky glass in her door. "Hopefully her insurance will pay for a new window. It can be pretty expensive to repair something like that."

Great. How could she afford that? Maybe he could organize a bake sale for her or something. At least he could find some wood planks or cardboard to board up the door.

He clenched and unclenched his fists. "Who do you think is doing this?"

John sighed and ran a hand over his smooth, bald head. "I don't know. It's tricky with stalker cases, unless they're sending you identifying information. Which really only the terrible ones do." He shrugged. Patrick wanted to scream. "And she doesn't have cameras." John waved at a group of bystanders across the street. "None of them saw anything. The neighbors on that side are gone"—he gestured next door to the antiques shop—"and the ones over there only heard the glass breaking. They thought they had left the downstairs TV on, so didn't see anything either." John scratched at the stubble of beard on his chin. "Can you think of anyone? An ex who wants you back? Someone pursuing you or Anita?"

Suspects. Patrick kicked himself. He should have thought of that. "I mean, there are a couple of women who have been more persistent lately, but they don't seem like stalkers. I don't know about Anita. Her ex is a bit of a meathead, but I don't think he would do something like this. He's more the kind to stage a dance off."

"Make me a list." John flipped open his notebook again and jotted something on one of the spiral-bound pages. "It's better to check it all out."

Patrick nodded. "Hey, John. Look, I don't know if Anita mentioned it, but she got really sick last week. She said it was food poisoning, but she hadn't eaten anything out of the ordinary. What if someone—" John was going to think he had gone completely paranoid, insane. Maybe he had. "What if someone, like, actually poisoned her? Dropped something in her drink or her food at the studio?"

He flushed. He had definitely become delusional, but John just pensively ran a hand over his jaw. "Do you think there's a list of everyone at the party tonight? Everyone who was there the day Anita got sick?"

"I think so. Anita keeps pretty good records of attendance and the lesson schedule."

"Let's get copies of those, and then I'll let you guys start cleaning up."

Patrick thanked him and watched as he packed up and got into his car. Anita was standing in front of the wreckage, arms crossed over her chest, tears glimmering in her eyes.

New blog post idea: how to ask your jumpy friend to do something after you've just kissed like the world was ending.

He figured simple and direct was best. "Anita— look—" But she ignored him. Without any acknowledgement of his existence, she went inside.

He followed her, tagging along like the good little

spaniel he was. It wasn't fair.

He fetched the broom, swept tiny crystals of glass into a huge pile.

He heard the dying wheezes of her ancient printer chugging along. It was practically a mimeograph. He could buy her a new one. She would have to look at him then.

She swept past him again in the hallway, her hands laden with papers.

He really couldn't sweep any more glass into the decent size pile he had accumulated. He pushed it into a heavy-duty garbage bag, tied the ends together, and hefted it outside to the dumpster.

He needed to find something to board up the door. Yes, that was it. Be useful.

As he turned back toward the studio, a glint of metal sparked in the periphery of his vision. *There*. On the sidewalk between the parking lot and the studio. He leaned over and picked up a tarnished silver lighter, the kind with the flip top. It was embossed with a growling cat of some kind. Wildcat. It reminded him of lazy weekend mornings practicing with Anita in an empty classroom at Villanova.

Weird. Maybe it was a good luck charm or something. He could use a little luck.

****

Damn it. Thump. *Stupid stupid.* Thump. *I never should have* Thump.

Anita banged the hammer harder against the nails. One more nail. One more board.

Fuck.

Patrick emerged from the shadows, flipping the top on a lighter open and closed. The sound drilled into her brain like a thousand angry hornets.

"Can you stop that?" she snapped. God, was that her voice? That harpy-ish crunch?

He slipped the lighter into his pocket, his movements slow, like he was worried she was going to explode.

Well, she had every goddamn fucking right to explode. She pounded another nail into the boards across the door.

"Can I hold the boards at least?" His voice was soft.

That soft voice against her neck, in her hair—

No. Another nail, another board.

"No." She pounded in another nail. She could not look at him, could not see that expression of concern, of pity on his face. Tears pricked in her eyes. Her father had been right.

She grunted and struck the hammer against the board, missing the nail entirely. A shock traveled from her fingers to her arms, and she almost lost her grip on the hammer.

She needed to slow down, needed to focus.

"We need to talk about this," Patrick said softly behind her.

She wiped at the tears with the back of her hands and focused on covering up the shattered glass in the door. "There's nothing to say." It was destroyed, completely destroyed.

"Anita, look, I—I don't think you should be alone tonight—"

She whirled on him, brandishing the hammer in one hand. "Are you fucking insane?"

He held up his hands in the universal gesture of

surrender. "Jeez, Anita, just to sleep! Not—not anything—just to sleep. I'll stay on the couch, okay? I just don't think it's safe for you to be alone."

Anita choked on a sob. "Don't you get it? I'm not safe *with* you." His eyes widened, and he seemed frozen in place. "Someone *saw us*. Someone saw us in here, and that's why they broke my door. It's because of what we did." Even if it had been one of the best moments of her life, she would shove it down deep and throw away the key. "We can't, Patrick. Not anymore." She turned back to the door and hammered the last nail into place halfheartedly. "I can't risk anything else."

She knew he had not left, could feel the heat of his gaze on her back. If only things were different. If only she could lean into the warmth of his arms.

"Anita, no." His voice was hoarse, rough. Broken. "You can't—look, you don't know how long I've lov— how long I've waited for this. How long I've waited for you. Please, please don't push me away."

He put a hand on her arm then, and electricity jolted through her. The tears ran freely now, she wasn't strong enough to contain them.

She pushed him aside and grabbed her purse and keys from behind the check-in desk. "I'm going to my parents' house."

Patrick blocked her exit, arms out by his sides. "Anita—"

Nothing else could be said. Nothing. She ducked around him and rushed outside to her hatchback, barely able to see through the curtain of her tears.

What a mess of a night.

Chapter Twenty

"More sex!" Nigel bellowed across the floor.

Anita stopped halfway through the hip twist she was attempting and crossed her arms over her chest. She blew hair off her forehead. "Seriously, Nigel?"

"You know I'm right, love." Nigel held up a bored hand. "Again. More sex this time."

She felt Patrick move behind her and shot him a cutting glare. He stepped back, hands up in mock apology. "I didn't say anything."

She hated this. It had been strained, and that was putting it conservatively, between them all day. He had every right not to be there. He *should* not have been there, not after how she had acted. Instead, he had installed video cameras at the studio and had waited with a cup of green tea to carpool to Nigel's studio in Philadelphia.

It wasn't right. None of this was. She could barely touch him without remembering the heat of his body on hers last night. She never could have imagined that passion caged inside his playful exterior.

She needed not to imagine it. Repress. Push it down. It would help if Patrick would stop looking at her, that concerned smile on his face which somehow made him more impossibly handsome. Her walls were crumbling, and it was freaking her the fuck out, and it was not her fault that she had tossed and turned all night last night because—

She stifled a yawn.

"Are we boring you, love?" Nigel called from the sidelines.

"Do you have anything more constructive to add?" She scuffed a spot out on the floor with the toe of her dance shoe.

"You pay me to be honest." Nigel sipped languidly from his coffee cup. If Anita had any more caffeine, she would likely explode into a fuzzy ball of frenetic energy. "You look wooden. You keep staring out at the audience. Rumba is not about them—it's about *you.* Engage more with your partner, Anita. This is not how you win. Deal with your shit, and put more sex into it."

"We are not going to win anyway." She did not need to think about this right now. Did not need to think about sex, especially sex with Patrick.

No matter how close they had come last night.

Nope, shoving it down.

She glanced at the clock and groaned inwardly. They still had forty minutes left of the session. If Keystone were not starting in four days, she would beg off tonight and soak her troubles in the tub.

"At least give me a chance before you doom us to mediocrity," protested Patrick.

Now everyone was pissed at her. *Perfect.*

Nigel shook his head disparagingly. "I don't know why I'm telling you things you already know, love." He turned another song on the stereo, Enrique Iglesias's "Ring My Bells."

They started the choreo again, but Nigel stopped them after only a few bars. "Crikey, Anita, you look like a fish. More sex!"

Patrick whispered something under his breath.

"Want to share with the crowd?" Anita barked at him. She needed to get a grip. Even Patrick, he of the infinite patience, was on edge. It was her fault, all her fault.

He raised an eyebrow at her, and her hackles raised. "I was just saying, maybe the problem is that you haven't had great sex."

Anita pushed him away, furious. Of course, she had. There was—

She did not have time for this. "That is absolutely none of your business."

Patrick smiled wickedly. "One might say that is exactly my business right now."

"Children, stop fucking around! More dancing!" Nigel stood at the edge of the floor, tapping on the face of his fitness tracker with a fingertip. "Time's ticking, loves."

Anita frowned deeply and turned back to Patrick, who was standing there, all innocent and adorable. *Bastard. Men. AAAAAAAARRRRGH.*

She moved into their starting position, avoiding his gaze. At least it played into the role of the choreo. "Just don't," she murmured, feeling his presence behind her.

"Yup, sorry, wouldn't dream of it."

Focus. She could do this. She had to do this. Anita closed her eyes and concentrated on the music. 2-3-4-and-1. 2-3-4-and-1. Her heartbeat settled into the rumba rhythm, and she synced her breath to the movement.

Now. She spun into Patrick's arms, then leaned away for a prolonged extension before a series of spins and then into his arms again, gentle but strong, his face near enough to kiss. After she wrapped one leg around his waist, he put a hand on her thigh and lifted her into a turn, his face inches from hers, her hands splayed across his temples. His breath warmed her skin, inviting her into a cozy cocoon.

"Open your eyes," he whispered, and she followed. She rumba-walked in shadow position, finding him with her hands. A quick connection, hands fleetingly together, heat burning through their palms, and Anita whirled back to face him. He turned her into a closed hip twist. The movements were quick-quick and then slow and elaborate, precise and luxurious. The entire dance felt like seduction, with Anita unable to resist his gravitational pull.

The dance had wrapped her, transported her away from everything. This world was better. This world was just her and Patrick, moving as two parts of one whole, there for each other.

The music slowed, and Anita leaned into Patrick, his arms supporting her as he dropped into a lunge, and she extended one leg into the air, keeping it slow and sultry.

Last night, his body pressed against hers, his hands in her hair, his mouth on her neck. *"Can I take you upstairs?"* Fire burning out of control within her—

Then that awful, sickening shatter of glass.

The magic music bubble popped.

Anita scrambled away from him. Water. She needed water.

Nigel clapped once. "Better."

Anita's breath came in hard pants, her ears still ringing with the clinking sound of glass cascading onto the floor of her studio.

"You really think we can't win?" Patrick reached

past her and collected his own water bottle.

She stepped away from him, determined not to inhale his scent.

"Who knows? I swear one time the judges marked us lower because they didn't like Mikhail's chest hair." At least he wasn't talking about sex anymore. She grabbed a towel out of her bag to wipe away the sweat from her brow.

"That's fair. It does resemble a mangy toupee. The best we can do is try, right?" He smiled. "I'm just going to go to the bathroom, and then we can get going."

Anita nodded and sank into a chair. Too much. It was all too much.

She heard a squeak as Nigel sat on the chair beside her. Great. More pity. Just what she needed. She covered her face with her hands.

"So what's up?" Nigel asked.

Hah. She must be more exhausted than she thought because her internal monologue went external. "Someone is stalking me and Patrick."

Nigel, he of the placid expression, blanched. "You're joking."

She shook her head. "Someone broke the studio door last night." The hot bite of tears stung her eyes. "I don't know what to do."

He put a comforting hand on her shoulder, and she thought she might melt into the floor. She hadn't been this much of a mess when she had told her mother. "Are you still going to Keystone?"

She shivered. Of course, Nigel understood. "I can't afford to miss it. You know how much money is tied up in the comps. If I backed out, I wouldn't be able to afford to have the door fixed." Her limbs felt leaden, but she straightened her back when she heard the bathroom door open. She sniffed abruptly and straightened her ponytail. She could get through this on her own. She had to do it. "Thanks, Nigel." She forced a tired smile. "I know we're helpless."

Nigel kissed the top of her head softly. "You'll be all right, love," he whispered. "You let me know if you need anything."

Chapter Twenty-One

How many push-ups did it take to erase the memory of kissing your best friend?

Patrick still hadn't figured it out by the time he reached seventy-five, and his arms felt like they were slowly being torn apart by a medieval torture device. One more part of his body ripped to bits by loving Anita.

He hadn't been able to sleep, so of course here he was in the wee hours of the morning, trying to exercise away his demons. *I am an idiot.*

Groaning at the pain in his arms, he stood and folded his yoga mat. Maybe a glass of water would help. Hell, maybe he could just have a whiskey neat and go back to bed. Though he had to meet Anita for practice, and he had at least three deadlines before he left for the competition on Thursday. Whiskey would have to wait.

Work. There was an idea. At least he could drown himself in that for a while as opposed to his own misery and aching muscles.

He grabbed two ice packs from the freezer, one for his back and one for his left hip. He would work for a bit, then maybe get out his foam roller.

Patrick leaned backward in his chair, tipping the front two legs off the ground to balance on the rear, while he waited for his computer to load.

What were they going to do? There were only four days until Keystone started, five days until the open professional Latin heats. His high school kids were competing on Friday morning, and he needed to make sure they were in good shape.

His high schoolers were the least of his problems.

Finally, his computer dinged to life, and Patrick yawned as he brought the front of his chair back to the ground.

He had to help her. That was it. The stalker's actions had taken away part of the vitality that he loved. He could not let her live in fear.

He found a yellow legal pad, an extra pen, and turned on the coffee maker. If he couldn't fix his love life, he could certainly delve into an internet troll.

****

"Wait, you did what?" Anita leaned over his shoulder and peered at the computer screen. Patrick was seated in front of it to show her what he had already been working on. "I understood literally five percent of what you said. What is a burner account?"

"You're so analog, it's adorable." Patrick yawned. He absolutely could not stare at the hollow at the base of her throat, the curve of her collarbone. *Nope. Firewalls, activate.* "A burner account is an account someone creates either because they want to do something that they don't want traced back to them, or you want to segregate the information you're getting. A lot of celebrities have them, either so they can act like a normal person online or behave inappropriately without it getting linked back to them."

"Doesn't it always get linked back to them?" Anita picked up a folding chair and positioned herself beside him. "I mean, I've seen a gossip magazine. Now and again."

"I always knew you'd admit it one day."

"A lot of people read it. And it's a good thing to leave lying around the studio." She brushed an imaginary piece of lint from her gray top. "For research and whatnot."

"Right. Research." He pointed at a spreadsheet. "Anyway, I started out first by identifying people that we know here IRL. Do I need to translate?" She rolled her eyes in response. "Good. So that's the list here. I figured most likely it's someone we know, someone local because they definitely know about the studio. Then I made a list over here of the burner accounts that have sent me weird messages. I then listed who those burner accounts interact with, especially the ones they interact with frequently."

"Interact with?"

"Seriously, Anita?" He stifled a laugh, unsure if it had arisen out of fatigue or frustration. Not the only part of him frustrated lately. *I need to stop.* "Do you even have a social media account?"

Gotcha. She examined her manicure. "I have chosen to spend my time in other pursuits."

"Like what?"

"I just find it all overwhelming. Like there's all this pressure to post and be viral and get likes." She sighed and shook her head. "Feels like a good way to be rejected."

"Not necessarily." In his early days of blogging, he had encountered more than a few asinine comments. "I get what you're saying. There are a lot of people out there with good intentions, and then a lot of assholes who take advantage of the relative anonymity."

"And which one are you?" She arched an eyebrow at him, her blue eyes sparkling. This was worth the hour of sleep and the four Americanos that had brought him here.

"I can't believe you even asked that." He raised a hand to his chest in mock horror. "*PhillyProud* is one hundred percent authentic, thank you very much."

"Doesn't this all take a long time?" She gestured vaguely at the computer. "Can't the police do it?"

"It's hugely time consuming." He hadn't made too much headway on his deadlines that morning after falling deep down the catching-an-internet-troll rabbit hole. "I don't think John or Sheriff Forbes has the time."

"If only Lewis rated a cybercrimes unit."

"Wouldn't that be nice? Maybe they can repurpose their Old Lady Crossing the Road Squad. Anyway, after we identify who the burner accounts follow, like, etc., then I can work on geotagging their photos, see who's around when. All that."

"Is there a computer program that could do all of this?" She placed her hand on her temples, smoothing back her hair, her this-is-giving-me-a-headache gesture.

"I have no idea," he replied. "I didn't really have time to look into that, I suppose."

"Really, Patrick? You mean you lost valuable time sleeping when you could have been reverse cyberstalking someone or internet troll hunting?"

He guffawed loudly, shocking himself, and she even cracked a smile, too. "Yeah, wasn't too much sleep last night." She tortured him in his dreams. In them, he replayed their kiss over and over and over, and never did it go any farther.

She quieted. "Me neither."

He glanced over at her. He was just so goddamn lucky. Lucky even to be in her orbit. But a planet in orbit never touched its star.

The room fell silent, the only sounds the humming of the desktop, the faint whirr of a fan in the nearby studio.

He should go. The ancient Greeks' knowledge of torture had nothing on Anita Goodman.

Instead, he felt the soft press of her lips against his cheek, tasted the salt from her tears. He glanced up, surprised.

"Thank you." Her eyes were cast down. Her hands trembled. "For this computer stuff. For the security cameras. For everything." Her eyes flicked up, and her gaze burrowed into him, a light in the tunnel.

"You matter to me." His voice was hoarse and cracked. *Please. Please.*

"You—you matter to me, too." She smiled shyly through her tears. "You always have, Patrick. Your friendship matters more to me than almost anything."

The lightness in his heart deflated abruptly. Of course, friends. Friends. He could be her friend, right? He had a lot of practice at that. It wouldn't be for much longer, at any rate. He nodded, trying to hide his discomfort. "I'll always be your friend, Anita."

"Let's get back to this." She gestured to the screen. "Who are the usual suspects?"

Chapter Twenty-Two

Deputy John Flaherty sang along to Mumford and Sons while sipping from the black Japanese travel mug that his fiancée, Katie, had given him for his last birthday. She had made fancy coffee that morning, adding orange peel and cinnamon to the brew. He took cautious sips, disliking the bitterness and wishing she would just let him add the cream and sugar he actually preferred.

John pulled his cruiser into the long driveway leading up to a three-story red brick Tudor with wide, black window shutters and framed in the front with large hydrangea bushes just starting to bud. Around the rear of the house, there was the outline of a red barn with a white roof, and he spied the glimmer off the surface of a pool in the backyard. A gardener, busily planting bulbs at the base of an oak tree, eyed the police cruiser warily. John just nodded to him.

He knew Melanie Templeton's husband worked for one of the pharmaceutical companies, but this house was practically palatial, even for Lewis. Rich people. Erecting nouveau plantations in the Pennsylvania woods.

He parked beside a paneled truck full of gardening tools and two white SUVs, one a slightly older version of the other. He made a note of the makes, models, license plates. He would check with Anita and Patrick later, see if either of them could identify the vehicle that had chased Anita. Privately, he doubted it. White SUVs were a dime a dozen in Lewis.

He made his way up the shingled path to the front door and pushed the buzzer beside the seemingly-freshly painted bright red door. A gargoyle-shaped door knocker? *Jeez.*

Melanie Templeton herself opened the door, in a thin, white cashmere Dolman tunic that hugged her narrow hips, expensive-looking black leggings, and three-inch heeled boots with metallic details. Her blonde hair was blown out in waves around her face. She smelled like gin and jasmine, and she held a new phone in one hand and a glass of white wine in the other. "Can I help you?" she slurred slightly.

"Hello, Mrs. Templeton. I'm Deputy John Flaherty of the Lewis Police Department. I have a few questions for you. May I come in?"

She didn't move from the door, but her body seemed to tense slightly. "Is this about my husband?"

Her husband? He kept his expression bland. "I'll explain inside, ma'am."

"God, don't ma'am me. Call me Melanie." She appraised him quickly. "All right. Come in, but take off your shoes. I literally just had the floors waxed."

He stepped inside, removed his shoes, and placed them next to the door. The foyer was spacious, dominated overhead by a large crystal chandelier. He followed the path of a fluffy white carpet runner along the highly polished wood floors.

Melanie led him into the kitchen, sipping from her wine glass. "My friend Kim is here, too." At the island there were two high-backed bar stools, and in one of them was a muscular, short blonde woman wearing a slim white top and black jeans. The woman did not smile but eyed him with immediate suspicion. *Interesting.*

"Kim," Melanie said. The other woman was all smiles for Melanie. "This is Deputy, I don't know, something or other."

"John Flaherty, Mrs. Templeton." He resisted the urge to tap at his prominently displayed name tag. "And you are?"

The other woman glanced quickly at Melanie, then leveled her gaze at him. Her brown eyes narrowed. "Kim Smith," she replied, her voice tight.

"Thank you." He jotted down her name with a question mark next to it in his notepad. God, he fucking loved a spiral notepad. "Mrs. Templeton, would you prefer to speak in private?"

"I don't see why we should bother. Kim knows practically everything."

The woman—Kim—seemed to glow under Melanie's praise. Interesting. *Always follow your instincts,* Sheriff Forbes had told him. His instincts were telling him that something was not right in this house. What was it Melanie had said about her husband?

"As you wish. I'll make a note that you declined to speak privately."

"Whatever." Melanie tipped her wine glass toward her mouth, clearly realized it was empty and headed to the massive subzero refrigerator. No doubt for a refill.

He could not stomach watching her drink herself into a stupor. That was no way to conduct an investigation. "Mrs. Templeton, could you please tell me your relationship with Patrick O'Leary?"

She startled, but he would have missed it if she hadn't spilled the wine she was pouring. "Patrick?" She mopped up the spill with a brisk twist of a hand towel. "He teaches our Zumba class sometimes. Kim and I go to the same Zumba class."

John would wager the cost of his wedding that Kim did more than share the Zumba class with Melanie.

"Have you ever met Mr. O'Leary outside the class?"

"Once or twice. I think we ran into him downtown, and then of course we saw him at the party last Saturday." She was being careful with her words, clipping each one, as only a day drunk can when trying to appear soberer.

"Did anything happen Saturday night?"

A shadow passed briefly over Melanie's face. Kim watched the proceedings from her bar stool, a carefully schooled bland look on her face. She swirled the wine in her glass but didn't drink.

John made another mental note.

"Not really," Melanie finally replied. "We went. There were too many women. I danced a couple of times, but it was boring. So we left to find something more fun to do."

"Do you recall what time you left?"

"No. A watch didn't really match my outfit."

"You would have had your phone with you. Didn't you need to text or call anyone that you were leaving the Saturday night party early?"

Melanie's eyes narrowed in an attempt at looking seductive. "There wasn't anyone I really needed to tell."

"Did you attend the party with anyone else?"

"Just Kim." Melanie yawned and examined her expensive French manicure.

"What did the two of you do after you left the party?"

"We came back here. Had a few glasses of wine, gossiped, watched TV." She gestured vaguely with one bejeweled hand. Katie would have killed for a diamond like that. "Not my best Saturday night, for sure."

"Where were you last Thursday?"

Melanie set her wine glass down hard on the marble island, the ring of the glass sharp and trilling. "I don't remember. Was that the night after the snowstorm?"

"Yeah," Kim interjected. Her voice grated, mouselike and affected. "There was a huge storm Wednesday night. I remember Melanie telling me how she couldn't even get out of her driveway."

Melanie shot Kim a cutting look, but because she was more than a little tipsy, it came off looking like a caricature.

One more sip of wine and this woman would not be able to hold the conversation. He turned to Kim. "And Miss Smith? What is your relationship with Mr. O'Leary?"

She rearranged her features into studied nonchalance. "Same as Melanie. We're acquaintances, I suppose." She took a sip of wine. At last. "And before you ask, I was snowbound last Thursday. They couldn't clear my driveway for ages."

"And where do you live?"

She had nondescript features, neither pretty nor plain, though she had clearly been shopping through

Melanie's castoffs. "Not far from here. Just a short drive down a country lane."

"Are you from this area?"

Melanie drunkenly slapped the marble island, missed, and hit her thigh. "I thought you came here to speak to me."

"Yes, Mrs. Templeton." He pasted on a patient smile. "But it's my job to conduct this investigation, and I thought I might avail myself of the opportunity to speak to Miss Smith while I'm already here."

Melanie rolled her eyes again and dropped dramatically and inelegantly into the other bar stool, nearly missing the edge. He was simultaneously glad and bereft that she hadn't fallen straight onto her ass.

Kim eyed her friend, but not with concern. "I don't think this is a good time, Deputy," Kim clipped, her dark-brown eyes staring straight at him. "I need to help my friend to bed."

Sure she did. "Of course. We'll be in touch."

Kim nodded. Melanie would have as well, but she had lain her cheek on the cold marble of the kitchen island. She had the aura of someone who had mixed her medications. He made a note to check with the pharmacy for prescription information.

John took down their phone numbers, and Kim moved toward Melanie in an overly solicitous manner. "I'll be fine here, Deputy," she said pointedly. "Safe drive."

He glanced around surreptitiously as he moved toward the door. Where was the husband? He saw a glass of water, condensation pooling on its sides, on a coaster in the living room between the kitchen and foyer. There was a black wool woman's coat hanging next to his on the coat rack. He didn't know much about women's fashion, but took note of the brand, color, size.

He walked back out to his cruiser, again looking around, trying to be casual. The recent snow had melted with the spring thaw that had closely followed. He didn't see anything overtly suspicious, but he wasn't really sure what he was looking for. Just a vibe. He was a man who definitely believed in vibes.

Chapter Twenty-Three

"How long do you think this will take?" Anita frowned at the contractor who was measuring her door. He was a squat, grumpy little man with a significant plumber's crack that she was determined not to see.

"Could he be more of a cartoon?" Patrick murmured behind her.

She swatted at him. The door repair was taking up far too much valuable time. "Don't you have somewhere to be?"

His lips tilted, and that goddamn dimple winked at her. "I'm all yours, Anita."

The back of her neck prickled at his words.

She turned back to the contractor and placed her hands on her hips. "Mr. Erickson, do you know about how long this will take?"

The little man sighed, dusting off his Phillies cap and then settling it again atop his tangle of grayish-brown hair. "Well, now, Ms. Goodman. Not too long, I should say. I have the piece of glass in my truck. Should be done before tomorrow."

"Tomorrow?"

She had to leave for Harrisburg in two days to ensure she would be there in time for the youth competition on Friday. If just one goddamn thing could go according to plan—

"Yup, not too long, not too long." Mr. Erickson

adjusted the beltline of his pants.

The strains of Frank Sinatra's "Witchcraft" suddenly pealed from across the studio. Anita's stomach dropped, and she wasted no time running for her cell phone.

"Hi, Maria." It was not wise to keep Maria St. John waiting. A petite and efficient woman, she had run the Keystone competition for the past three years. The open secret in the Dancesport world was: What Maria St. John giveth, she can take away. And she had given Anita a lot in the last few weeks.

"Anita!" Maria drawled, her voice sounding tinny. Anita turned away from Patrick, who was following her and clearly determined to drive her even farther into insanity, and sank into her desk chair. "How are you? How's Patrick? Good Lord, we were all devastated when he quit. I can't quite believe he's out of retirement just to dance with you, but thank goodness, right?"

"Yes, well, thank you for making the exception." Anita wished she had a fresh cup of coffee. Or a large glass of wine. Or maybe earplugs.

"Of course!" Maria's voice rose three octaves. "ANYthing for you, darling."

"Is there something I can do for you, Maria?"

"Well, now—" the woman's voice lowered in a conspiratorial manner and Anita frantically pushed the volume button on her phone "—I'm hoping you and that handsome fellow can help me with a little problem I have."

Here it comes. Anita tried to prepare herself without breathing into the phone like a serial killer. "Sure, of course. Whatever we can do." Patrick's gaze burned into her. Maybe she should just climb underneath her desk and hide like a six-year-old.

"Wonderful! Well, you know we have dear Nikita's tribute scheduled, and her assistant Chris was supposed to coordinate with Robbie and Talia to do a special showcase dance for it, but now Chris has completely dropped off the face of the earth, Robbie and Talia got booked in Vegas, and I need someone to dance the showcase."

Anita gripped the phone with white knuckles, willing herself not to drop it, not to start crying, not to scream, *"Are you batshit crazy?!?!"* All of which she would rather do. Instead, she breathed. 2-3-4-and-1. 2-3-4-and-1.

"Anita? Anita dear? Did you hear me?"

Oh no oh no oh no oh no oh no.

Her lungs and stomach twisted. She couldn't breathe, she was going to throw up, she could not see anything beyond—

Patrick's warm hand on her back. His wonderful, trusting, confident face. She met his gaze, and her insides slowly unknit themselves.

"Okay." Thank God she had managed even that.

"Good. Pick something sassy. You know how Nikita loved the rumba." And with that, Maria hung up the phone.

Anita stared at it, afraid it might burst into flame. She hoped it would, though none of that would erase the promise she had just made.

"Do you want to talk about it?" Patrick asked quietly, no sarcasm or pretense. His hand was still on her back. She should move, get out of his way. But it was the only thing holding her together.

Breathe. Just breathe. "She asked us to dance the showcase for Nikita's memorial on Friday night."

Patrick blanched. "Fuck no! Is she batshit crazy? She knows we only started dancing together a few weeks ago. We're barely managing our Latin choreo."

"I couldn't say no." She put her head in her hands. "I just couldn't. She controls the whole thing. She could make my students' lives hell. She could make my life hell. Why can't anything be easy right now?" In the past, before competitions, she had limited stress, maximized her sleep and healthy food intake, cut down on outside problems. Now all she had were distractions.

He knelt beside her again. It was a bad idea, to look at him. To see him there, all comforting and warm and smelling of home. It made her want.

"We will be okay." His fingertips grazed her chin, traced the line of her jawbone. "We can do that one we did in college, for the Ohio Star Ball."

Her body tensed and heated in an entirely opposite reaction to Maria's request. Not Hozier. They were not even supposed to dance together that night, but his partner had come down with mono, and—

She couldn't. She couldn't think of it. She was hyperventilating as it was.

"Anita? Are you okay?"

Perfect. Just perfect. Not about to burst into flames at just the thought of that dance.

Pull it together. Keep it together.

"Yes." Okay, at least her voice worked. "Of course. Good idea. At least we don't have to come up with something new."

"Great." He stood and extended his hands to help her. "I think I even still have that costume."

His touch paralyzed her. There had been this moment all those years ago, the two of them, cocooned in this sensual bubble created by the dance. Anita had not thought about that moment in years, but now, here it was. Wrapping her in heat and promise and lust.

This was not going to go well.

Chapter Twenty-Four

Not wanting to be distracted by the studio construction, they moved their practice to the Lewis High School gym. It coincided with Patrick's class, and he had a feeling watching Anita dance would be excellent motivation for his kids before the competition.

Though after two and a half hours of trying to perfect a show dance in record time, Patrick wondered if it would be better just to cancel his class. If only for the sake of his glutes, which were one step away from rioting for an ice pack.

This had been either the best or worst idea of his life.

He had thought originally he could contain it. Keep his complete schoolboy undying love separate from the dance.

He was a complete and utter idiot. At this point, he just needed to tell her how he felt and run like hell if she did not feel the same. He only had a few more days before his self-imposed deadline.

The showcase was working. He was surprised so much of it came back to him. It was impossible not to get swept into the drama, the romance of the music itself. Still, it was incredibly physically challenging, almost all tricks and lifts and complicated footwork. Particularly for Anita.

She dropped into a split and let out an "oof!"

"Are you okay?" Patrick panted. He reached out a hand to help her.

She rubbed the back of her right thigh through her black leggings. "I'm fine, just pulled it a little too tight. I forgot how complicated this routine is."

Complicated and so sexy it was difficult to keep his hands to task.

He motioned for a break. They rested on the metal bleachers, the cold soothing his sore muscles and— other sore parts. When he was in high school, he had always wondered if cold bleachers were somehow a method of enforced abstinence. It was not entirely unhelpful at the moment.

Anita sipped deeply from her water bottle. "Can I ask you an awkward question?"

Do I love you? Yes. "Shoot."

She looked down at the ground, her long ponytail falling over her shoulder. "Do you think it's too...I don't know, risqué? For a memorial showcase?"

The air sparked around them. Did she remember? Did she remember how the world had contracted to just the two of them, the air between them so electric it felt like firecrackers on a hot summer's night? They had been so young. He had found himself outside her room later that night, trying to work up the courage to knock on her door, but never doing it.

Missed possibilities and timing. He was an idiot.

"Honestly, Nikita would have liked it." He smiled at her in a way that he hoped was reassuring. "She would have loved the burlesque aspect."

Anita laughed. "The costumes would definitely have appealed to her."

"You don't still have that dress, do you?" He

vividly remembered the lines of her body in the crystal bustier, the feel of the red satin negligee skirt whispering through his fingers. God, he hoped she had kept it. And also no, because he needed to be an educator to impressionable youths in a very short period of time.

"Nope. It was Gabriella's dress. I gave it back to her."

Something tickled the back of his memory. Gabriella had torn apart her dorm room after that weekend, looking for that costume but never finding it.

Anita tilted the water bottle to her mouth, and the memory faded before he could analyze it. That curve in Anita's throat, like Nefertiti. She had tasted of mocha and buttery shortbread.

Get a damn grip. You are a professional.

Maybe there was something about high schools. All of the hormones just leeched into the air until you were as powerless around them as the adolescents who actually attended the school.

Fortunately, at that moment, the school bell tolled like a military call to arms. The gymnasium doors clanged open with a squeak and squawk, and four teenagers in various attire interrupted.

Showtime. Repressing the ache in his glutes and back, Patrick clapped his hands boisterously. "Jess! How are the jive flicks coming along? Tim! You ready for Friday? You guys are going to be great."

Before the second bell rang, the group swelled to eight, five girls and three boys, all eager, hormonal, looking for somewhere to fit in and finding it here.

This was the best part of his week. Apart from every single moment spent with Anita, obviously.

"Should I head out?" Anita packed her bag. She didn't seem to notice how the kids all stared at her, murmuring excitedly in their tightly knit group. So he might have built up her skills a little. He had not been exaggerating.

"No." He reached for her hand. "Come on, let's show them what ballroom is all about."

He pulled her beside him in front of the kids. "Everyone, a lot of you already know Ms. Goodman, from Lewis Dancesport downtown." Anita waved shyly, somewhat uncertain. If she believed in herself the way he believed in her, she would be a world champion. "She will be heading to Keystone as well on Friday, and so we will see ALL of you there." He gave them all a fake stern look. They all already had their tickets, even if they weren't going to be competing. He made sure his group knew how to support one another. "Ms. Goodman and I will also be competing there this year, for the first time. Up to now, she has always refused to dance with me." A few of the kids tittered politely. "I thought maybe today we could give you guys a little preview."

"Patrick, what are you doing?" Anita hissed at him.

"Go put your skirt on." He pulled out his phone and cued the sound system. "Hurry up."

She arched an eyebrow at him, but did as he had asked, pulling a black skirt with an asymmetric frill out of her bag and over her leggings.

Patrick smiled wolfishly at her. "All right, kids, enjoy! The sssssssamba."

The drum beat of Sergio Mendes thumped through the gym, filling the wood floors and metal bleachers with rhythm. Anita and Patrick both posed, smiling, moving their hips, until the song began in earnest and they did batucadas reversing away from one another. As the song sped along, Patrick swirled closer to Anita. Nothing brought out her inner goddess like samba. The bass of the drumbeat seemed to control her hips, her arms, the staccato punctuations of her head movements and flicks. He ducked her into a samba roll, promenade and counter promenade runs, turn-turn-turn-cruzado walks. Dimly, he could hear the kids cheering, but he was too in the zone. The music moved too quickly to think. Patrick relied on muscle memory and the electrical hum of Anita, spurring him onward.

The dance finally ended with a huge dip, and as the drums faded away, Patrick realized he and Anita were laughing, and his kids were on their feet for a standing ovation.

****

"It's not a problem," Anita told the teenager. Lucy Knight was fourteen, and Keystone was going to be her first competition. "I fixed the paillettes and sequins so it's all ready for you. You're going to be wonderful."

"Thanks, Ms. Goodman." Lucy gave her a quick hug. She was shorter than Anita by about five inches, her tidy brown hair streaked through with hot pink. Anita hoped her enthusiasm would last—the girl had talent and drive. "And you'll be there on Friday?"

"Of course! I wouldn't miss watching you all for anything."

"You too, Mr. O'Leary?" She turned to Patrick, who had just finished coaching Lucy's partner, Daniel Riley.

"Absolutely. Wild horses couldn't stop me from coming."

It had been a while since she had seen Patrick in action. She waved as Lucy and Daniel left the gym, then turned to Patrick. "You have a bizarre and inspiring talent with today's youths."

"Everybody's good at something." He threw his shoes and extra brushes into his dance bag. "They're good kids. I just let them dance."

"Well, there is something to be said for giving them a safe space to work out their hormones."

"As we know from experience."

A thrill shot through her, and Anita grimaced in order to try to control her blush. "I mean, when we were teenagers, of course."

"Right, right, of course." Teenage hormones must be contagious.

She kept her hands to herself as they walked outside the gymnasium, neither saying a word.

In the parking lot, Deputy John Flaherty reclined against the closed door of his police cruiser.

"I had no idea how fun it is to drive a police car at a school." A huge grin crossed his face, crinkling the corners of his dark-brown eyes. "I swear I saw one kid literally dive behind that tree when I pulled up." There was a rather terrified-looking freshman pretending to play a video game, hunched behind a large chestnut and furtively checking on the deputy every few seconds. It would help if John were built less like an NFL linebacker.

"So glad you take your civic responsibility seriously," Patrick joked.

"I heard you guys were over here and wanted to give you an update. I went by the studio first. It looks like the new door is almost done."

Something loosened in her chest. At least that was heading in the right direction.

"We weren't able to pull any fingerprints off anything," John told them. "I'm working now on some of the names you both gave me. It's a whole cast of characters, isn't it?"

"Did you find out anything?" Patrick asked.

"Nothing concrete yet. The two women are unusual to be sure, but I still need to do some digging, verify some things. I tried calling your former partner a few times, Anita, but no word yet."

It would be just like Mikhail to ignore a police officer. He tended to discount anything that did not serve his personal image of himself as a living god.

"Hey, John." Patrick glanced over at Anita. Was he nervous? It was stinking adorable. "Look, I've been doing some social media dives into a few people. Nothing too in-depth yet, just trying to cross-reference likes and tags and geotags and all that."

John's eyes widened. "Wow, I didn't realize you had the blog, the brawn, and the brains, O'Leary. Triple threat, am I right, Anita?"

She smiled weakly and tried not to yawn. If they were going to have a male self-congratulation session, she would rather be napping.

"Anyway, I'll send you what I have," Patrick responded.

"Great! You two have a good evening. Keep your eyes open and your doors locked." He waved to them both, then climbed into the cruiser. He pulled slowly out of the parking lot, doubtlessly turning on the cruiser's lights just to torture the teenaged populace.

Anita smiled. "It's like some men never leave the

sixth grade."

"John's a good guy, just a little immature at times."

They climbed into Patrick's car for the short ride back to Main Street. Anita tapped her fingers rhythmically on her thigh, watching the familiar sites of her hometown flick past.

"A quickstep, maybe?"

Her fingers stilled at the joke. "It was clearly a cha-cha. That's how out of practice you are."

"I'm sure you can whip me into shape."

Her mouth went dry. Did she imagine the sultry huskiness of his voice when he had said that? He couldn't possibly have meant it that way. This was all way too confusing. Things had been so much easier when she knew exactly how to define their relationship.

Before she had much more time to ruminate, they arrived at the studio. "Can I come in?" he asked quietly, his eyes on her. "I still don't really like the idea of you being alone with the stalker out there. And we need to figure out costumes, maybe work on the suspect list."

Anita barked a nervous laugh. Could she be more of a spaz right now? He was so calm, and that samba and those kids…She had forgotten how much fun dancing could be when it wasn't all work. "Suspect list? Is this the Lewis Detective Agency now?"

"Hey, I'd make a damn fine Sam Spade." He smushed his face into his best impression of Humphrey Bogart. " 'I don't mind a reasonable amount of trouble.' "

Anita could not help herself from giggling.

"That's okay, I don't need a knight in shining armor to protect me."

"I know you don't. But I like being there for you."

Anita sat in the passenger seat, gazing out at the new studio door, the brand-new, very expensive glass covered in brown paper tape.

"Thank you." The sound of shattering glass thrummed through her once again. "I'll be all right. I have to finish Lucy's costume and hem a pair of pants for Shawn. It will be a quiet night, just me and my sewing machine."

He paused, then took her hand gently in his and brought it to his lips. "You know I'm only a phone call away."

It took her an age to pull away from him, but at last she opened the door, straightened her spine, and went up to her apartment alone.

****

She watched from the safety of her car across the street. Good, that bitch was going in alone. Not trying to seduce him today. She frowned at the new studio door. It had gotten fixed sooner than she had anticipated.

Her phone buzzed insistently, but she refused to look at it. That damned deputy would not leave her alone. She wouldn't be surprised if he were following her, the dick. She had been so careful to this point. Just another few days and everything would work out. She just needed to avoid the deputy and any trouble.

She fought the urge to leave the blonde bitch another message, but the thoughts of him, of PATRICK, would not leave her. Even now, slouched in her car so he could not see her, her fingers itched to message him. She had to talk to him, had to make him see her. He was the only one who would understand that everything she had done had been for him.

That bitch would not do ANYthing for him.

She glanced at the phone. Four missed calls. Four voicemails.

Maybe just one quick look. She had a new account that he hadn't blocked yet. She could see what he had posted that day, what he had eaten, any inspirational quotes or sly jokes. Just one. A little taste to whet her appetite.

Chapter Twenty-Five

Wednesday passed in a blur of rescheduled lessons, last-minute costume fittings, and practice with Patrick. Anita ended up canceling dinner with her parents because of the time crunch. By the end of the day, her feet and low back were killing her.

Her bathtub and foam roller called to her.

Anita ran the tub and poured in a handful of peppermint-scented bath salts. She pulled her long hair up into a bun, even the slight motion causing her to wince.

Just as she was sliding into the tub, her cell phone pinged with a text message.

Great. The first chance all week to unwind and release some tension, and of course her cell phone would ring.

She couldn't ignore it, though. The days leading up to a competition were hellish for her students. They needed reassurance, hand-holding, costume and cosmetic advice. She raised herself halfway up to grab her phone from the bathroom sink. Anything could happen this close to comp.

Patrick.

—call me—

Cute. Simple. Warmth flooded through her, from the bath, of course. The thrill of excitement was definitely not that she had gotten a message from him.

Anita smiled, settled back into the tub, and pressed the speakerphone button.

"Hey." His voice sounded rushed.

"This had better be important." She rolled her ankles under the warm peppermint- and lavender-scented water. She would love just to doze in here, the warm bath surrounding her, buoying her aching back and legs, relieving some of the tension. Not all the tension.

Damn Patrick.

"Have you heard from John today?"

"No. I haven't heard anything." She closed her eyes and focused on the gentle motion of the water around her body.

Patrick exhaled, and she could picture him running his hands through his hair. Classic Patrick. "Okay, well, look, he called me a few minutes ago. You know that I sent him that spreadsheet I've been working on?"

"Yes."

"Well, he looked through it too, and thinks he has narrowed it to two suspects." Patrick paused, and she sat up straight in the tub, causing the water to slosh. "Wait a minute, are you in the bathtub?"

"I've had a long day," she grumbled over the speakerphone as she reached for a towel. Thank God they weren't video chatting. "I needed to soak my muscles."

"Right," he replied quickly. Anita wrapped the towel around herself and tied it in front. Was it her imagination, or was his voice a little strained? "Anyway, he gave me some other things to look into. I was wondering if I could pick your brain tomorrow morning? Either before or after practice, whatever works best for your schedule."

Anita sighed. She cradled the phone against her ear and pulled the drain in the tub. *Goodbye, relaxation.* "Before, probably. I have to leave tomorrow afternoon for Harrisburg."

"Great. I'll be there at seven. Don't worry. I'll bring the coffee."

Chapter Twenty-Six

Anita rolled her shoulders and did some relevés against the barre set along the wall of the studio. She stretched her leg long into the air and then rested it against the wood. Her hamstring stretched and pulled, the fire in it warm and inviting.

"How do you always beat me?" she heard Patrick ask.

She did not look up from her exercises. He did not need to know that she had woken up at two in the morning, dreaming of bathtubs and him.

"I avoid the internet before bed so I can get a good night's sleep." She raised her other leg to rest on the barre and stretched out the other hamstring.

"Well, it is my job," he grumbled. "Besides, you live just upstairs."

Anita snuck a peek at him. He had taken off his jacket. It had been raining that morning, and his hair was slick with raindrops. Even slightly mussed and grumpy, Patrick was impossibly handsome.

He was certainly handsome enough in her dreams.

Keep it together. "So what did you find out?"

His normally sardonic face had tightened into seriousness. "I looked into Melanie. She seemed the obvious choice."

"No argument." Anita sipped at the cup of green tea he had offered. Since she had gotten sick, she had lost a little of her coffee fervor.

Patrick had a look of boyish pride on his face, like a kid showing his school project to his parents for the first time. Her heart tugged in her chest, reaching for him, but she mentally slapped its greedy little hands. "She has kind of a normal online print. She's tagged in a lot of the burner account photos, but it doesn't seem like the accounts belong to her. Though some of the messages I was able to geotag to this location."

"We knew whoever it was had to come here to the studio. I mean, they saw us the night of the dance." Whoops. She should not have brought up what the stalker saw, what almost happened.

He frowned. "But the weird thing is that I don't see any mention of her husband."

"He does seem on permanent trips abroad. I realize how stupid I sound, but I never really bothered to understand what he does."

"I looked into it. He's an executive at a pharmaceutical company. He also has social media accounts, but he hasn't posted anything in three weeks."

Sounded like a vacation. "Is that unusual?"

He sighed. "Social media is an addiction. For someone who goes from posting pictures of every cocktail and cheese plate every single day and then nothing, that's kind of a red flag."

The nerve endings on the back of her neck tingled. "Did you tell John?"

Patrick nodded. "Late last night, right before I called you. He's looking into it."

"It's so bizarre," Anita said. "Odd that Melanie doesn't mention her husband vanishing off the face of the internet."

"So I also looked into Kim. I stupidly did not know her last name."

"It's Smith." Anita had checked her name off enough Zumba rosters. "Kind of generic."

"Yeah. And I don't know if that's the reason or something else, but I cannot find her at all on social media."

"Isn't she in Melanie's posts? They've been all over each other the last few months." Some friendships burned hot and heavy. She gulped. She could not think about anything hot and heavy at the moment. Not when he was standing so damn close to her.

"No, she's not in any of the pictures. She isn't tagged in the comments. I looked through the people who comment frequently on Melanie's posts, but none of them matched the burner accounts, and none led back to anyone named Kim. It's curious, too, but Melanie seems to have just recently met Kim. She had this other friend in all her photos a few months ago."

"How on earth do you have time for all this?" Anita yawned. He had certainly not convinced her to increase her social media presence. She did not like the idea that so much information could be found out by just about anyone.

Patrick grinned at her. "Coffee and confidence."

****

Later that day, Anita lugged her suitcases down the stairs and dropped them at Patrick's trunk. "Carpool, save the planet, safety in numbers," he had said.

There went all her excuses.

"I called the hotel," he said as she climbed into the front seat. "They had adjoining rooms available, so I asked if they could switch us."

Her hand froze on the seat belt. "Why is *that* a good idea?"

For many, many reasons, she did not want him so close to her at night. Lately he had filled her dreams, and she had woken up sweaty, panting, needy. If he were so geographically close, she did not know if she could be in charge of her actions.

"Practice." He tuned the radio to her favorite station. "We want to squeeze in every moment, right? We still need to nail work on the tuck turn in the show dance, and our cha-cha needs more syncopation. Plus it will make it a lot easier for the stalker to find us." He grinned broadly. "Hey, I absolutely promise to knock first. Wouldn't want a repeat of Stuttgart, right?"

She had a sudden and intense urge to hit something.

Stuttgart and *Giorgio*.

Adjoining rooms were a terrible idea.

She should have known. That's all. She should have stuck to her guns, not confused a dance partnership with a romantic relationship. Then maybe she would not have to live with the memory of Stuttgart, walking in to see her naked boyfriend Giorgio atop Eva, Patrick's partner.

"At least it had a silver lining." Patrick squeezed her hand. "We were both free of them after that night."

"Giorgio was an ass." Why had she ever agreed to dance with him, date him, sleep with him? Giorgio was nothing compared to Patrick. Whoops, she had to get off that slippery slope. "I thought that you had really liked Eva, though. You two certainly seemed…compatible."

Patrick laughed. "Eva was a sociopath. She used

me to get what she wanted, just like Giorgio used you."

Sighing, Anita leaned her head back against the headrest, her eyes shut. "Just tell me this weekend is going to be okay."

"Better than okay. It's going to be spectacular."

Chapter Twenty-Seven

The hotel in Harrisburg had been decorated for Easter, with giant pastel bunting hanging from the walls in the lobby and bushels of tulips and lilies arrayed on every table. When they drove up under the arrival portico, a large banner across the front doors proclaimed, "Welcome Keystone Dance Competitors!" in large gold-and-black script.

If ever a font looked ominous…he should really talk to Maria about her graphic design choices.

Patrick helped Anita load their luggage onto a cart before handing his keys over to the valet. "What on earth did you bring?" He grunted, hefting one deceptively small case that had to weigh at least forty pounds.

"Costumes, make up, supplies for fashion emergencies, shoes, things my students may have forgotten," she ticked off on her fingers. "Shall I go on?"

"Nope, I'll just unload it and be grateful when I need something."

****

The buzzing in her ears was so loud it drowned out what they were saying to each other, but she could see him, turned toward that bitch's filthy lies, see her with her overly red lips curled into a smile. Shitshitshitshitshitshitshit.

193

Now they were heading for the elevators. They couldn't see her past all the goddamn tulips. Making her itchy all over, which just made her angrier and more frustrated. Why hadn't she been able to figure out earlier where he was staying? She hadn't realized he would want to be there for the Friday part of the competition when all the kids danced. She admired it, honestly she did, helping those goddamn reject kids. He had such a big heart.

Still, though, she hadn't been fast enough and hadn't figured out where he was staying, hadn't been able to request the adjoining room in time. And now he was sharing it with that whore. She would need to keep her eyes on them, make sure that blonde bitch was behaving herself.

She could adapt.

He looked so good today, in snug jeans and a plain heather-gray T-shirt. All those muscles, rippling just out of reach. He didn't really want that blonde woman. Not like I would, she thought. Not like I will.

"Chris?" she heard someone call. She was intently watching the elevator, willing him to come back down to the lobby, so she must have missed the first few times the woman called the name, as the woman was now hurrying over to her.

Shitshitshitshitshit.

She pulled herself up straighter, pasting on what she hoped was an appropriately vacant expression. The woman who approached her sighed with relief and exasperation. She was petite and in her mid-fifties, wearing a designer black tweed sheath dress and three-inch stilettos. Her black hair, clearly dyed, was pulled back into a neat chignon, and she was clutching a clipboard like it was an extension of her arm.

"Chris!" the woman exclaimed, finally stopping before her. "Where have you been? I've called you almost a hundred times."

She stammered, keeping her voice demure, trying to remember the other woman's name. She wanted her gone. She had things she needed to do. "I just—I just had to go do something else after everything that had happened."

"Of course." The other woman pursed her burgundy lips. "Nikita was such a bright light, and the two of you were so close."

She nodded, dipping her head, hoping she had remembered to color her roots. The motion helped her see the name on the top of sheets on her clipboard.

Ah yes. Maria, the organizer for Keystone and the Pennsylvania Dancesport Association. Officious bitch. Always calling Nikita, never remembering names.

"But, Chris, you had promised to find the showcases for Nikita's tribute. We tried calling you, then tried calling Robbie and Talia directly, but they didn't know anything and had booked another competition out west. I had to call in last-minute replacements."

Her ears suddenly perked. "I'm so sorry, again, it's been a really hard time for me. You know how much Nikita meant to me." She paused, trying to will tears. "Um, who did you end up getting?"

Maria's eyes widened eagerly, and she brushed an imaginary piece of lint from her clipboard. "Do you remember Patrick O'Leary? He was the journalist who covered the Jersey Classic. Well, he just came out of retirement."

She couldn't move, was paralyzed in this spot on this stupid, ugly, gray, uncomfortable lobby chaise. A showcase? Patrick and Anita? What kind of showcase? She tried to tell herself it would be something jazzy, upbeat.

"Really?" She tried to sound disinterested. Maria did not seem to notice her distress. She was already searching the lobby for someone else to chat up. "Do you know what they're dancing to?"

Maria sighed, clearly annoyed, and flipped through a series of pages, drawing one perfectly French-manicured nail down lists of names. "I think this says Hozier."

Her heart seized in her chest. He couldn't do that dance with Anita. Not her.

"I see," she said quietly. "Well, I'm grateful you could find a replacement."

Maria made a noncommittal noise, looked around, gratefully seeming to find someone she recognized. "Well, I must be off. See you at the tribute tomorrow, Chris."

She wanted to scream, tear out her hair, throw the fucking allergenic tulips on the ground, and stomp on their rainbow-colored blossoms.

She needed a new plan.

Chapter Twenty-Eight

"This lift is not working." Anita rubbed her hip. The sting of falling never got any easier.

Patrick frowned and held out his hand to help her stand. "I know. It's kind of at a crucial moment, though. I don't think we can take it out."

"We don't have time." She put some weight on the hip and winced but managed to stand. "The showcase is tonight. If we keep this up, I won't be able to walk, let alone dance."

Patrick looked about how she felt. "I could use a break."

They moved off the dance floor to the folding chairs where they had stashed their water bottles. A junior couple across the room practiced a quickstep. They were about fifteen, the girl in a long blue dress with marabou across the bottom. She needed to pull up her elbow in her dance frame, but no one had asked Anita.

"Can I offer some unsolicited advice?"

The tension in her shoulders eased almost immediately when Nigel stepped out of the shadows. "Thank goodness."

Maybe she wouldn't be as tense if Patrick were being a little less sweet and attentive. It rankled like an itch she couldn't scratch.

****

Nigel asked them to show him the lift, and they obliged. Patrick led Anita into slinky swivels, then lifted her while she bicycled her legs. When he tried to rotate her into the next move, though, their rhythm fell apart.

"Shit!" It would certainly be a fashion statement to show up with a giant ice pack taped to her ass.

She lifted her gaze to Nigel, who was rubbing his gold-tip-frosted hair contemplatively.

"You're not going to like what I have to say," he finally said.

Her heart sank.

"Well, we don't have a lot of time, so I'll just have to deal."

"All right, come here." Nigel gestured brusquely.

Great, now she was in trouble with the headmaster.

"Stand here." Nigel moved Patrick behind Anita. "You need to put your hands here." Nigel took Patrick's hands and wrapped them underneath her breasts. A current of electricity and heat nearly stole her breath. "You were positioned too low before. Try it now."

"Are you okay?" Patrick whispered.

Of course she wasn't okay. She was suspended less than a foot from the ground, and he was about to flip her over, and all she could think about was how the heat from his hands—

And she did not fall.

The lift worked?

She caught his gaze, the fire of triumph burning in his eyes, the dimple winking back into existence. Something feral and wild coursed through her—lust? It had to be. Images flashed so quickly through her brain she wondered if she had indeed fallen and now was concussed. Images of her and Patrick. Laughing together, grooving to the Jackson Five, tossing pieces of popcorn into each other's mouths. His body, pressed so firmly to hers that she could not tell where one left off and the other began.

"Great!" Nigel clapped his hands, and Anita staggered to her feet, trying to regain her composure. "Now do that fifteen times so you don't muck it up tonight."

****

Patrick excused himself half an hour later.

Thank God and all that was holy. She absolutely could not manage another moment with him without breaking into an ugly flop sweat and/or tearing off his clothes.

Neither seemed appropriate for the venue.

She winced and unbuckled her shoes from her ankles.

Nigel sank into the seat beside her, his posture unhurried.

"Go on, say it." She rubbed at her feet, brushing over and massaging the calluses. "I know; it's lacking. It's—it's too juvenile."

"That's not it, and you know it, Anita."

Anita straightened her back. What did he know? She ached all over. She had barely slept for weeks now. As if she would have any rest knowing Patrick was sleeping just across a thin partition.

"I don't know what you're talking about."

Nigel leaned back in his chair and sighed. "I've known you since you were twelve. You would see a challenge, work hard, do well, repeat. I'm so proud of everything you've done. You're one of the best students

I've ever had." Anita felt tears well up, but no. No, she would not cry in front of him. Not Nigel. "But I never understood how you chose your partners. None of them were good enough for you. I knew they would always let you down, and part of me sensed that you knew it, too."

That seemed unnecessarily harsh. Her father had been right. She would never make it as a dancer.

Nigel wrapped a warm arm around her shoulders, and despite everything, she leaned into it. "Then I see you with Patrick. And now I know what it was, now I know why you were so bloody stubborn." He smiled at her and put a comforting, paternal hand on her shoulder. "It frightens you. You worry he is going to leave or maybe that you don't deserve him, which is bollocks. But when you find a partner like him, you need to commit and trust in him completely. Patrick will never break a promise, never let you down. Let your inhibitions go, and the two of you can be champions."

Anita barked a laugh to cover her sob.

The junior couple had left finally, and she was immensely grateful for the privacy. "He won't stay." Anita examined a rent in the carpet. "This was temporary. He's just doing me a favor."

Nigel laughed, so long and so loud that she worried she had broken him. He wiped a stream of tears from his cheek. She crossed her arms over her chest and frowned. "You're a smart woman, love. Don't be daft. Now tell me, what's your get up for the show dance?"

"I'm not sure. I gave back the original one. I have a gray one I thought I might wear."

Nigel winked at her. "Keep it. I have just the thing."

Chapter Twenty-Nine

John Flaherty parked his car again in front of Melanie Templeton's enormous house. The grounds were quiet, only one white SUV in the driveway today. High-end. Looked like dark-gray leather seats, too. John inspected the tires, the mud packed in the treads. She must have driven somewhere after the recent snowmelt.

He looked up at the house, squinting in the sunlight. The snow had all melted now, except for a deep patch by the woodpile. The house seemed ominously empty, the black shutters on the windows gaping like dead eyes.

A big house for one person.

Katie wanted him home early tonight. She was making her famous lasagna. He wanted nothing more than to sit at their neat little dinette with an open bottle of wine and his fiancée's home-cooked dinner.

But nope. Instead, here he was.

She didn't answer at the first knock, nor the second. For his third attempt, he rang the doorbell and heard a terse "I'm coming!" in response.

Melanie looked slightly more composed today than at her last visit, though it would have been obvious to anyone with a pulse that she had been crying. She was, as last time, impeccably dressed in narrow, black ankle-length pants and a silky blue top that hung loosely over her too-thin body.

"Can I help you?"

"Deputy John Flaherty, Mrs. Templeton." He smiled, and she nodded, clearly irritated.

"I remember who you are." She over-enunciated each word.

"May I come in?"

She did not answer, simply stepped away and led him this time into the sitting room. She perched in the corner of the dark-gray designer sofa, tucking her legs underneath her. Next to her was a thin glass-topped side table holding her phone and an empty wine glass. "Have a seat." She gestured him to the beige club chair opposite her seat.

John felt the kiss of the luxurious fabric even through his uniform. "Mrs. Templeton, thank you for speaking with me again. I just have a few more questions for you."

"I'm really not in the mood, Deputy." She ran her fingernails through her long hair and sighed dramatically.

"I notice you're alone today." She huffed and tapped her phone, looking to see if she had any notifications, no doubt. "Where's your friend?"

"My friend?"

"Kim Smith, the woman who was here with you last time."

Melanie sneered. "She's not my friend."

"She certainly seemed to be."

"She hangs around, tries to be like me." Melanie swatted a hand in the air as if swiping an offensive gnat. "She vanished a couple days ago. Probably off to Single White Female someone else."

"Why do you let her hang around?"

Melanie didn't look at him, but he could see tears in her eyes.

"Mrs. Templeton?"

She took a deep breath, and her voice cracked.

"Are you all right, Mrs. Templeton?" He reached into his pocket for a handkerchief and handed it to her. She stared at it for a moment, as if unsure what it contained, then took it. She held it in her hands for a moment.

"Thank you," she said, her voice husky. "I'm sorry. I don't know what's come over me."

"It's all right." Curiosity burned even down to his fingertips. "Mrs. Templeton, I need to ask. Have you perhaps been stalking Patrick O'Leary?"

She laughed suddenly, her entire face contorting, as she did not laugh kindly. "Are you insane, Deputy? Stalking Patrick?" Her eyes welled again with tears. "Is showing interest in a healthy, handsome man now called stalking?"

"Do you follow him on social media?"

She waved a hand nonchalantly. "Of course I do. He writes about places to be seen in Philly. And I know him personally, of course. But that isn't a crime, liking someone's posts." She sniffed and stood. "I need a drink. Would you like anything?"

"I'm fine, thank you." He followed her toward the kitchen. "Do you know who would be stalking him?"

She removed a liter bottle of French white wine from the fridge and poured a full glass. "No. I didn't know he was being stalked. It happens, though, to those who live out in the public eye." She took a large drink from the glass, and John could see her shoulders lower slightly, but her interest in him had clearly waned.

"Actually, may I have a glass of water?" He smiled broadly at her. "With ice, if you have it." He sat on one of the bar stools at the island, watching her movements. "This is a beautiful house."

"Yes, I suppose so." She slid the frosty glass toward him. "My husband bought it as a wedding present for me. I would have rather had diamonds."

"My fiancée loves houses like this."

"Oh?" Like he had just told her how moss grows.

"What do you like, Mrs. Templeton?" John sipped the water carefully, keeping his eyes locked on hers. Her posture changed, her shoulders slid back, a grin played along her lips. He needed to keep the desperation out of his voice. He had tried calling Kim Smith several times, but the numbers she had given him were all clearly fakes. He had also tried going to her house yesterday, but it was silent as a grave, the windows dark. No warrant, no entry. Melanie Templeton was his only link left.

All that time chasing down noise complaints that turned out to be unruly raccoons, and now this. Something real. A real case, a real challenge.

"I like lots of things, Deputy." She simpered and sipped from her wine glass. "Lazy days by the pool, a cold glass of Chardonnay, a handsome man by my side…" She scrunched one eye, appraising him. "You're not too bad yourself, by the way. Let me guess, a good Catholic Philly boy like you…I'll bet you went to Villanova."

"Navy for me. And you?" He bet Bryn Mawr.

"Bryn Mawr." She sipped again at the wine, not breaking eye contact with him. "I wanted to go to

Wellesley, but my parents didn't want me to leave the state."

"Family, right?" He paused. "Is that where you met Kim, at Bryn Mawr?"

She rolled her eyes, but this time in a playful manner. "God, no. Kim at Bryn Mawr? Please, she would have been eaten alive." She ran her fingernails through her hair, combing it into gentle waves. "You know, I don't know if she ever mentioned where she went to college."

She probably did not pay attention. It was the Melanie show or bust. "I know they never would have let me anywhere near Bryn Mawr. So how did you meet Kim?" Keep it light, innocuous.

"I think it was at a wine bar, you know that new one that opened in Wayne? I was there one night, waiting for my husband, who was late as usual, and she sat next to me. One thing led to another. We had a couple of drinks." Melanie shrugged. "Suddenly, she was everywhere. At the coffee shop, at Zumba, at yoga. I guess I got used to having her around."

"Doesn't she work?"

Melanie sighed. "Who knows? She said something at one point. I think she mentioned working in an office. She must have money, though. We'd go shopping, and she would buy whatever I advised." She tossed her hair, pride shining through her. "I have a good eye for fashion."

He felt like he was right at the cusp, like he was back on the submarine, and it was time for an emergency blow.

"I'm sure you do."

Melanie had finished three quarters of her wine,

but the alcohol sharpened the light in her eyes. "She's just using me, like everyone else," she muttered bitterly. John cocked his head, listening. "Always 'yessing' me and trying to kiss my ass. At first I thought she was gay, but then I found all these erotica novels in her car. Kim's such a fucking packrat. It's disgusting." The bitterness changed her in a way that was more appealing that her faux veneer of self-confidence. A beautiful woman with an ugly soul.

"Sounds fucking exhausting." He drank the last of his water.

She rolled her eyes, nodding. "Do you want a real drink? I need something stronger."

"I'm all right. I'm on duty."

She pushed her thumbs clumsily together, extended her pointer fingers into the sky in the shape of a W. John hadn't seen that since the playground in elementary school.

Melanie turned to open the fridge again. John wondered if this was the right time, wished he had more experience so he would know he wouldn't lose this interview thread if he pushed now.

But Katie was waiting at home. Katie, with her long reddish-brown braid that smelled like citrus and sunshine, and her homemade lasagna, and her gentle rolling laugh that couldn't help but make him smile. He felt tarnished by entering this house a second time, like everything was just slightly mildewed. He had read Dickens in high school, a lifetime ago, but it was hard to get rid of the image of Miss Havisham's environs. Was that what this place was? The designer living room set, the faux-vintage light fixtures. Maybe they were all something that once was beautiful, now past its sell-by date.

Or maybe not. That chair had felt like heaven. He'd talk to Katie about adding something like it to the wedding registry.

"Mrs. Templeton?" Keep it casual, he reminded himself, as she poured the last of the wine bottle into her glass. "Where is your husband?"

He did not hear a reply, just the sound of the bottle crashing to the polished kitchen, shattering into a thousand tiny shards of crystal. Melanie stood at the counter, her mouth slack, staring emptily at the mess, her posture now limp.

Bazinga. Now he was getting somewhere.

Chapter Thirty

Junior competitions were the best. The participants all had so much energy, little balls of hairspray and mascara writhing and jiving and spinning.

And they were short. Thank God in Heaven they were done by four.

"You ready?" Patrick asked her, high-fiving one of his kids and shaking hands with their parents.

"No." She pasted on a smile for Lucy Knight, who had come in first in the quickstep. "This is insane. I have never competed with so little preparation."

He glanced over at her, and he really needed to stop doing that. She could hardly sit still as it was. His gaze on her just made her more restless.

"It will be okay. I'll catch you if you fall."

Her heart pounded in her chest. Damn Nigel and his perfect outfit. She could feel all the hairs standing up all over her body, a delicious heat building inside of her.

Shut it down, get it together.

"I've got to get ready." She ignored his questioning gaze and headed upstairs to her room. He would find out soon enough.

****

Patrick wrung his hands and bounced on the tips of his toes. Where was she? He had knocked on the door around five-thirty, offered to get her something to eat, but she hadn't opened the partition. Patrick had wolfed down a small bowl of soup and an apple from room service, finished gelling his hair and touching up his spray tan. He had forgotten how much grooming was required for a competition, but the routines had come back to him, like they were waiting for him to find them again.

But now he had been biding time for an hour, and he was tired of schmoozing with people who were calling this—somewhat mockingly—"his great return." He didn't feel like his smile could stretch any wider. It was making his teeth hurt.

Besides, he really, really needed to talk to Anita.

She had been so jittery all day, unable to meet his eyes, her movements frenetic even as she feigned interest in the proceedings.

Not that Patrick had been any less tense. Adjoining rooms had definitely been a mistake.

Maria St. John was still giving a speech, but he and Anita were up after a group showcase dance honoring Nikita Ivanovna. He saw the six dancers all dressed identically in white-and-gray Standard attire, chattering quietly to one another and waiting in the on-deck area. Patrick checked his phone again. Damn it. No service in the ballroom. Damn hotel ballrooms and their—

"Hey." Anita sidled up next to him, and his mind went still.

Her long blonde hair was down, held back by a Dutch braid with a crystal ribbon running through it. Her eyes were rimmed with silver eyeshadow and black eyeliner that turned into wings at the corners, and her lips were Rockette-style red. She was stunning.

"Is that the costume?" The top was a formfitting,

black, glittery bustier, and then she had on a long, asymmetrical black skirt cut through with lace. He would have chosen something slinkier. The skirt was going to get in the way during several of the tricks.

"Yeah." She smiled wryly at him, twisting the glittering silver crystal bracelet on her wrist. "Don't worry. The skirt tears off."

Patrick whipped his head so quickly that his neck creaked. "Beg your pardon?" Was he a man or a mouse?

He could hear the laughter in her voice. "When we do the first lift, after the tango section and the *Amen* drops, you tear off the skirt."

He collected his mouth from where it had fallen on the floor. *Shit, was it hot in here?* Usually they turned the ambient temp way down, but he must have a fever. "Is it complicated?"

"No." She turned to show him the tearaway tab at the back of the skirt, and his gaze arrested at the small dip in her lower back. She would taste like sugar and spice there, he was sure. "Just make sure you throw it far enough so we don't trip." She turned around, forcing him to look anywhere, everywhere else but at the perfect curves of her ass.

"Should we practice it?" He had said that remarkably well for someone who was currently wolf-panting on the inside.

"Probably, but I don't think we have enough time." Indeed, Maria had finished talking about Nikita's contributions to Dancesport and was finally introducing the Standard showcase group dance.

Patrick heard the opening of "The Saddest Song" and rolled his eyes at Anita to cut the tension he felt building inside of him. "Ballroom's never subtle."

Anita laughed quietly. "Nervous?"

He felt the fluttering in his stomach, but it evaporated as he took her hand in his. *There.* He looked straight into her eyes, her lashes elongated, her makeup flawless. He could look at her forever.

"Not now."

The audience applauded for the group showcase, and Patrick led Anita to the on-deck area, her hand tight in the crook of his arm.

"And now, dancing to Hozier's "Take Me to Church," Pennsylvania's own Patrick O'Leary and Anita Goodman!" Maria and the crowd started cheering, applauding, and they stepped onto the dance floor.

She took her position, head bowed, expression seductive, then started to move as the song began. Patrick stepped into her backlight and took one of her hands. A few moments of hands meeting and pushing away, then he pulled her into a tango section, feeling the warmth and strength in her body pressed to his. At the prelude to the first chorus, he dipped her low, turning her slowly as she reached a hand up to his face. At the last *Amen*, she placed her head on his shoulder, he wrapped his arms low around her waist, and as the chorus commenced, he whipped the overskirt off and lifted her high into the air. Underneath was a short, silver negligee that accentuated her hips and legs. Dimly, he could hear the crowd roar its approval, but he and Anita were now deep into the conjoined rhythm. They spun, performed sliding doors, moved into some Argentine tango, some waltz, some rumba, and with each chorus there was a lift, a trick, each building on the last. With one, he flipped her up onto his back, where she curled into a tuck as he spun her slowly. With another, he took one outstretched leg and curled it around himself, loving the feel of his hands on her body, the way she instinctively responded to him. Every movement was sensation, instinct. Reach and pull and slide and spin.

The last chorus was a rapid succession of mixed dance moves, spins, all with her pressed against him, so close he could taste her breath mixing with his, and then there was the final spectacular star lift. He held her on her side, her arms and legs extended as he spun her two, three, four times, then tucked her into both of his arms, still spinning, gaze fixed on hers, slowing gently until he set her feet to the ground. He knelt before her, reverent, arms around her waist and her palms extended against his temples.

Patrick was aware of nothing else for a few moments more, not that the music had ended, not that the crowd was on its feet roaring with applause. In that moment, it was just him and Anita alone on the dance floor, bathed in a single pool of light, wrapped around each other. They were one, two parts of the same whole, two wings of the same bird. That instant stretched and bowed like a galaxy around them, the pair nestled in the other's gaze. He wanted this to be forever. He wanted to kneel at her feet, worship at her altar. Did this mean she would let him? Hope fluttered tentatively in his chest.

She broke eye contact with him with a slight turn of her head, and he crashed back to the ballroom in Harrisburg. Winded as though he had just leapt from an airplane, he stood, pasting a smile on his face. He turned Anita out and bowed with her several times, the audience still cheering and chanting their names.

As he took Anita's hand to lead her off the dance floor, she whispered, "That went surprisingly well."

"Yeah," he panted. Focus. He needed to focus. What had just happened? He wasn't naked, was he? Usually he only felt like this when he woke up from an erotic dream.

"I really need to talk to you." Adrenaline flooded him, but he could not hold back the gate any longer. This was it. This was his moment, his one perfect, shining moment. She had felt it, too. He knew she had. They could not have danced like that otherwise. "Can we find somewhere quiet?"

Anita turned and gazed intensely at him. *Yes*, her eyes said. *Yes.*

Patrick could not run from the dance floor fast enough.

****

"Oh my goodness!" *Maria. Shit, Maria.* Fanning herself dramatically with her clipboard. Excellent timing, as always. "You two certainly delivered."

"Hello, Maria, thank you for the opportunity." Was her heart still beating? It was so fast she could not tell if it was racing or at a standstill.

She was acutely aware that Patrick's eyes had gone dark, nearly black like the sea during a hurricane. For a moment on the dance floor, for the whole dance, really, she had never felt so connected with someone. It was the most sensual foreplay she had ever experienced, and she forced herself to focus on the task at hand. Not on the heat of his gaze burning through the thin fabric of her costume. Not on the way his hand clutched at hers like she was his life preserver, and they were caught in a riptide. Not on the way that sexy dimple of his kept winking at her, calling to her, like catnip.

"I knew it. I just knew it!" Maria gushed. "I knew the two of you could pull off something amazing. Patrick, thank goodness!"

Maybe if Anita was super pleasant, Maria would just leave, and she and Patrick could get back to— Whatever the hell it was they had been about to do. Make out on the dance floor? Strip Patrick naked and have her wicked way with him? She wasn't into exhibitionism, but she was so heated at this point she might have agreed to anything.

Patrick pulled his eyes from Anita, leaving her feeling strangely unmoored. "I didn't do anything. It was all Anita. She's the real professional here."

"Don't be so modest!" Maria put a hand on his arm, suddenly flirtatious. Anita wanted to smack the hand away from him, then inwardly chastised herself for her unkind thoughts.

"I'm not." He slipped an arm around Anita's waist, and she almost died. "I retired, remember? Anita works at the studio every day, she teaches fellow champions. She is incredible." Her knees wavered, but she managed to stay upright.

She needed to eat something more than a granola bar. Maybe Patrick.

"I think I need a cold shower after that performance," Maria said conspiratorially. "Well done, you two. Can't wait to see what's in store tomorrow night." She blew them a kiss with her fingers.

Alone again. Good. No, no bad. Bad. Alone with Patrick equaled bad.

215

But the still, soft voice at the back of her mind did not want to cooperate. The still, soft voice reminded her that they had adjoining rooms and nowhere else to be for the next eight hours. The still, soft voice that remembered every single curve of Patrick's body, the taste of his kiss, the way it had felt pressing her lips to his dimple.

"You didn't have to say that."

"This isn't my triumph." The color had seeped back into his eyes as the intensity had left. Damn it. They had lost the moment again, hadn't they? *Shit.* "You deserve all the credit, Anita. You really are amazing."

"Yes, she is," said a thick, dark voice.

Perfect, just perfect. Of all the *zasranets*—

"Hello, Mikhail." No greeting was too frosty for him. He looked shorter all of a sudden, particularly next to Patrick. As Mikhail was not performing tonight, he was dressed in a light-blue button-down shirt and dark-gray suit with black highly-polished Oxfords. He had slicked his hair back in a nouveau pompadour, and Anita was certain he was wearing gray eyeliner.

She just kept making the same bad choices. She couldn't drag Patrick down with her.

Patrick shook the hand Mikhail extended tersely. At least this time he had acknowledged Patrick's presence.

"That was quite the performance." Mikhail set his hands on his hips and jutted out his chest. An image of a preening blue jay popped into Anita's mind, and she choked on a giggle.

"Thanks." Patrick tightened the arm around her waist.

Ugh. If anything could kill the mood—

"You never danced like that with me, Anita. If you had, maybe we should not have broken up."

"It's lucky you did," Patrick replied, his gaze steely. "Now you can finally get out of her way."

Mikhail whipped toward him, and Patrick dropped his arm from her to adopt a more offensive stance. "What did you just say?" Mikhail demanded, fists clenched at his sides.

"I said, now that you are out of the way, maybe Anita can start winning again."

"Boys, please." She crossed her arms over her chest. The fire from the dance had fled, leaving her chilled and ticked off and frustrated. She was so done. Men and their idiotic pissing contests. "You two are being ridiculous."

Neither paid any attention to her. Their voices had risen as well, drawing a crowd.

She bristled at the tension in the air and wished they could go back a few moments in time so they could have just left the ballroom. *And gone where, Anita?* Her heart pounded. She told it to hush.

"You are just some halfwit writer, dancing on the weekends. You think you can do better than me?" Mikhail thumped on his puffed-out chest.

Patrick smiled languidly at him. "Yeah. Yeah, I kind of do. I may be a halfwit writer, but even I can see that you can't tell your mambo from your cha-cha."

Mikhail moved so quickly, Anita almost missed it. Patrick dodged the first fist, but Mikhail brought a second uppercut into his chin.

"Stop it, you goddamn idiot!" She pulled at the back of Patrick's shirt, but he pushed her away from him and threw a wild punch at Mikhail's ribcage.

The crowd that had gathered oohed and aahed, their collective breathing rising each time a hit landed. Anita tried again to intervene, but they seemed lost in their own world of the fight.

Idiots. Men!

Two security guards from the hotel rushed into the middle of the circle and pulled the two men apart. Both were bleeding, disheveled. Mikhail's shirt had come unbuttoned, and Patrick's was ripped across the front, exposing his tanned and muscular chest. Both men had their teeth bared at the other, and neither noticed Anita's anger or the crowd's presence.

Anita watched for one more moment as the security guards broke up the fight, then, seething, spun on one heel and left them to themselves.

Chapter Thirty-One

Anita paced her room for nearly an hour. At one point, she tried to remove her makeup using her beloved cold cream, but then she tore one of her false eyelashes, which just added to her irritation, and she tossed her makeup towel on the floor of the bathroom with disgust.

Boys. Children.

After what seemed like an eternity, she heard the gentle click of the neighboring door closing, and she stood by the adjoining partition, tapping one foot repeatedly on the floor.

No. She was not going to do it. She was not going to open that damned partition. This was his fault and his mess. He had gotten into a stupid bar brawl instead of staying with her.

She could hear him, breathing too loudly. Of all the inconsiderate, shitty things a person could do.

She whipped open the door, prepared for a full-on headmistress drilling, and immediately her ire deflated.

Patrick looked awful. His carefully gelled hair now pointed every which way, and his hands were cut and bruised. She could see the cut above one eye, the shiner making its appearance underneath the other. He had stuffed tissue paper into his nose which was now crusted with dried blood.

"I'll call room service for ice," Anita said stonily

when it became abundantly clear he wasn't about to say anything.

He moved shyly into the room behind her as she called for ice and food.

Stupid, stupid men and their games. "Sit down." She opened one of her suitcases and removed a large travel case.

He perched in the armchair by the window. What an ass. He wasn't even going to apologize.

She busied her hands by removing bandages, antibiotic ointment, arnica, and ibuprofen from the travel case.

Never. Never again.

"I'm sorry, Anita," she heard him whisper. The crack in his voice stilled her movements. "I am so, so sorry."

He was sorry? Sorry for what? Getting into a fight the night before a professional competition? Sorry for being her friend? Sorry for the most sensual dance she had ever experienced and then denying her satisfaction?

No, she didn't want satisfaction. Not *that* kind. No. Of course not.

She didn't move for a very long moment, then sniffed and took a seat beside him.

"Let me see."

Patrick just watched her as she ministered silently to him, checking his wounds, applying arnica here, bandages and ointment there. She traced the laceration on his eyebrow with her fingers before cleansing it with a damp hotel washcloth. The water washed over her hands, and the tumult of the night drifted away with the blood and grime.

Patrick didn't say a word. She no longer expected

it of him. He had told her he was sorry. That was enough. For now.

Room service arrived, and Anita brought the tray to the desk. She filled a napkin with ice and handed it to him. "Are you hungry?" She removed the silver lids from the plates, showing a chicken Caesar and a club sandwich.

"Why are you being so nice to me?"

She saw now the tears in his eyes. She hadn't noticed before, but his ribs looked bruised. Through his ruined shirt she could see the purple starting to throb against his muscles. "I don't deserve it."

It reminded her of all of the moments he took care of her. The soups and the ginger ales and the witty rejoinders and the easy companionship, the effortless aid.

She sat beside him and took his injured hand in hers. "You're an idiot. But you're still my friend."

A shadow darkened his features, but he put the ice pack over his face to hide it. "Your friend, right. Right, of course." His voice sounded thicker than usual. Anita wondered if he had hurt his mouth in some way. God, she hoped not. An injury to a mouth like his would certainly be a shame.

She pulled herself away from him, trying to keep the rising heat in her body to a minimum. She preferred fury. It was a cleaner emotion than desire.

"You're not mad, then?" he finally asked.

"Mikhail kind of deserved it." Though she kind of wished she had been involved in the battle. She busied herself packing up the supplies, setting them neatly back into the travel case.

"Yeah, but I went and got a black eye the night

before a competition." He winced, and Anita wasn't sure if it was his admission of wrongdoing or the injuries that caused it.

She suddenly realized she was still in her costume. Oh God, the way his hands felt as they tore off the overskirt. The ridiculously short silvery skirt hardly seemed to cover anything. Maybe she should surreptitiously find her sweatpants.

"Tanning spray and cosmetics can hide a lot. I've basically got a beauty store in my luggage." Good job, Anita. Keeping it easy.

"I just—what he said about you." Patrick looked straight at her then, and her heart caught in her throat. He looked so intense, so unlike the gentle man she knew. But it thrilled her, too, this side of him. This protector, this serious man. Patrick would never let her down. "How he insulted you. I couldn't let it go. He was making it out that he was the good in your relationship, and I know that's not true."

"So do I. But I can fight my own battles."

She filled another cloth with ice and pressed it to his ribs. His breathing increased suddenly, and heat flushed across his skin. "Are you okay?" She placed the back of her other hand against his forehead. "You don't have a fever, do you?"

****

Patrick couldn't breathe. Not because of the pain. The pain was a bitch, for sure. But she was so close to him, her hands on the sensitive skin of his ribs, her face solicitous, caring, open. *Anita.* Patrick found he could not break his gaze from her eyes. The light in them sparked something in him, sun shafting across a lake.

"Are you okay?" She pressed the back of her hand

to his forehead.

No, he wanted to reply. *I got punched by a guy who probably knows Capoeira. I feel like my insides are on the outside.*

Patrick also had never been in a fight before. Plenty had taunted him over the years for his interest in ballroom dance, the small-minded bigots, but he had always been able to one-up the other guys verbally. Clearly he had lost his mind.

He was losing it again.

He was just so tired, and she was just so close to him. He could smell her perspiration that had settled into her clothes. Her fingers had whispered lightly across his skin as she ministered to him, and he knew his body thrilled at her touch.

The whole thing was exhausting.

He didn't want to fight anymore. The thought entered his fatigued brain, and he could not shake it, could not dislodge it. He could not escape the memory of her kiss, the way her body had molded perfectly to his. How could he when it felt so much like destiny? He could not leave town without telling her, at least once.

He reached a hand out and gently cupped the underside of her chin. "I'm in love with you."

Patrick felt her stiffen beneath his touch, but he couldn't look away from her. He had not quite known the words would actually leave his mouth this time. Maybe at times he had implied it, but he had never told her directly. And now it was out there. A real, true fledgling thing, seeing the sun for the first time.

It felt like relief.

"What are you talking about?" Anita whispered, her body still. God help him, she was still wearing the costume, the glittery bustier and short skirt that showed way too much of her skin.

"I love you." His shoulders relaxed. "I've been in love with you since we were teenagers."

She moved away from him then, and his broken body suddenly felt crushed anew, like an elephant had sat on him. He was an idiot. Hadn't he known that she didn't feel the same way? Otherwise, wouldn't she have said something earlier? Although when they had kissed last week, he had thought she felt it. She had kissed him back, deepened it, wrapped herself around him. That wasn't nothing. He was sure he had felt it tonight. Or maybe she really was that good of an actress.

"Anita?" He stood, looking at her back, his hands slightly outstretched as if he could grasp something as elusive as her.

She turned her back to him, and his heart deflated again. She was crying, tears welling in her eyes and coursing silently down her cheeks.

"I'm sorry, Patrick, I'm so sorry. I just—I just can't."

Chapter Thirty-Two

Anita closed the door and sank along the wood frame. She put her head in her hands and indulged in a good, solid cry. He *loved* her? How could he tell *her* something like that?

He didn't mean it. That had to be it.

She ripped the crystal headband from her hair, tearing at the braids held taut with hairspray.

She stood up abruptly, her hair now long and wild around her shoulders. She needed to move on. She had to compete tomorrow. She had students who needed her in the morning, pro/am competitors who would be waiting. Anita had to do her job.

He loved her.

She could feel the makeup running down her face in little rivulets. *Routine.* She could manage that at least. Pulling in her abs and straightening her back, she moved to the bathroom and turned on the faucet.

Her face in the mirror looked like a Salvador Dali painting, colors melting in different areas. "Cute, Anita, real cute."

Patrick loved her, little Anita Goodman. Anita, who never could go to the party because she had dance practice. Anita, who disappointed her parents by following her own foolish dreams. Anita, who had terrible taste in men.

Anita, who was tired of being alone.

In every single one of her past relationships, even when she was intimate with her partner, she had never really felt that sense of simpatico, that belonging. Except with Patrick.

She shook her head to stem the tide of tears and applied cold cream before wiping it off in large swaths with a washcloth. After each swipe, she could see her own pink skin underneath, and it made her oddly, unbearably sad. Underneath the mask of foundation, bronzer, and cosmetics, her face was blotchy and raw.

Fighting back tears again, her face now stripped of its adornments, she was suddenly desperate to be in her cozy sweatpants, wrapped under the covers where she could wallow. Moving out of the bathroom, she reached around to the back of the costume to tug at the small hidden zipper on the bustier. It wouldn't budge. Anita pulled on it, again and again, the tears now falling freely. "Seriously?!!?"

Shit. Shit. She was a bitch and an idiot, and Patrick loved her.

She collapsed in front of the partition to Patrick's room, her arms around her fishnet-stockinged legs and her forehead resting on her knees.

This night honestly could not get worse. Stuttgart be damned. Mikhail breaking up with her via text three weeks before Keystone be damned.

Patrick loved her.

A timid knock came at the partition, and Anita looked up. "Anita?" She heard his voice, muffled through the door. "Are you okay?"

For a moment, she considered lying, considered telling him she was fine. She could keep up this whole charade and likely drive him away forever. What else could she say? Could she tell him she was confused and tired and frustrated and her goddamn zipper was stuck on this ridiculously cut, borrowed dress? Could she tell him how even now she longed for him, really yearned with something deep and primal that she had not known existed inside of her?

Patrick loved her.

"Anita?" He knocked softly again.

She raised her hands to the doorknob, and before she was fully aware of it, she was standing before the partition, her hand on the lock. Tears still cascading down her face, she flipped the lock and pulled the door open a few inches.

Patrick looked unbelievably handsome, all scruffy and disheveled, an undeniably masculine scent about him. And his face, his wonderful face, was set in a look of concern. "What's wrong?" He brushed his hand across her cheek, wiping away a tear.

She inhaled sharply at his touch, and he dropped his hand as if burned.

She was doing everything all wrong.

"I'm so sorry, Patrick. This is ridiculous." She breathed deeply for a few moments, summoning whatever courage she had left. "But my—my—" Her voice hitched as she choked on a sob, a cry of humiliation. "—my zipper is stuck."

The excuse hung between them for a moment, its feeble wings flapping ineffectually.

"Okay," he replied at length, his voice stilted, his eyes darkening. "Turn around. I can get it."

She inhaled and turned so her back faced him. She lifted her hair off her shoulders so he could access the zipper.

She shuddered as he warmed her back with his breath. His fingers traced the backs of her arms, then clutched the zipper. A tug and realignment, and the zipper slid slowly, sensually down her back, exposing her flesh. She clutched the front of the costume to herself, thought to turn to thank him, but stilled as he slid his hands across the tender skin of her spine.

"Patrick?" She didn't dare look at him. Not now. A long moment passed.

"Please." His voice was ragged, his breath hot and lush. He flattened his palm against her lower back, leaned down, and kissed the base of her spine. The sensation of lips against skin rocketed through her, igniting along her nerves. "Is this okay?"

Anita arched reflexively into his touch, biting her lip, closing her eyes. *Stop this. Stop this, you can't do this, Anita.* But she wanted it. She had denied herself for so long, denied this for so long. She couldn't hold back anymore.

"Yes. God, yes."

It was like she had unleashed a tiger.

Patrick breathed out hard against her skin, moving his lips up her back, kissing her shoulder blades. Now he was licking the base of her neck, and she loosed a deep moan. Emboldened by her response, he slid his hands from her spine to the front of her stomach, beneath the thin fabric of the costume. She arched into his touch, the delicious heat of him filling her, and her head fell backward. His mouth moved slyly from her neck toward her ear as one hand moved just below her navel. The other started tracing tiny circles just underneath her breasts, firing her nerve endings, making her yearn and moan.

"Patrick," she gasped. His mouth had moved to the side of her neck, where he kissed, licked, nibbled the soft spaces. "Oh my God, Patrick."

"Do you have any idea how long I've waited to hear you say that?"

She felt him smile against the base of her jaw, and she reached a hand up behind her to run her fingers through his hair. She just wanted to tangle herself in the soft, curly plush.

He turned his head to kiss her palm and then took the proffered hand, spun her, and pressed her backward into a deep and luxurious kiss.

The kiss was hot, dark, full of need. She felt blown backward by the force of it, but two could play this game. She would not yield. His tongue darted into her mouth, slid against hers, and she matched him stroke for stroke. She would take what she wanted, if only for tonight. She did not want to exist outside of that kiss that tasted of coffee and chocolate and something spicy and exotic and so utterly him. At least no existence that she wanted.

Anita leaned into the feelings, leaned into Patrick. She wrapped her arms around his neck, releasing her costume to the floor. He scooped her up and carried her over to the bed. She was light, light as an ember floating in the air, but his breath made her catch fire anew.

And then she completely lost the ability to think as he covered her mouth and her body with his.

Chapter Thirty-Three

John Flaherty felt at loose threads. Sheriff Forbes had not yet authorized the search for Mark Templeton, but John couldn't let it go. His gut would not let him rest. Katie had eventually kicked him out of bed at four in the morning, kissed him lovingly on the cheek, and told him to figure out whatever was making him toss and turn so she could get back to sleep.

John stood in the kitchen, brooding over the coffee maker while it percolated and grumped and dripped.

Melanie had told him, while sobbing thick Chardonnay tears, that she had not heard from her husband in almost three weeks. She thought he had been traveling for work, had been up in Rochester, New York. The last time he called her, they had argued. She had complained that he traveled too much, she was lonely. Mark Templeton had called her some names (Melanie wouldn't say, but her cheeks had gone bright red), told her he needed some space, and they had hung up. She had tried calling, texting, but no response.

Three weeks was a long time for radio silence.

John poured his coffee into a souvenir mug from the Franklin Institute, added just a splash of almond milk, and sat down at the small kitchen dinette with his notepad and laptop. It was early still, not even six, but at least he could organize his thoughts.

He made a number of bullet points on his notepad.

Mark Templeton disappears 3 weeks ago—Rochester NY
Hotel—Regency Elite
Confirm check in/check out
Need airline info/GPS on car
No SM updates in that time—Patrick
Melanie—whereabouts on night of studio party
Went to party with Kim Smith
Afterward—Kim dropped her back at her house per her report
Confirm—Kim (???)
Studio—3-4 weeks ago, Patrick back from NYC
Dead bird
Patrick SM stalking
Message on mirror
Broken door—night of studio party
Connection—Melanie/Kim/Studio—Zumba
Regular Zumba teacher?
Coincidence Patrick back from NYC?

Here John paused, setting down his pen, and sipped at his coffee pensively.

The real question was how to find Kim. She wouldn't answer any of his calls or texts and had gone AWOL from her house. Sheriff Forbes had told him he didn't have nearly enough evidence beyond "idle suspicion" to obtain a warrant, but John's gut and common sense told him it wasn't a reach.

Oh well. He rubbed his hands against his face. Someone at the hotel would be up. He could check about the airlines as well. Thank goodness they kept long hours. He listened intently to Katie's soft snores echoing through the quiet house. He had some time.

****

She sat in her room on the utilitarian hotel bed, tearing pieces of paper rhythmically as she fumed.

Last night. Goddamn it, last night.

That tribute for Nikita? All those people saying such nice things about her. None of them had known what she had really been like. None of them had been forced to respond at three in the morning to her whims, pick up her dry cleaning all the way across town when she was supposed to be off, help yank her into those skimpy dresses she chose to squeeze into despite her advancing age. Good riddance. Nikita had deserved it after relentlessly pursuing Patrick.

Patrick. Oooooooh God, Patrick. It had been so much better than the one at the Ohio Star Ball. Sex in motion. She doubted she had been the only woman in the room in love with him last night, but she, she had loved him the longest. He would know. He would remember.

It wasn't fair that bitch got to feel his hands lifting her into the air. He was just a good actor, that was all.

And that fight? She had hung back initially after the showcase, not wanting to crowd him, wanting to find a moment alone with him later once the well-wishers had spoken their piece. But then there had been a murmuring in the ballroom, people whispering "fight", and she had to see. She had to make sure Patrick was okay. Anita, of course, had already turned and left. That blonde bitch had stormed right past her, not even noticing.

Watching the blood and sweat pour off the two attractive men locked in a primal dance…well, she would be forgiven for feeling a little warm. She was sure Patrick would forgive her. Unless he was into role play...

But she had to focus. She didn't like that he was still sleeping in the adjoining room beside that woman. That woman who had abandoned him in his hour of need.

She got off the bed, paced the room, biting her fingernails. Stupidstupidstupid. She couldn't keep letting Anita get him to herself. It wasn't fair. She had never had a moment alone with him. She was sure if she could just talk to him, tell him about how she felt and how long she had loved him, he would understand. He would feel exactly the same way. She was absolutely sure of it.

Now she just needed to figure out how to get him alone.

****

"Look, Sheriff," John said and handed over two sheets of paper to Allison Forbes. "He never checked out of the hotel in Rochester. I called. They said after he was supposed to check out, housekeeping went to his room, and his clothes were all gone. They figured he had done a runner and charged the card on file. His car had GPS. I tracked the coordinates, and it's parked in the back corner of a rest stop outside Scranton. Looks like it's been there for weeks."

Sheriff Forbes pushed her salt-and-pepper stick-straight hair out of her eyes and tapped down her silver wire-framed glasses over her eyes from their perch on her head. "Did you call Scranton PD? It's too far for you to drive up on your weekend off."

John shrugged. "I don't mind the drive."

"I'm sure Katie would." The sheriff smiled, running her finger over the pages. "How does she feel about you being here when it's your weekend off?" John was always surprised at how much she knew without ever having asked him. He supposed it was one of the benefits of being in a small department. The only other deputy was currently sitting at her desk, pretending that she was not playing Minehunter like it was 2004.

Sheriff Forbes looked back at John, her bright-blue eyes locked on his. "Call Scranton. Have them look for the car. Report back to me afterward."

Chapter Thirty-Four

Anita awoke abruptly and disoriented. *Shit.* Had she missed her alarm? She opened one eye furtively and noted that it was still fairly dark outside.

Good. Great. All was good. Nothing out of the ordinary.

Except.

Suddenly keenly aware by the chill of morning across her bare skin that she was completely naked, she pulled the hotel sheet up to her chest and turned to her cell phone to check the time. Five forty-five. At least she wouldn't let her students down.

Still using the sheet as a shield, she surreptitiously glanced over at the other side of the bed, and the smile spread from her toes to the crown of her head.

Patrick was sleeping, turned toward her, his hand reaching for her even in repose. The bedsheets had pooled around his waist. God, he was handsome, an Adonis with his toned torso and sexily disheveled mop of hair. Even with the bruises blossoming around his eyes, his chin, his ribs, Anita felt a stab of desire that quickly cooled with a rush of embarrassment.

She could no longer say she had never had great sex. No, not great. Mind-altering, life-changing sex. It would be so easy to slide into this, nestle into him. Every nerve on her body screamed for her to do it. She was more awake, more alert than she had ever been.

Her phone pinged and buzzed. Still thinking about Patrick, she turned her head and stifled the scream in her throat.

—YOU FUCKING BITCH STY AWAAAAY FROM HIM HES MINE MINE MINE—

Her breath caught in her throat, but there was a photo attached. Hesitantly, she tapped at the text, and a photo of her smashed studio door covered her phone. She clasped a hand over her mouth, stifling the cry.

Another ping and buzz.

—YOO THINK THAT WAS BAD WORSE IS COMING I KNOW WHERE YOUR MOM LIVES YOU FUCKING TALENTLESS BITCH—

The sobs choked through her despite her hands clamped over her mouth.

Patrick stirred beside her, and she felt as though she were being sucked into a vacuum.

What had she been thinking? She needed to delete the texts before he could see them.

As quickly and silently as she could, she gathered her dressing robe out of the closet and fled into the bathroom. How could she have done that to Patrick? How could she have let her guard down?

Once safely ensconced in the small bathroom, she sank to the cold tile floor and focused on trying to find her breath.

This had been a mistake. A huge mistake. Not only was someone threatening her mom, but how could she have forgotten that she was toxic in relationships? None of them had ever worked out in her favor. And Patrick, Patrick was the best man in the entire world. She would ruin him. He would be better off without her.

Tears falling silently down her face, she tucked her

hair up into a shower cap and turned on the water as hot as she could manage, letting the steam rise to the ceiling. She hoped it could cleanse her, take away the memory of his hands hot on her body, his mouth teasing her, his weight on her.

After all, it wasn't as if it could ever happen again. The text vitriol had only set everything into perspective. Last night was an aberration.

And she really ought to have opted for a cold shower if she were going to dwell on last night's escapade.

Once out of the shower, she wrapped herself in her blue-and-green peacock-embroidered dressing gown and set to work on her hair and makeup, the movements so practiced they were muscle memory. *This is better.* She applied toner, moisturizer, eye cream. *Let that set.* She shook her hair out of the shower cap and busied her hands by brushing it, sectioning it. *Makeup prep first, then do hair, then complete makeup. Leave lipstick for last. Eat and drink. Routine. Don't think about Patrick's hands, his tongue, his mouth.*

Patrick.

No.

Routine.

"YOU FUCKING TALENTLESS BITCH"

No. She would not give that more power.

So focused was she on her pre-comp ablutions that she literally jumped in the air when she heard the doorknob turn and the door creak open. She had forgotten to lock it. It had been so long since she had needed to lock a bathroom door.

Patrick leaned against the doorframe, clad only in boxer shorts. "Hey." A wicked smile curled across his lips, sleep still burning out of his glittering blue eyes. "I didn't realize you would be up quite this early." He scratched idly at his bare stomach, and Anita felt her eyes drawn to the thin line of hair on his toned lower abdomen, leading beneath his boxers.

Focus! Her body was having difficulty cooperating, judging by the rush of heat in her belly. *Tell yourself he is not devastatingly sexy right now. Shut it down shut it down.*

"Oh." If ever there were a lame, flustered response. She was never flustered. Just because she had lost it last night did not mean she had to succumb again. Even if a niggling part of her brain really, *really* wanted to succumb again. "Well, I have students competing this morning. I don't want to be late."

He smiled, and her breath caught in her throat. That goddamn sexy little dimple. She wanted to perch on his lap just like she had when they were seventeen, coloring it peacock blue. His smile lightened something in her, and she did not want to chase that feeling for fear of where it would lead. "I like your hair like that." He gestured to her coif. "Very alien invasion."

She glanced in the mirror. She had only completed part of her final look so far, so half was crimped and teased, and the other had been brushed back and slicked with hairspray. "Haha." He stretched, providing her ample view of his eight-pack as well as his blossoming bruises. Anita averted her eyes and focused in the mirror on her hair. "How are you feeling?"

He ran his finger over his jaw, assessing. "Like I've been in a fight."

Maybe everything would be all right. Nothing had really changed between them. He was still just Patrick.

The text message didn't mean anything. Her mom wasn't in danger.

But then he straightened from the door frame and moved closer to her, his smile now sheepish, endearing, a little sultry. Tears pricked in the back of her eyes, and her spine tensed.

They spoke simultaneously.

"I thought you and I could—"

"About last night—"

They both stopped at the same time. She cringed at the flash of pain across his face.

He was just staring at her. What could she do but stare back at him, try to keep her gaze level, convince him that she was right? Not only was having sex— amazing, life changing sex, but she was *not* going to dwell on it any more—the night before a major competition ill advised, but ruining a friendship? He was the best thing in her life; she did not want that to change. Three weeks of a roller coaster of trauma and emotions had just led to a moment of weakness. That was it. Absolutely.

Her heart reared in protest, but she forced it to be silent.

"Look, Patrick—" She hesitated, unsure what she was going to say.

"Don't." His voice was hoarse, his beautiful, kind eyes full of hurt. "Don't. Don't 'about last night' me."

"It was a mistake." Even she could hear the lie, could hear it tearing a deeper rift between them. Maybe it could open a hole in the fabric of the universe, and she could dive into that. That would be preferable to having to look at him.

He put his hands over his face, but his mouth

contorted with pain. He ran his hands through his hair instead. "You don't mean that. You—you can't mean that."

Her heart sank lower in her stomach. She would really appreciate a wormhole. "I do. It's just—it's all too much. I don't know what I was thinking last night. The dance and the fight and this whole stalker thing, and there were just all these emotions, and I-I think I got carried away."

He turned away from her, and she grimaced at the bruises and cuts on his back. Then she realized he had not sustained all of those in his fight with Mikhail, and a flush rocketed across her skin.

"Patrick—"

"I'm in love with you." He turned back to face her, his features set in an expression of pleading. "Last night was the single greatest thing that has ever happened to me."

She recoiled as if he had slapped her, felt the words settle somewhere deep in her heart, her brain.

"You pretending it was a mistake..." He swallowed deeply. "I was there last night, Anita. You can lie to yourself, but I know you."

"Patrick—" Seriously, she wasn't going to throw up, was she?

He suddenly moved toward her, took her hands in his, looked straight at her. Fear and desire pounded in her chest, and her hands burned where he touched. But fire burns out. Fire doesn't help set up the studio for the Saturday night party or pay the bills or get more ice when you run out in the middle of an event. Fire doesn't want to hear about a bad day or accept mistakes.

"Ani," he whispered, his voice soft and endearing. She couldn't look away, she couldn't. "Ani, just tell me. Tell me you don't feel the same way, and I'll—" He swallowed, the look on his face full of grief. "—I'll try to go back to being friends. I'll try. But tell me the truth. I deserve at least the truth, right?"

No, no.

Every memory from the last few weeks, the last umpteen years, crept along her skin and etched itself into place. He was her best friend. He loved her, *loved* her. He deserved only the best. He did deserve the truth.

"I'm so sorry," she whispered, and he backed slowly away. "I'm so sorry, Patrick, but I—I don't love you."

He stalked away, slamming the adjoining door behind him.

Thank goodness she hadn't yet finished her eye makeup. It would have been hell to have to clean up the mascara running free down her cheeks.

Chapter Thirty-Five

Patrick stormed down the hallway toward the hotel gym.

What the actual fuck had just happened?

He used his hotel room card to enter the small gym, grabbed a towel and a bottle of water from the entryway, and headed straight for the elliptical machine.

He chose a pre-programmed HIIT routine, probably a mistake given the extent of his bruising, but he was past caring. He needed something else to throb besides his broken heart.

He ignored the television. He cranked up the volume on his earbuds to drown out the panting of the middle-aged gentleman next to him, and the even breathing of the toned twenty-year-old with the long brunette ponytail across the room. *She* had looked at him as he had entered. That woman he had never met, who was pretty and nubile, had eyed him from her peripheral vision, was eyeing him now as he started moving on the machine.

If that random woman wanted him, why didn't Anita?

A crush of grief flashed through him, so he subjugated it into the ache of his muscles. Which both a good idea and an incredibly bad one. How was he ever going to compete tonight if walking at a level four was making him wish he had an oxygen mask? Patrick slowed the pace on the machine to give his ribs a bit of a break.

He was an idiot. A true and complete idiot, and not just for forgetting to take ibuprofen before storming out of the room.

Blog post idea about all the ways he sucked: First, he had gotten into that ridiculous brawl with Mikhail, which he regretted more and more as the pedals on the elliptical moved faster and faster. And then, just when he thought he was broken and would never be whole, Anita had asked him to unzip her dress. How could he have resisted touching her? He had been imagining that moment for over a decade, and every scent, every touch, every part of her was better than he had ever imagined.

He had been mesmerized at the proximity of her skin, the way she had responded to him. Even now, trying to sweat out his anger and frustration, he could remember the addictive heat that had grown between them. Being together with her like that, it had finally been his way out of the Friend Zone, his one chance to prove to her that they belonged together, that he did love her. And last night, with her hair strewn out across his chest and her body in his arms, it had felt like she understood. Like she wanted it, too.

But she hadn't.

The HIIT program on the elliptical cranked up the speed to six. Patrick tried to move with it, but the incline was too steep, and the bruises on his back screamed for him to slow down. Now he was a failure at this, too.

After everything they had been through, she had

reduced that monumental night to a mistake. A *mistake.*

Though he tried usually to be as steadfast and honorable as possible, there was a brittle and shattered part of his psyche that wanted to spite her. Leave now, head home, abandon her before the competition tonight. Hell, his bruised ego wanted to move away from Lewis, maybe out to California or overseas, shut her completely out of his life.

Not that it had worked when he went to New York. He had seen her everywhere. Buying a blue cup of bad coffee from a stand, running down the steps to the subway to catch her train, turning up the collar of her coat against the wintry chill of the city. He had tried to escape her before. He had tried dating other women, but he had realized quickly how futile and empty it made him feel, trying to learn someone new when all he wanted was back home in Lewis.

Maybe he had not run far enough. Mozambique was supposed to be nice.

The brunette was finishing her program. She pertly checked her fitness tracker as she walked, then cast him a shy smile when she caught his eye. The middle-aged man huffing along next to him was also staring unabashedly at the brunette and seemed disappointed that she would not meet his eyes and his reddened face.

"I feel you, bro," he whispered.

His phone buzzed. A text from Anita.

—*can we talk??*—

He had pined for Anita long enough. He had prioritized her over his own work, his own needs, his own life. He had needed a kick in the pants, and this was it.

Breathing more heavily as the HIIT program hit

eight with a hill, he reached out and deleted Anita's text before slowing the program back to a four.

California wouldn't be far enough. Maybe Fiji.

****

"Hello." John Flaherty answered the cell phone with one hand. He had the other around Katie, who was perusing a wedding magazine and showing him items she swore they needed for their ceremony and reception. Did anyone really need eight-foot-tall centerpieces sparkling with diamanté?

"Hi, Deputy Connell, Scranton P.D. Just calling in with an update."

John could hear the grind of policework behind the other officer. He stood from the couch, held up a finger toward Katie to indicate he wouldn't be more than a moment, then stepped out into the hallway. He hooked one thumb through the belt loops of his jeans as he leaned against the hideous 1970s wallpaper. Personally, he thought they should spend the money on repainting their house instead of huge floral centerpieces.

"Thanks for calling me back."

"So we found the car, and the guy was inside. Templeton, right?"

John felt his pulse quicken. "Yeah, Mark Templeton. Can you tell me what happened?"

"Keep it on the DL, but he was shot from behind. Looks like the perpetrator was sitting in the seat behind him, fired straight through his headrest. We'll know more once we get the report from the M.E."

John let out a low whistle. "Poor guy. Any leads?"

"Not yet. Crime scene unit's out there now processing the scene. Did find some long hairs, likely female, but can't confirm until CSU finishes their analysis."

"Interesting," John replied. That itch scratched at the back of his mind again.

"Is the wife blonde?"

"Yeah. So are a few others that may have been involved."

"Again, it's not the most specific clue. And sloppy, too, of the perp to leave it. Could be the wife's, after all."

"Right, thanks. Well, keep me posted. I'll let the sheriff know, too."

"Sounds good. Have a good day."

John hung up and immediately called Sheriff Forbes to update her that they'd found the body. He told her his suspicions as well.

"Whoever's been stalking Patrick and Anita hasn't always been the wiliest criminal, either," Sheriff Forbes remarked after John had given her the rundown. "Leaving hair at a murder scene isn't their first strike. I'll bet there's a lot more DNA in that car, too. Sounds like someone likely to make mistakes, be emotional, impetuous. Stalkers escalate, especially if they're provoked."

"That sounds like a dangerous combination."

"Yes," she replied crisply. "Maybe warn your friends if you haven't already."

****

Patrick left the hotel gym an hour later, drenched in sweat, his bruised body aching terribly. He downed the rest of the bottle of water in the hallway while waiting for the elevator, while trying to convince himself it did not make the lift come any sooner if he pressed the button repeatedly. It was just so tempting, though.

"Oh, hey, Patrick," a soft voice purred beside him.

Startled, he lost his laser focus on the elevator buttons. "Kim?" he asked, confused.

Kim stood before him in a thin white cardigan and dark-purple leggings. She had her dyed-blonde hair pulled back from her face in a high ponytail. Similar to Anita's. How long had she been standing there?

"Hi," she replied quietly.

Where was the damn elevator? His phone buzzed in his pocket. It might be Anita. Fuck if it was Anita.

He ignored it.

She pointed at the buzzing sound in his pocket. "Important call?"

"Nope." Yeah, he could do this. Life without Anita. Life with a massive hole in his heart. "Not right now, I guess."

She turned to face the elevator with him, standing just a hair's breadth too close. Patrick felt suddenly ashamed that he wasn't being politer. "I'm sorry, you startled me." He flashed a quick smile. "I wasn't expecting to see you here."

"Oh!" She seemed to open up, a smile broadening across her face. She did have pleasant features, he supposed. A bit sharp around the eyes, but overall she could be quite pretty if she hadn't tried to copy Melanie Templeton to a T. The style just didn't suit her. "Well, you know, there were posters for this all over the studio, and I've never been to a ballroom dance competition before. It sounded so exciting!"

"Yeah, it's a lot of fun." What was Anita doing? Maybe he should try talking to her again. A lot of people said things they might not necessarily mean when they were tired or stressed out. God knew they had been through a lot the last few weeks.

His phone buzzed again.

"Are you competing today?" Kim was asking, staring at him.

She had somehow unbuttoned the top three buttons of her cardigan when he wasn't paying attention. "Tonight, yes. Actually, that's where I'm headed. Have to meet Anita for practice."

A shade fell over her features but just as quickly disappeared. "That's great. You two dance really well together. I saw the showcase last night."

He smiled back at her. "Thanks." He paused, still wondering where the goddamn elevator was. Oh, Kim was still there, too. "So, what about you?"

"I was going to get something to eat and then watch the show, but then I tried to open my suitcase, and the zipper is broken! Can you imagine? So I was going to go find a locksmith or something—"

His phone buzzed again while she was talking, and he tried to remove it from his pocket as incognito as he could. A text from John Flaherty.

—call me ASAP. —

Patrick shoved the phone back in his pocket, as now Kim was gesticulating. He had already been so rude.

"—so anyway, that's where I'm headed," she concluded.

"That sounds rough."

"Hey, do you, like, know anything about that?" Kim asked. She tossed the long ponytail over her shoulder so it fell over her back. It reminded him of Anita.

Get her out of your head. She doesn't want you.

"About?"

"Well, zippers and suitcases and the like." She laughed, gesturing to her clothes. "I mean, I've been wearing this since last night, if you can imagine."

No, no, he definitely did not want to imagine that. "Um, I mean, I guess so." *I mean, I had done just fine last night when Anita's zipper was stuck...*

He shifted from foot to foot uncomfortably, suddenly far too warm. His brain was a traitor. Maybe he could go to Mexico and get some sort of illegal brain and heart transplant.

Her smile lit up her entire face, and she grabbed his arm. "Perfect! Oh, thank you! It would mean so much to me!"

She continued to babble as she led him away from the elevator and down the hallway. What was happening? He did not want to offend her. She and Melanie were regular clients at the studio. Losing them would mean a loss for Anita.

Still chattering, her nails now firmly digging into his arm, she opened the door to a hotel room and led him inside.

"Kim." The hackles on the back of his neck raised. "I don't know—"

But that was all he could say before she pressed a cloth to his face, and he collapsed sideways onto the bed.

Chapter Thirty-Six

Anita politely curtsied to her pro/am partner for the silver Latin competition. Her student was a forty-two-year-old bespectacled man named Dennis who had initially started dance lessons with his fiancée before the latter broke off the engagement. Dennis had decided to keep the lessons as a way to meet other women. So far, though, he had only managed to talk to Anita. She was not particularly concerned—the ballroom community was good for the shy.

"Thanks, Anita," he said quietly before moving to the table where he had stashed his things. She hoped he hadn't gone far. He had danced fairly well. There was a high likelihood he would get called back for the finals round. Anita made a mental note to introduce him to one of Rodrigo's students, Tabitha, a forty-four-year-old single marketing executive who was quite pretty and very accomplished. She had a feeling Dennis and Tabitha would hit it off. They both had similar—and loud—views about suburban Philadelphia real estate.

She grabbed a sip of water, mentally checking off the rest of her students. Distractions. That was what she needed today.

"Calm down." Rodrigo stretched out in one of the other chairs at their table, arms behind his head, watching the next heat. "Everyone has enough hair spray."

"Their performances are the best advertisement for the studio. They have to look good." She completed her mental canvass. All well and good. Everything in order. Not thinking about Patrick. Check. Check. "Don't you have another heat coming up?"

Rodrigo lazily checked his schedule. "Not for another fifteen minutes. Where's Patrick?"

Nope. Not thinking about Patrick. Anita's pulse quickened, but she tried to keep her voice neutral. "Probably sleeping off his idiocy."

"He'll need an hour to conceal those bruises." Rodrigo picked imaginary lint from his long black trousers. "Hope he iced them last night."

Something deep inside Anita curled and flared at the memory of Patrick's actions last night. "Hopefully," she replied coolly. "I have to check on a few things. There's no reception in here. Can you man the fort for a bit?"

Rodrigo waved a perfectly-manicured hand toward her. Anita grabbed her phone and stepped out of the ballroom.

She nodded at the vendor selling crystal jewelry and hairpieces and paused briefly to peruse the gowns from a local custom dress shop. The dark-green one with royal blue would match her dressing gown. Stalling. Stalling was a perfectly acceptable age-old diversion.

Patrick probably didn't want to talk to her. Not now, or ever again. He had a right. If he had done the same thing to her, rejected her—

Tears stung. She needed somewhere quiet.

She found an empty practice room and shut the door.

Time to face the music.

She thumbed through the texts, sure one of them would be from him. She just wanted the chance to apologize. That was all. Nothing else.

Unfortunately, most of the texts were from her students, who had already arrived and had their questions answered. At last, though, her thumb paused over the last one from John Flaherty.

—*Call me ASAP.*—

The sinking, roiling feeling in her stomach blossomed. Her hands shook as she held the phone to her ear.

"Hi, Anita." He sounded busy.

"Hi, John," she replied, holding one finger from her other hand in her opposite ear so she could hear better. The partition between the practice and competition rooms was too thin, and the din from the music and crowd was deafening. "I got your message."

"Great. Is Patrick with you?"

"No." And he was not answering any of her texts because she was a monster. A heartless, talentless monster. "He's still asleep, I think."

"I've been trying to reach him."

"He's supposed to meet me around lunch time to practice." Not that she knew for sure he would turn up after the complete ass she had been.

"Maybe you can pass this message along? Let him know we found Mark Templeton's car."

Mark Templeton's car? She had a feeling she was supposed to understand the significance of that. Probably something she and Patrick ought to have discussed the previous night instead of—

She made a noncommittal sound.

"Look, Anita, I don't want to freak you out. I know you guys are pretty busy today, but just be careful. I have an idea of what's going on and who's doing this, and I'm worried she's going to come after you."

Anita's mouth felt uncommonly dry. "Really? What do you think is going on?"

John exhaled, the sound amplified by the speaker on his phone. "I can't really say anything until I've confirmed it. But just lay low, keep an eye on each other. You're safer together. Can you pass it on to Patrick for me?"

A knot twisted again in Anita's stomach. "Sure, of course. And you'll let us know if anything else comes up?"

"Absolutely." John paused. "How are things going there? Nothing unusual?"

Anita briefly considered the sight of Patrick grappling with Mikhail, those same hands wrapped around her body. The text from this morning. Everything would be fine as long as she stayed away from Patrick. "Nope." Nothing except the absolute dumpster fire that she had made of her life. "Usual ballroom drama."

"Great. Take care. I'll update you guys as soon as I can."

Anita murmured her thanks and hung up the call. She tried calling Patrick, but it went straight to voicemail. Apologizing would be easier without caller ID.

She sent Patrick a quick text telling him to call John, then leaned against the wall of the ballroom lobby, ujjayi-breathing to ward off the fatigue of lying. Would it have killed John to be a little more specific?

Duty called. She roused herself and headed back into the ballroom, forcing herself to smile, be calm. He was fine. She was fine. Everything was just fine.

Chapter Thirty-Seven

Patrick groaned. His eyelids were glued together. Had he gotten himself into another fight? Everything was foggy, like he had been drinking heavily, passed out, and then woke up still drunk. Not to mention he ached everywhere. What had happened? He would kill for a glass of water, even just a sip.

He attempted to open an eye, found it too painful and stiff, groaned again. Wait, why couldn't he put his hands on his face? His arms stretched, his shoulders tense. And cold…

Patrick tugged experimentally, then shocked himself fully awake. Handcuffs?

"Oh good, you're up," said a cheerful voice. A cloud of too-strong tuberose engulfed him, and the mattress beside him sank.

Patrick whipped his head around, then regretted it immediately because of the throb in his temples.

"Kim?" he whispered, his voice full of gravel and fatigue. "Kim? What the fuck is this?" He tugged again at the handcuffs.

Kim giggled, lay down beside him, and rested her head on his chest. Seriously, had she bathed in the perfume? Patrick tried not to gag. "Oh, my God, Patrick." She sighed contentedly. "I can't tell you how long I've waited for this."

The heat of his anger suddenly iced into fear.

"What?"

She lifted her head and tilted it toward him coquettishly. "Oh, Patrick, like you haven't known!" She ran one hand down his chest, which he noted was now bare. What had happened to the shirt he had worn to the gym? He checked quickly, noted that at least he still had his shorts in place. He had loved that shirt, damn it. He and Anita had picked it out in Tokyo.

"Seriously, Kim, just let me go." His impassioned plea would probably have benefited from some water.

She sneered at that, her face turning on a dime from blushing rose to Annie Wilkes. "Why?" She thrust a hand against his bruised ribs and pressed hard, like squeezing water out of a zucchini. Pain lancinated through him. "So you can run back to your little blonde whore?"

"I don't know what you're talking about," Patrick gasped. The pain, oh my fucking God, the pain. "Please, can I just have some water?"

"Poor baby!" The insipid debutante had returned, all solicitous and cooing. She slid off the bed, grabbed a bottle of water, and inserted a straw. "Here, baby." She held the straw out for him, and despite his misgivings, he drank as much as he could tolerate. Poisoning seemed better than thirst. "Baby needs to drink."

Gross. "What did you do to me?" At least his voice was better, buoyed by the water. He tested the handcuffs as quietly as he could.

Kim laughed, tossing the long blonde ponytail behind her shoulder. She had changed into a bright-yellow sundress with little bows on the shoulders, and she tucked her bare feet underneath her as she perched next to him on the bed. "Sweet, silly Patrick," she cooed, running her finger down his cheek. "I'm saving you."

"Saving me from what?" Patrick hated the thrill of desperation in his voice. He tugged again at the handcuffs. The last time he had used them, they had been covered in neon pink marabou, and the experience had been far more pleasant. Less fraught with peril. "Kim, I have to get back. I have to compete tonight."

A storm crossed her features, darkening them. She leapt from the bed and crossed her arms over her chest. "Back to *her*?" Her eyes spat fire. "Why? Because she's so pretty and smart. All the boys like *her*." She turned on her bare feet, stomped over to an open suitcase, and started shuffling things around.

Had he stumbled into a horror movie after he had left the gym? Patrick needed a different strategy, needed to get his mind working properly. Where was his phone? Probably useless since he couldn't use his hands, but still…

She was still throwing items of clothing, lingerie, black rubber tubing on the floor from her bag of crazy.

Patrick cleared his throat. "Kim?" She whipped around, her loam-colored eyes now murderous. "I'm sorry, Kim." The tension visibly released from her body. "Look, I know you're a really nice person." She approached the bed again, quietly this time. "I'm just, um, having trouble understanding why you've tied me up."

She had calmed. She climbed onto the bed beside him again, put a hand on his cheek. "Isn't it obvious?" She bent close to him and brushed her lips gently against his. "I'm in love with you."

****

"Stop jiggling the table." Rodrigo rolled his eyes.

She stilled the rhythmic tapping of her knee with her hand.

"What's with you today? I would have thought last night's showcase success would have calmed your nerves, not made you into a knotty ball of them." Rodrigo had a low tolerance for frailty.

Patrick still hadn't called, and she had run out of excuses to leave the ballroom to check her phone. "I don't know. I just feel like something's wrong."

The announcer called out a new heat, and Rodrigo smirked. "The only thing wrong is that you and your students have been mopping the floor with mine. And this program is going too quickly." He grimaced. "At least we should be able to break early for lunch, right?"

It had been nearly five hours since she had argued with Patrick. Five hours was enough to cool off, right? Her leg resumed its rhythmic tapping.

She noticed Rodrigo staring at her closely. "What?" she barked. A few of her students were seated at the table near them, watching the performances and chatting, but they all turned to stare at her. "Sorry." She needed to get a grip on herself. This was not the professional behavior she needed to display.

Anita picked up her phone and strode quickly out of the ballroom. One more call, that was all she needed. Just one more call. Patrick couldn't avoid her forever.

"Anita, wait!"

She turned to see Rodrigo following closely behind her. He put his arms over his chest and stared at her. "Are you going to tell me what's going on?"

"Nothing." She fixed a small wrinkle on the plain black dress she wore for pro/am competition. She wished she could talk to her mom, or even her dad. But they wouldn't understand. Her mom would tell her she was being an idiot, and she should just be with Patrick, like it was an easy decision. Her dad would probably tell her this never would have happened if she had gone to medical school. "I just, um, I just haven't been able to reach Patrick, that's all."

Rodrigo's face softened. Though he had at least a couple of decades on her, he had few wrinkles to speak of, likely due to his fondness for retinol and sunscreen. But despite his affected sneer, his eyes had always been kind. It was why Anita had hired him.

"Look, Anita." He placed a comforting hand on her shoulder. "Patrick is the very definition of a good man. He is not going to leave you high and dry."

"But, I—" Unbidden, the tears welled in her eyes. She couldn't do this, not now. She most definitely did not have time to fix massive mascara mistakes. "You don't know, Rodrigo. I—I said some things to him."

"You two have been friends since you were teenagers. You've never fought before?"

"Not like this." Anita crossed her arms over her chest, the memory of Patrick's heartbroken and bruised face scarred into her memory.

"He cares a lot about you. And he is definitely not the type to run from his commitments. So give him a little time." He gestured back toward the main ballroom. "After all, the professional competition doesn't start until six, right? And that's only if things run on time, which we know they never do."

He smiled and then, clearly bored by the exchange, reentered the ballroom.

Anita stayed, arms still crossed protectively over

her chest, while she chewed on her bottom lip.

Rodrigo was right. That in itself was a bit of a miracle. Patrick would not run away from a promise. But if that were the case, where was he? Why hadn't he at least returned her text or John's call?

She saw a sudden stream of people exiting the ballroom, heard snatches of conversation. Early lunch break.

Her heart clenched. Not all these people, not the hustling and schmoozing. There was only one face she wanted to see.

Patrick would help her if she was in trouble. She owed him the same courtesy.

****

"What?"

Kim had tried kissing him again, tried pressing his mouth open with her tongue, but had found it too dry. Now she was busying herself getting him a new bottle of water and humming to herself.

"Patrick! Don't be so shy. I know you've noticed it. There's just this—feeling when we're together."

Revulsion? Anger? Happy ignorance? He kept his mouth shut. She had the look of a kettle about to boil over.

Kim brought him the water and held the straw to his lips. "I don't think you ever noticed me back then. I didn't look like this. I was like thirty pounds heavier." She pulled one hand through the long blonde ponytail. "Extensions and dye. It's not really my color, I think, but I know you like it. But even back in Irish History, I knew. I knew that you were the one for me."

Now he did gag. "Irish History? You went to Villanova?"

She giggled with delight, kissed his cheek, and pulled away the water bottle. "You do remember! I tried joining the ballroom dance club, but I wasn't very good, and it hurt my back. You were so busy touring with Anita and Gabriella and all of them, you never really noticed me." Kim looked at him shyly. "Why would you? I had to become what you wanted, I knew that. Gabriella was so pretty, but God, she was so full of herself."

"Yeah." Patrick wracked his brain. Gabriella had been his partner for two years while they were at Villanova. She had been an engineering student and a wonderful dancer, better at Standard than Latin, from an Italian family in Rochester, New York. He had broken up with her because he thought she was too paranoid. She kept telling him someone was taking things from her, just little things, but they were noticeable. A hair clip, a shoe brush, the calculator she used for her advanced calculus courses. The showcase gown Anita had worn.

Pieces of a puzzle clicked into place in his brain. *Shit.* He was going to die here.

"Anyway, I went to all the competitions to cheer you on. And you were so wonderful. So strong and graceful. And kind. I'd never met anyone like you. But it was just so difficult to talk to you!" Right. No one could ever be introduced in a ballroom. Kim had positioned herself over him, her arms close together to enhance her cleavage and her hands on his chest. He had an almost uncontainable desire to scream, *"Get off!"*

"I'm sorry," he managed. Was he still to be held responsible for how he acted in college? His mother's

voice rang in his ear: *never stop being a gentleman.*
Oops.

"And then I lost track of you for a while." A
shadow crossed her features, and she was gone again,
reliving some past Patrick had no desire to know. "You
were off doing those international competitions with
Eva. I would watch them when they were on TV, but I
never had the money for travel." She turned away from
him on the bed. He wondered if she wanted him to
soothe her somehow, but then again, his hands were
manacled to the bedposts. So, fat chance. "I figured you
had moved on, and I had missed my chance."

"What did you do then?" He heard a phone
vibrating somewhere in the room, and his heart leapt.
Maybe he could tell her he had to go to the bathroom.
Anything to get unshackled. Then maybe he could find
his phone or call John or security or—something.

"I was around, odd jobs and such." The faraway
look in her eyes reminded him of a true crime
documentary he had seen once, where the sociopathic
female protagonist gaslit her competition before beating
them to a bloody pulp. "I missed you so much, though."
Her face brightened infinitesimally. "Then I saw you
were coming home, to Lewis. You were working with
Anita and started your website, which of course I
followed from your very first post." Patrick could
barely remember his first *PhillyProud* blog post; it had
the veil of something unreal and unfinished, like a
picture you drew as a child that you later found as an
adult. "You had just been to a Phillies game, and you
gave the most wonderful account of it!" She clasped her
hands together in reverie. "So I knew it was time to
come home. Just a matter of time before I'd find my

way back to you. I was willing to wait. Of course, Nikita was very easy to convince—"

"Wait, Nikita?" A light dawned in his memory. Good God, he was an idiot. "Chris. You're Chris, her assistant."

Kim whirled in delight, whooping, and kissed him again on the lips. Her breath smelled like diet cola and strawberry lip gloss. "You are so wonderful! I knew you would figure it out, even though I changed my hair and I was wearing color contacts at the time. I called it my Clark Kent disguise. I wasn't sure how to get you to see me. You had retired from dancing. But then I saw your articles in the *Inquirer.*" Her features settled into a self-satisfied expression. "It was so easy to convince Nikita to do an interview with you. She was always such a vain person."

Patrick could remember the quiet assistant talking with him on the phone, trying to joke with him as she set the interview particulars, standing in the back of the room with her clipboard and phone clutched to her dress.

"I didn't quite figure how much she would like you," Kim now said quietly. "I should have. How could she not want you? She kept asking me to call you back, arrange a drinks meeting, book a hotel." She spat out the last word. "Every word was like a dagger in my heart. Here you were, finally, right in front of me. And Nikita wanted to take you away and keep you for herself."

Patrick's stomach tautened, and his arms stilled in the handcuffs. He did not know what to say, because what did someone say to his kidnapper who had chained him to the bed? Uh oh.

"Fucking *bitch*!" Her entire face tightened into the scream. "She never cared about anyone else. She never really cared about you. She saw that I liked you, and she wanted to take you from me." She did not lose the hard mask as she clipped, "She got what she deserved."

Damn it, he was a grown man, and he was about to wet his pants. Of all the people the ballroom community had debated as potential murderers, no one had really considered Chris. Chris had always seemed an asexual being, a humanoid drone, plain and sinking into the wallpaper. And then she had disappeared, lost to the investigation, forgotten to all who had ostensibly known her. Patrick wracked his brain, tried to remember conversations, events, anything that could link Chris to the woman currently in front of him. Normally he was better at remembering faces.

Now, reminiscing through her lens, Patrick could see how she had tried to show him her feelings. There had been the innocuous chit chat on the phone, the way she always had his Americano on hand, how she had tried to keep him by her desk instead of buzzing him straight through to his interview. Mentally, he kicked himself for just assuming this attention was routine. He was not just an idiot, he was a vain idiot.

"Well, anyway." Kim literally shook away the more intense veneer from her features. "After Nikita died, you disappeared, and I couldn't figure out where you'd gone. It was difficult to find a new boss, someone I knew you would be drawn to. A conduit." Her eyes snapped to his. "That's what I needed. And then I found Melanie Templeton. It was almost too easy. She was so lonely, she just wanted to be adored." Kim sneered again. "But she seemed like just the kind of person you would want. Blonde, statuesque, controlling. So I became her. And then her dickhead husband tries to tell me to leave her alone? I wasn't doing anything. I was just being her friend." Kim spat the words, lost in her reverie. "I had to clear my path back to you." Her voice iced over. "And then I saw you with that bitch."

"Anita?"

"Don't you *dare* speak her name! She doesn't deserve you, doesn't want you." Kim rubbed her hands up his sides, her fingertips pressing into the bruised muscles.

"You left the lighter?" Patrick remembered the small tchotchke with the engraved Wildcat he had found outside the studio, the night he and Anita had kissed.

"Yes! I was so pleased you had found it. I thought for sure you might recognize me then, little Christina Blake." Her features clouded. "But you didn't."

"Did you poison Anita?" Maybe he could somehow wiggle his wrists from their binding. Nope. Metal handcuffs were a bitch.

"She deserved it." Kim stared at him with eyes that had turned black. Ice chilled Patrick's spine.

"Why are you telling me all of this?" This never ended well for guys like him.

Kim grinned widely and clasped her hands together in a ludicrous romantic gesture.

"Patrick!" She curled up again beside him on the bed, nestled her head into the angle of his shoulder. "Oh, my darling, darling, sweet, sweet Patrick." She pressed her cold lips to his cheek. "I'm telling you because I love you. We are going to be so happy together."

Fuck.

Chapter Thirty-Eight

Sheriff Forbes closed the door of her police cruiser, and John followed suit. They were both in plain clothes today, since technically, John was supposed to be at home watching basketball with four of his soon-to-be brothers-in-law.

"Tell me a little more about her." Sheriff Forbes tilted her head to examine the house. There were no cars in the driveway, the windows were dark. John noted the black paint beginning to peel on the shutters, the front hydrangeas looking a little too beleaguered despite the recent rains. It was a single-story ranch-style home, more like the starter homes Katie was eyeing than Melanie Templeton's mansion.

"I haven't gotten a good read on her yet." John ran his hand over his bald scalp. "She gave her name as Kim Smith. Ran her through the databases but so far, no hits on that or Kimberly Smith. According to Melanie Templeton, Kim showed up about three months ago, glommed on to her fairly hard. Doesn't appear she owns the house."

The sheriff gazed up at the house pensively, her posture strong. Some things from the service never left a person. "A rental."

"Maybe. Haven't been able to track down rental records or anything like that. House was registered to Ivanocorp, a multinational corporation with its hands in just about everything, including real estate. The wife of the founder actually was murdered a few months ago." The sheriff turned to look at him, her gaze sharp. "I haven't found a connection yet between Nikita Ivanovna and Kim Smith."

"There will be one. What does Ms. Smith do for work?" The sheriff approached the front door while waiting for his answer.

"Unclear." He joined her on the stoop, his shadow dwarfing her. "She was not very forthcoming in the interview. Clearly she gave us an alias."

They knocked several times, but there was no answer. Forbes pointed silently to a security camera tucked discreetly into one of the eaves. The red light was off. "Police," Forbes said sternly, knocking again. Then she bent over, reached down, and lifted the plain brown welcome mat.

"Not the smartest place to hide your key," John remarked as the sheriff picked up the small silver key with the hardware store logo embossed on one side. "It's like she's asking for us to enter."

"We have reasonable cause." She unlocked the door and pushed it open. "Police!" she called out again into the echoing foyer. There was surprisingly little furniture in the front rooms. They moved through the first floor, following the foyer through the empty living room, then into the kitchen. There was a single wine glass on the dish rack, but also a distinct smell of funk. "Tell me about the owner who died."

"It was the founder's wife." John absently opened a door, noted a powder room. "Nikita Ivanovna. She was shot during a ballroom dance competition three months ago. I spoke to the local police. No leads yet on suspects."

"Hmm." The sheriff turned to the other hallway and headed toward another door. "Police." She knocked at the door but, when there was no answer, pushed it open.

Sheriff Forbes hit the light switch on the wall, illuminating its contents.

John sucked in his breath sharply.

"That's your friend, right?"

All over the walls of Kim's bedroom were photos of Patrick. Some were printouts from websites, some seemed to be candid shots taken from a distance. It was worse than clutter, manic and disorganized. It felt like stumbling across a dragon's hoard and smelled about as bad. "How far back do you think these pictures go?" There was a collage of photos clustered by her bed. In them, a shirtless Patrick posed on a campus green, wearing athletic shorts bearing the Villanova logo.

"Call your friend." Sheriff Forbes took her own phone out of the pocket of her khakis. "I'll put out the BOLO."

****

Anita decided to avoid the elevator and headed instead for the stairs. She didn't have the time for any distractions.

As she ran down the hallway toward their adjoining rooms, she clutched the phone so tightly her nails dug into her palms.

He had to be there, he just had to be there.

She fumbled with the key card for the electric lock, but it finally blinked green.

"Patrick!"

But the word died in her throat.

He wasn't there.

Tousled bedsheets, a lingering hint of his aftershave mingling with her body lotion, but not him.

Suitcase. He must have taken his suitcase if he was leaving the competition.

She dashed into his room, but no. There it was, splayed open on the bed, his clothes all neatly folded inside its leather walls. His toiletries were still on the shelf in the bathroom. But no Patrick.

Patrick was gone. Tears burned in her eyes, and she didn't care if it smeared every single ounce of makeup. Patrick was gone, and it was all her fault because she had lied to him when he deserved—

He deserved to know that she loved him.

The shock wave of the realization nearly toppled her backward onto his bed. She was in love with Patrick. Wildly, madly, passionately in love with her best friend, and she needed to stop lying to herself and to him. She needed to take a chance. She could not run from this, could not shove it down or lock it away.

Where was he?

Her phone buzzed in her hand, and her heart fluttered and crashed when she saw it was from John.

—Is Kim Smith there?—

Kim? *Oooooooooh.*

Anita sank onto Patrick's bed. She had missed it. She had gotten so distracted she had forgotten about the danger. Ridiculous, stupid error.

Now Patrick was radio silent.

An image came to her, a quick meeting of the eyes as Anita had pushed her way out of the ballroom last night during the fight.

She texted back.

—Yes.—

Three dots.

—Calling Harrisburg PD. Don't worry.—

Anita threw her phone across the room. *Don't worry?* What a ridiculous platitude. Men. As if she were some damsel who needed them to come to the rescue.

Patrick was missing. She was in love with him and would never have the opportunity to say anything, because he had been kidnapped by Kim, apparently a psychotic internet stalker/bird killer/poisoner and—and bad hair-dyer person, and Anita was not proficient enough in sleuthing to figure out their location.

Internet. A person could do an internet search on anything, right?

She knelt and searched wildly for her phone. There it was. It had somehow nestled itself into one of Patrick's well-worn T-shirts, one sporting the logo for a cat café in Tokyo.

She shifted her weight back on her heels, holding the phone in one hand and the T-shirt in the other. Tokyo. Patrick had drunk way too much sake and left his phone at that cat café. She and a very wobbly Patrick (who would not stop screaming "Sssssssake!" with progressively more slurring of the S) roaming the streets of the city until they had found it. Of course he had to buy a T-shirt. Never again, Anita had vowed. Not never to roaming streets with a drunken Patrick, because she had never laughed harder than she had that night. Never to losing his phone. They had just needed a faster strategy to track it down. So they had added his phone to her GPS tracking app.

How had she not realized she was in love with him

then?

Adrenaline and hope flooded through her. With a few quick swipes on her screen, there it was. The reassuring homing beacon ping of the GPS phone locator. She squinted at the direction.

Patrick was still in the hotel. Kim. Kim was in the hotel.

She frantically pulled outward on the map, trying to narrow it down.

There.

She allowed a smile to tilt her lips and dashed from the room as quickly as her sneakers could take her.

Chapter Thirty-Nine

Patrick's eyes were shut tightly, his mouth uncomfortably dry again. Kim paced at the foot of the bed, checking her phone repeatedly and muttering to herself.

Fuck was the only word he could muster. How long had he been there now? Would Anita even be looking for him after this morning? His chest clenched at the memory of her words. How had last night meant so little to her, that she could just write it off as a mistake? Patrick had fallen asleep last night, breathing in her shampoo on his hands, feeling for one of the few times in his life completely content. Whole.

Then she shattered his heart.

Not to mention he was then drugged, kidnapped, and tied to a bed by a woman who had been stalking him since college. So, yeah, fuck. *Fuckfuckfuckfuck.*

"Oh, baby, you poor, poor baby," she cooed. She moved to the side of bed, knelt beside him, and a cool drip of water touched his lips. He drank as greedily as he could from the paper hotel cup, sick at his delight of the water coursing down his chin. His stomach growled at the influx. He wondered if maybe she could order him a cheeseburger. All she had allowed him to eat was half of a protein bar.

Kim didn't seem to notice his audible hunger and ran a finger down his cheek. "Sweet Patrick." She bent forward to kiss his eyebrow, and he caught another whiff of tuberose and something that smelled musky, like mushrooms or aged ham. Yup, he was officially starving.

"What are you going to do to me?" Hopefully it did not involve disembowelment or breaking of his appendages, but after what he had seen in her suitcase, he could not rule anything out.

She looked at him, nonplussed, as if she had not even contemplated how he would not understand her wishes.

His was to eat.

"Patrick, I think you know the answer. Now that you know how I feel, I'm sure you feel it, too. We have such a history together. We can be happy." She clapped her hands together, like a toddler getting a chocolate cupcake.

Patrick pushed thoughts of dessert from his mind and did his best to sit up, but it was impossible with his arms pulled out to his sides. He slid back down the sheets. "Kim, I can't."

"What do you mean?" A storm clouded her features, her voice thickened with ice. "What's wrong with me?"

"Nothing! Nothing! You're a wonderful person. It's just, I-I'm in love with someone else."

Kim lunged toward him, wrapping her hands around his throat. The shock hurt almost more than the choking, but no, no, being choked was definitely the worst thing that had ever happened to him. The pressure on his throat was a vise, clamping and gripping, and the light at the edges of his vision dimmed.

"Please—" he attempted, but all that came out was

a gawk.

"You have to love me!" Kim tightened her grip.

He was passing out. Shit, he was passing out, and everything was going dark, and it all hurt so fucking much—

And then there was a firm and rapid series of knocks at the door.

****

Anita tapped her foot impatiently and knocked again. And again. Patrick was in there. He was definitely in there. She could smell him.

At last she heard footsteps inside the room approaching the door. She posed and pasted on her "ditsy blonde needs a favor" smile.

She could do this.

Kim opened the door a mere inch, and Anita resisted the urge to shove the door into the other woman's face. Patrick was in there. She couldn't make the wrong move, or Kim might kill him. She should have seen it earlier.

"Hi, Kim!" She kept her voice bright. "I'm Anita, from the studio?"

"What do you want?" Kim's loam-colored eyes were rimmed with red, and she had a trickle of spittle in one corner of her mouth. One of the straps of her sundress hung off one shoulder.

What had they been up to?

She pushed it from her mind.

"I'm such an idiot." Anita moved closer to the door. "I completely ran out of hairspray. I saw you last night at the showcase, and I thought maybe you had some?"

"No." Kim tried to close the door. Anita put out a

hand to stop it closing completely and smiled wider.

"Please, Kim." Her smile was probably too brittle, but she could do this. She had to do this. "Let me in."

Kim's eyes narrowed, and she tried again to shut the door, but Anita was prepared. She thrust the toe of her sneaker into the jamb and pushed back against the door with both of her hands. It popped open.

Kim fell backward into the room and stumbled but tried to regain her footing.

No. The bitch had kidnapped the man she loved, and she was not going to let this go any further.

Anita sprang forward and planted a firm uppercut into the other woman's chin. Kim's head popped backward, blood flying from her nose and lip. She gasped, her hands going to her face and tears falling from her eyes.

"You *bitch!*" Kim screamed. She flailed a wild fist toward Anita, but Anita dodged it easily.

She planted her feet in a solid fighting stance, grateful for the give of a dance skirt. When Kim rushed her again, she stepped to the side and planted an elbow in her sternum and a side kick in her stomach. A satisfying whump and thwack as muscle hit flesh.

Kim collapsed to the ground, gasping, sobbing. Anita whipped off the belt looped around her waist and quickly tied the woman's wrists together.

"No!" Kim sobbed, but her voice was more distraught than angry. It dulled to a whisper. "You don't deserve him."

Anita sniffed, and the adrenaline rush faded from her muscles. "I know."

"Holy shit!" Anita heard a tight gasp from the bed.

Patrick. Patrick was alive.

She stood up and went immediately to his handcuffs, blinking the tears out of her eyes. He was strapped to the bed, shirtless and bruised, tired, dehydrated, and his breathing was rough and fragile. But he was alive. She wanted to wrap her arms around him and suck all the pain from his body and absorb it into her own. Not that anything would be possible while he was still handcuffed.

"Where's the key?" Anita wheeled on his kidnapper, fists clenched at her sides.

Kim sniffed, then gestured with her bound hands toward her suitcase.

Anita dug through the clutter until she found the handcuff key in a pile of ominous-looking black rubber tubing. She unlocked the cuffs and helped him gently pull his arms back toward his center. She rubbed at his stiff, swollen shoulders. He was okay. Patrick was okay.

And she loved him.

His eyes met hers. His gaze stopped the breath in her throat, so bare and desperate it was. She had never seen Patrick so vulnerable.

She couldn't say it. This wasn't the time. He didn't need her adding to his drama.

"I—I need to call the police."

He nodded and sat up tentatively, casting a quick glance at Kim, who was still sobbing in a ball on the floor.

"I don't suppose there's any ice for her face?" he asked.

Anita went to the ice bucket in the bathroom, wrapped a few half-melted cubes in a washcloth, and handed the bundle to Kim. The woman inspected it like it was napalm.

Whatever, she had things to do and not enough time. She called the police and hotel security.

"They'll be up here in just a minute." She turned back to Patrick. He was still staring at her as if she were a demon or a goddess. Great, good start. Great way to tell someone how you feel, go ninja on their stalker. She did not think this was how the movies had ended.

His gaze was still on her, even as he massaged the muscles of his shoulders. His hands. Those wonderful hands.

A flush swept through her. "I'll get you some water."

She grabbed the cup on the bedside table. As she filled it from the bathroom sink, she heard him ask, "How did you find me?"

"The GPS locator app." She handed him the cup. He tossed it down in one go, and she went to refill it. "Remember Tokyo?"

Patrick groaned, and she wasn't sure if it was the memory of the hangover or his recent physical trials. "How could I forget? A cat café? I never could touch sake again."

"That's a shame. You told several Tokyo citizens how much you enjoyed it." Patrick looked like he would smile but winced instead. "After that, you were so worried you were going to leave your phone somewhere, or it would get stolen. So I added it to my GPS phone tracking app. I didn't know how to take it off afterward." She shrugged. "Must be fate."

On cue, Patrick's phone buzzed across the room. All three of them glanced over at it, but she could not move to find it. Every nerve and muscle in her body wanted only to be beside him, never leave him.

"Well, I have never been so grateful for your inattention to technology," Patrick said quietly, reaching out a hand and covering hers. Anita's heart pulsed loudly in her ears.

"As I've said before, I've chosen to focus on other pursuits." Her mouth felt dry, her eyes unable to break away from the sight of his smooth, bruised hand covering hers. Form the words. *I. Love. You. I'm sorry.*

Nope. Wasn't happening.

"Like kung fu lessons?" His mouth curved coyly in a smile.

Her own laugh surprised her. "It's not kung fu. It's kickboxing."

"When did you ever have time to learn kickboxing?"

"I'm a single businesswoman who often travels alone. I have to protect myself."

"My knight in shining armor. Well, sneakers and a black dress." The broad smile restored his features to themselves. He was okay. Bruised and hoarse and tired, but he was still Patrick. Her Patrick.

He reached his hand toward her face and ran his thumb along her jaw, then opened his mouth to say something.

From the hallway: "Hotel security!"

Chapter Forty

Harrisburg police arrived about ten minutes after the bewildered security team. Patrick and Anita sat beside each other on the bed, his hand still covering hers, despite the din of people shoved into the room. He ached everywhere, but everything hurt a little less as long as he had her with him. Poor Kim never stopped sobbing as the police officers Mirandized her, exchanged Anita's belt for the cold steel of handcuffs, and led her from the room. Patrick and Anita answered the questions they could, directed the police to John Flaherty, and then, after a surprisingly short amount of time, they were asked to leave so the police could process the room.

He could not let go of her hand. She had saved him. She had gone all Chuck Norris and had surely missed hours of the competition. For him.

Besides, he felt less like he'd been wrung through a dry cleaner's machine when he held her hand. His throat still burned from when Kim had choked him, his shoulders still ached, but he felt surprisingly…calm. Lighter than he had that morning before Kim had chloroformed him.

They stood in the hallway together for a moment, watching the proceedings in the room before being shooed away by the officers.

"I'd like to get changed," Anita said, somewhat

indecisively. "I think Kim bled a bit on my dress." She pulled the black fabric away from her body to scrutinize the small stain.

Patrick nodded and followed her down the hallway to the elevator. "What time is it?"

She glanced at her phone. Patrick saw at least fifteen unanswered texts on her lock screen that she was clearly ignoring. "Four thirty."

He hung his head. "I'm really sorry, Anita."

"For what?" They stepped into the elevator. Patrick convinced himself to drop her hand. He felt its loss acutely.

"You missed your whole afternoon."

She must be devastated.

Instead, she shrugged. "Ricardo handled it. Everyone will understand." A long pause. "They—they all care a lot about you."

He had disappointed her. Damn it. "What about the professional comp? Doesn't it start at six?"

Anita's gaze was steel, and she would not look at him.

"Anita?" He tucked his hands into the pockets of his gym shorts so that he could tame his impulse to reach out to hug her. The elevator pinged again. Their floor this time.

"It's fine." She took the room key card out of the pocket of her dress. "The important thing is that you're all right."

"Maybe—"

"No!" She whirled on him and thrust a finger into his chest. "Patrick, you were in a fight last night and spent most of today literally with your arms tied over your head. I don't even think you've had anything to eat. There is no way you can participate in a professional competition tonight. I don't want you to hurt yourself more."

She moved into the hotel room and reached up to take out some of the hairpins holding her hairstyle in place.

Patrick reclined against the doorjamb, just watching her for a moment. He watched the firm set of her shoulders, the subtle set of what had to be disappointment in her low back.

"What are you doing?"

"I'm going to change and get you something to eat." She pulled out a sensible black sheath from the closet. Beside it, Patrick could see a deep-red dress embossed with crystals across the bra-style bodice, a fire-colored flounce. It was exquisite, reminiscent of a phoenix. A dress that should not be confined to a closet.

Patrick could feel the ache in every muscle of his body, the stiffness of his throat. But what was worse? Physical pain or the emotional pain from disappointing the love of his life? Besides, the adrenaline coursing through him was better than coffee, more like a battery.

"Wear the red one." He could not let her down, not now. Not after she had single-handedly saved his life.

"Absolutely not. There's no way you can compete."

"I refuse to sit on the sidelines. I'm the one who was kidnapped, so I get to decide."

"That's a ridiculous statement."

No, this felt right. Destiny. He was a master of his own destiny. He would compete, they would beat Mikhail, and then Anita would fall into his arms, and they would live happily ever after. Or something.

Hunger dulled his reason.

"Never underestimate the power of coffee and concealer, Anita."

Anita planted her feet and crossed her arms over her chest. "Patrick, you are not listening to me. I do not care about the competition." Her voice cracked slightly. "*You* matter. I—I care about you, Patrick. I was so worried I was going to lose you." She put her face in her hands, and Patrick went and wrapped his arms around her.

"You'll never lose me," he whispered. He felt like she had poured a little bit of her warmth into the spaces Kim had emptied. The aching in his back and ribs ebbed as she wrapped her arms around him, and he inhaled her scent. This was his home. Why did he ever think he could be away from her?

"You say that, but I could have lost you today." A sob wracked her, and he tightened his hold. She was better than ibuprofen.

He pulled slightly away from her to rest his fingers on the bottom of her jaw. "I know, but I didn't get murdered today, because you're a badass chick with wicked hot fighting skills." Anita laughed broadly through her tears. Patrick had a strong desire to kiss them from her cheeks, but instead used the pad of his thumb. "Right now, the only thing I want to do is jive kick Mikhail's stupid hair out of Pennsylvania. You got to kick Kim's ass. Let me have mine."

Anita could barely stop laughing long enough to agree. "Just make sure you eat a protein bar or something. Ballroom can be brutal."

****

They arrived back in the ballroom, both breathless,

while the announcer was halfway through the introductions. Anita ignored the many curious glances, the raised eyebrows of Rodrigo. *Focus, just focus.*

Patrick would not let go of her hand. "I'm sorry, Anita." They stood in the on-deck area behind Hanna and Markus, waiting for their names to be called. "I feel like I've let you down."

Anita felt like laughing. He looked better than she had anticipated. He had showered and applied a liberal coating of sunless tanning spray to cover his various bruises. He also smelled amazing, which was horribly distracting, and she needed to stop thinking about it. "I'm just glad you're all right. Pace yourself."

"In the cha-cha? Ha." He looked over at her, and she saw the relief in his eyes. "What are you thinking about?"

"That we're not going to win, because I chipped my nail polish when I hit that bitch."

Patrick barked a surprised laugh, but there was time for nothing else because at that moment the announcer called their names.

"And last but not least, Pennsylvania's own Patrick O'Leary and Anita Goodman!"

The applause drowned out Patrick's laughter, the sound of her own heart pounding in her ears, and this was it, this was the moment.

Electricity sparked off of her skin as she placed her hand in the crook of his elbow, and he led her out onto the dance floor. She stretched her arms wide, and then he turned her out into a spin and a bow. 2-3-4-and-1. 2-3-4-and-1. Across the dance floor, her gaze found his, and the cha-cha beat pulsed through the ballroom, traveling through her feet to her hips, her arms, her hair.

This was what she loved and who she was and who she wanted to be with, and it was glorious.

Show time.

Chapter Forty-One

"I blame the nail polish."

Patrick laughed, and Anita swatted at his arm playfully. He couldn't keep the stupid grin from his face. There was nothing better than this, their post-comp ritual, sitting beside her with his long legs crossed on the floor. After the awards ceremony, they had found an empty ballroom for their celebration. They were both barefoot and had changed out of their costumes into roomy sweats. In front of them was a veritable feast of sandwiches, fruit salad, and brownies. He had made extra sure to request brownies. Chocolate healed most of her wounds.

"Why?" Patrick leaned forward and winced, repositioned himself. He sifted through the sandwiches until he chose a turkey hoagie loaded with lettuce, tomato, red wine vinaigrette, and oregano. It was his third sandwich. "We came in third. After everything, number three isn't bad. My jive kicks were decidedly lackluster."

Anita patted him on the arm reassuringly. "They weren't that bad."

Patrick grimaced. "I'm just grateful we hadn't choreographed any more challenging poses in the Paso. I had a chance to catch my breath."

"At least we beat Mikhail."

A wide, wicked grin spread across Patrick's face to

match the one on Anita's. Revenge definitely helped ease the ache. As did the ibuprofen he had taken twenty minutes before the comp. "I'll never forget the way his partner refused to hold his hand during the awards ceremony. What a fake smile. And why did he still choose to wear the shirt open to his navel? You could see all the bruises he didn't hide."

Anita bumped him on the shoulder. "I'm so glad to see you're taking the high road here."

He didn't need the high road. He was here, alive, with her.

"At least I finally get to eat," Patrick said at last, partially to his sandwich and the half-eaten bag of crinkle cut chips. "If Kim had really wanted to keep me alive as her love slave, shouldn't she have bought me lunch first?"

Anita stilled beside him. He shouldn't have said anything.

John Flaherty had arrived at the ballroom shortly after the awards ceremony for the professional contestants, bearing the smorgasbord and news of how everything had transpired.

"I can't believe she killed Nikita. And Melanie Templeton's husband. I don't understand why she would do that."

Patrick shrugged, mouth full of sandwich. "Maybe he was trying to tell Kim to back off of Melanie, and she didn't like that."

Anita shivered. "I'm grateful the worst thing she did to me was break my window. Although that poor bird…"

"Have you forgotten that she poisoned you?" Patrick's eyes arched.

Anita grimaced. "I blocked it out. Some things are better left forgotten."

They ate in companionable silence for a few moments. There was a slight smudge of mayo on the corner of her lip. He desperately wished he could lick it off.

But nope. All of that, and her feelings for him clearly hadn't changed.

"You sure you don't want to go to the after-party?" Patrick asked. "We always had fun."

Anita stuck out her tongue. "And be accosted by everyone wanting the latest gossip? Please. I'd rather just hang out with you."

His heart leapt. He leaned over and wiped the mayo from her cheek with the pad of his thumb. Her skin was as soft and delicate as he remembered. At least he could take that with him to Fiji.

He would take the memory of her smile with him right now, too. It would be like aloe on his sunburn.

Though now she was looking at him like he was insane. Which he might be.

"Me too. In the end, I'm glad she was kind of bad at being a criminal psychopath."

Anita raised an eyebrow, the very motion of it teasing. He loved her so much, and it hurt more than anything else that she didn't feel the same way. "Yeah, you should have tracked her down earlier." She grinned. "Aren't you supposed to be some kind of social media tech wizard?"

"I'm hardly a black hat."

"I don't know. Chris Hemsworth has nothing on you."

She wouldn't look at him, but his treacherous heart

was desperate for any sort of subtext. He couldn't put too much stock in it, though. "In my defense, I was balancing a lot of other things at the time."

"Well, I don't think we need to change careers just yet. Someone else can open the Lewis Detective Agency."

The air sparked, and he found her gaze.

All the hum and bustle of the party outside faded, and all he could see was her. All he ever saw was her.

"This was the most fun I've ever had."

Anita scoffed audibly. "Patrick, you were in a ridiculous fight, with Mikhail of all people, then got drugged and tied to a bed for several hours before I forced you to dance in a professional competition. You're insane. I would just want to take some ibuprofen and sleep for five days."

She had a point.

"Okay, yes, it was eventful. And painful. But I was with you. And that makes it all worthwhile." He looked down at his now-empty bag of chips. If he didn't go for it now, he never would. Life was too short for regrets. His voice softened. "Last night, too, was also pretty epic."

Her response, or lack thereof, told him everything he needed to know.

"Patrick, I—"

"It's okay, Anita." Patrick started gathering up bits of trash and putting them into an empty plastic bag. "It's okay if you don't feel the same way. I can just deal with it." Tickets. Packing. Subletting his apartment. Yup, this was it. They would have a friendship of platonic GIFs sent from faraway places. The end.

It was going to end in an empty ballroom filled

with sandwich wrappers. Fitting, since the first time he had ever seen her, she had been picking up trash in the high school parking lot.

Anita put her hand on his, her touch stilling his mind.

"Patrick, I'm sorry."

It wasn't helping. Could he get a ticket on one of those billionaire space missions?

"I'm sorry for what I said to you this morning. I was scared. Terrified, really. Last night was"—she closed her eyes, breathed deeply—"momentous. I felt like everything had changed, and it was overwhelming. I've never felt anything like this before."

The air abruptly left the room. His wandering mind circled directly back to her.

What was happening?

She continued, her eyes downcast, a flush across her cheeks. "You are the best person I've ever known. You are my best friend. I don't deserve you." His heart hitched. "And what I said this morning, it wasn't true, Patrick. I—I do love you. I think I've loved you since we were teenagers, but it scared me so much—"

Unable to contain himself any longer, he closed the short distance between them and pressed his lips to hers. He wrapped his arms around her waist, drew her against him. He breathed in every good thing that he loved, returned it all with promises.

He never wanted it to end.

Finally, his lungs desperate for air, he pulled back and leaned his forehead against hers. His entire body smiled. "I hope it doesn't take another crisis for you to dance with me."

Anita wrapped her arms around his neck. "I won't

make that mistake again."

She sealed her promise with a kiss.

Epilogue

"I just think it's a ridiculous term."

Patrick groaned and rested his forehead against the base of her neck, the heat from his skin melting through her costume. It never got old, being this close to him. Being happy, feeling whole for the first time in her life.

"Anita, who cares what it's called? The video of our show dance went viral, and it's helping the studio's popularity."

"But doesn't *viral* mean virus, and viruses are bad?" She turned and looped her arms around his waist. He leaned toward her for a kiss, but she put a hand between them. "Do you know how long it took me to fix my lipstick this morning?"

Chuckling, he bent and brushed his lips against the curve between her neck and shoulder. Twinges of heat and electricity fired through her skin, making her peacock-blue Standard dress feel even tighter against her skin, ruffling the feathers that comprised the skirt.

"I can make anything work." Patrick's smile was crooked, but his eyes shone brightly. "Come on, aren't you a little excited about your success?"

"It isn't my success, it's *our* success." Anita linked her arm with his and turned to watch the finale of Hanna and Markus's show dance. Since Keystone and the video of their Hozier dance going viral, she and Patrick had been invited to myriad competitions, showcases, master classes. Patrick had devoted the time he had promised to improving their social media presence, and it was working. Their relationship was working. She was happy, actually, truly content for the first time in a very long time. It all felt too good to be true, and she didn't want to take a single moment for granted. She didn't want to hear about Christina Blake's upcoming parole hearing. She didn't want to read about the drug wars escalating across the Pennsylvania border. She wanted only to live in this perfect, shining moment with Patrick.

Hanna and Markus finished their show dance with a series of sparkling spins and pirouettes, thrilling the crowd. Anita and Patrick whooped and cheered along with the audience. A thrill of excitement and passion sparked in her heart, and she nurtured it, let it grow, let it flow through her and into Patrick.

"Ladies and gentlemen, dancing to 'Tightrope,' Anita Goodman and Patrick O'Leary!"

Patrick led her out into the middle of the ballroom, and they took their opening positions. It had taken a crisis to bring them together, and she doubted it would be the last one. But she didn't care.

Nothing was better than Patrick and ballroom.

A word about the author...

A lifelong lover of the written word, Natalie used to spend her school recess hours reading Michael Crichton and Jane Austen. Not much has changed, except now she writes stories about smart, kickass women and the people who adore them. Sometimes there are even pirates involved. Natalie lives in Los Angeles, where she is married to a man who literally brings life into the world. She is mom to two lovely young munchkins who despise brushing their hair and eat way too much cake. She is unapologetically terrible at taking selfies. www.nataliecrosswrites.com

Thank you for purchasing
this publication of The Wild Rose Press, Inc.

For questions or more information
contact us at
info@thewildrosepress.com.

The Wild Rose Press, Inc.
www.thewildrosepress.com